MAY 1 3 2014

D1530483

THE SISTER SEASON

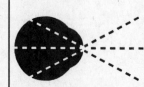

This Large Print Book carries the
Seal of Approval of N.A.V.H.

THE SISTER SEASON

JENNIFER SCOTT

THORNDIKE PRESS
A part of Gale, Cengage Learning

GALE
CENGAGE Learning·

Farmington Hills, Mich • San Francisco • New York • Waterville, Maine
Meriden, Conn • Mason, Ohio • Chicago

GALE
CENGAGE Learning·

Copyright © Jennifer Brown, 2013.
Conversation Guide copyright © Penguin Group (USA) LLC, 2013.
Thorndike Press, a part of Gale, Cengage Learning.

ALL RIGHTS RESERVED
This is a work of fiction. Names, characters, places, and incidents either
are the product of the author's imagination or are used fictitiously, and
any resemblance to actual persons, living or dead, business
establishments, events, or locales is entirely coincidental.
Thorndike Press® Large Print Women's Fiction.
The text of this Large Print edition is unabridged.
Other aspects of the book may vary from the original edition.
Set in 16 pt. Plantin.

LIBRARY OF CONGRESS CATALOGING-IN-PUBLICATION DATA

Scott, Jennifer, 1972–
    The sister season / by Jennifer Scott. — Large print edition.
        pages ; cm. — (Thorndike Press large print women's fiction)
    ISBN-13: 978-1-4104-6858-1 (hardcover)
    ISBN-10: 1-4104-6858-5 (hardcover)
    1. Sisters—Fiction. 2. Middle-aged women—Fiction. 3. Large type books. 4.
Domestic fiction. I. Title.
PS3619.C66555S57 2014
813'.6—dc23   2013050877

Published in 2014 by arrangement with NAL Signet, a member of
Penguin Group (USA) LLC, a Penguin Random House Company

Printed in the United States of America
1 2 3 4 5 6 7 18 17 16 15 14

For Scott

3 0053 01126 4994

ACKNOWLEDGMENTS

First and foremost, I would like to thank my agent, Cori Deyoe, for always being willing to read and champion my work, and for never wavering in her belief that I would someday write women's fiction.

Thank you to Sandy Harding for making my first foray into women's fiction safe, easy, and fun, and to everyone at New American Library/Penguin who helped bring *The Sister Season* to life. From cover design to copyediting, I couldn't have done it without you.

Thank you to my writing friends, with all the idea bouncing and manuscript reading and hand-holding and whatnot — especially Rhonda Helms, Michelle Zink, and Susan Vollenweider.

I'd like to thank my kids for being patient and understanding when the writing needs to happen and the traveling needs to happen and the speaking and the Skyping and

7

the reading need to happen, and for still being around when Mommy comes home and
the super-tight hugging needs to happen.
And especially thank you to my husband,
Scott, who is the other me, only usually the
better me. There would be no book without
you. I love you all.

Finally, I want to thank my parents, and
Hugh Bethards, for giving me the gift of
Sundays on the farm. Henry the goose and
Clawed the barn cat, you are as much a part
of this story as I am.

Prologue:
December 21

Blow, blow, thou winter wind.
Thou art not so unkind
As man's ingratitude;
Thy tooth is not so keen,
Because thou art not seen,
Although thy breath be rude.
— William Shakespeare,
As You Like It (Act II, Scene 7) (1600)

The tree needed tinsel.

Elise stood back and admired the great Colorado blue spruce that dominated the den, absently rubbing the raised scratches on her arms. She'd always been allergic to the damn things, but she felt too heart-warmed by their scent and the sleepy bluish tint of their limbs to care. The way Elise saw it, the spruce, cut from the ground by one of the sweet Boy Scouts who set up their tent on Highway 3, was the only way to go. A farmhouse with a fake Christmas tree was practically a crime in her book.

When Elise was a little girl, her daddy had always dragged the sticky things into the den, despite the protests of her depressingly pragmatic mother, who insisted that the house would burn down the minute he clipped the first twinkling light onto the first heavy branch. Elise recalled what seemed like a million Christmases, lying under the tree, itching and staring up into the faces of ornaments, winking in and out of motion, deep reds and supple golds, her kneesocks pulled up tight to her knees, her ponytail pushing painfully against the wooden floor while she tried to remember all the words to "Silent Night" (were the shepherds lowing, or was it the sheep? No, maybe cows. And what was lowing, anyway?).

God, how she missed her daddy. The firm, scratchy feel of his calloused fingers brushing up against the back of her neck so gently, the same way they stroked a horse's neck. She missed the way he would smilingly chide her mother, *Now, Bernie, this here tree is moist as a duckling's backside.* The way he'd spread his broad fingers over his chest while sucking in a lung-filling breath. *That's a smell God intended,* he'd say, and though Elise never quite knew what he meant by that, she felt certain she understood the feeling that must have been coursing through him while he said it.

So, itching or no itching, there would be a real spruce in her house.

And tinsel. The tree needed tinsel.

She quickly stuffed the flaps shut on the large box behind her, the one with XMAS DEKRASHIONS scrawled across the top in ancient Magic Marker. Which of the girls had done that? Claire, perhaps? Her spelling had always been atrocious. As she closed the box, a waft of stale cardboard puffed up her silver bangs. It was the scent of Christmas, *a smell God intended,* and she nearly buckled under the weight of memories.

Claire, dancing around the room on a stick pony all those years ago, whinnying and giggling, with no idea that Robert had tidily stashed a real pony out in the stable for her — Tilly, the damnedest horse to break, but Claire had done it as only Claire could, patiently, doggedly. Maya, baking cookies while wearing Grandma Ruby's ratty old apron, chatting nonstop about what she would be like someday when she became a mom, when she had a husband. And Julia — stately Julia, who practically came out of the womb coiffed and proper — sitting next to the fire, her knees tucked up into her nightgown, staring into the

11

flames as if she could see the meaning of Christmas in them. Julia, handing Robert a crudely wrapped aftershave, her fingers steadily gripping the paper, but her upper lip trembling. God, how Robert's approval had always meant so much to that girl.

Oh, the food they'd had back then. Home-made stollen. Carefully carved geese so juicy that whole tablecloths were ruined. Venison sausages and greens and casseroles and hot, buttery braided breads. The drinking. The music. The laughter. The visits from friends and relatives and the revelry through the night. The fire that smoldered for hours, Elise's nephews forever dredging up pocketfuls of acorns and tossing them into the flames just to hear the pops and watch the girls squeal when an errant shell would skitter right out of the hearth and rattle across the den floor. The shimmery garland that reflected the firelight and danced light and shadows off of cheeks, and the smell of pinecones soaked with cinnamon oil, with just a touch of the stench of melted lard from the bird feeders the girls had made prior to soaking those pinecones.

Elise brushed her hands together and stood, stretching her back.

The memories. It had all been so perfect. So just-so. So as she liked it.

12

Except for one thing.

Robert.

The stony silences. The hushed, drunken insults. The withheld intimacy and the yelling and the way he always seemed on edge, as if she'd ruined his life by tethering herself and her children to him.

"Can't you please just relax? Have a drink. Eat a cookie," she'd begged him time and again. "It's Christmas, after all."

"To hell with your Christmas," he'd growl, climbing the creaking steps to the bedroom, leaving her curled up in front of the dying firelight with itching arms and the garland shining onto her face in a darkened, empty room, her feet tucked under her, her shoulders shaking mournfully.

Robert hated tinsel. Thought it was trashy. Thought it beneath them.

She hadn't decorated with tinsel in years. Probably not since the girls had last come home for Christmas anyway, so what did it even matter?

"Well, to hell with you, Robert," she said aloud now, all these years later, shrugging off the memory and brushing her hands together once more, only this time with feeling. "I happen to think tinsel is beautiful, and this year, by God, we will have tinsel." She bent and hoisted the mostly empty box and lugged it down to the basement, where she scooted it back underneath the metal shelves. When it was in place, she stood and rummaged through a plastic tub on the shelf just above where the Christmas box went. After a few moments, and one panicky skipped heartbeat when she could have sworn she saw a telltale fiddle shape on the back of a spider tucked inside a broken ornament in the bottom of the box, she emerged, clutching a fistful of silver strands.

The phone rang just as she reached the top of the stairs, and she paused as if to answer it, then thought better of it and jerked her hand away from the receiver as if it were alive. It might be one of the girls. Calling to say they couldn't make it again this year. Calling to wish her a Merry Christmas a couple of days early. Calling to put their unwilling children on the phone to spit out an awkward thank-you for the mailed gift that they probably didn't like and most likely had already returned for money or a gift card they could use to buy something they really wanted.

It was Christmas — of course she wanted to talk to them. She would call the girls later. All of them. She had to. And she'd make some other calls too. But first, the tinsel. Before Robert had anything to say

14

about it.

She bent to check the oven on her way back through the kitchen. The cookies were browning beautifully. Just a few more minutes and they'd be perfectly soft in the middle with the tiniest crunch around the edges — just as the girls always liked them. The mulled wine she'd put on the stove in the morning had begun to percolate, sending a cloud of heavenly spicy orange scent into the room. She supposed she'd drink plenty of it later. She supposed she'd need to, when the weight of everything that had happened over the past several hours pressed in on her and she was faced with her own demons, demanding that she look at the truth.

"Well, good fortune," she announced to Robert as she passed him on the way to the den. She held up the tinsel and shook it. "I still had some from years ago. It's a bit dusty, but it will do."

She breezed right past his recliner and into the den, tossing strands of tinsel gleefully toward the tree while she was still steps away from it. Pieces that didn't snag on a limb fluttered to the floor, creating a shivering river of reflected tree lights.

"I know you don't care for it," she called. "But maybe just this once you'll leave it be."

She artfully arranged a few strands, cocking her head to one side to study her work. "Maybe you'll get used to it. I'm sure you will."

After a few short minutes, she was done. She placed her hands on her hips and smiled wide — something she rarely did (her mom had taught her from day one that farmers' wives have nothing but hard work and poverty to smile about, so what was the point?) — thoroughly enjoying her handiwork. The tinsel draped off the tree's branches like silver molasses, and for the briefest moment she had a mind to wrap her hair into a tight ponytail and pull on a pair of kneesocks and lie underneath, see if the magic was still there.

"Well," she said, wiping the corners of her eyes, not even realizing until she made the motion that there was wetness there. She swiped a knuckle past the tip of her nose as well. "I think it's beautiful. A tree all three girls will love." She kept staring at the blue spruce, even as she backed into the front room, and absently reached down and tweaked the stockinged toes of her husband's left foot, perched on the recliner, with a familiarity born of decades of marriage. "Don't you, Robert?"

But Robert didn't answer.

16

She knew he wouldn't.
He was dead.

■ ■ ■ ■

DECEMBER 22

■ ■ ■ ■

"Dear God, he's really gone."

ONE

Claire was the first to arrive.

Not really a surprise to Elise, as Claire was the most . . . unattached. No children, no home to button up for a few days, not even a goldfish to find a sitter for.

To Elise, her youngest daughter seemed to be hopelessly and perpetually fearful of making a commitment. The first sign of anything permanent, be it a kitten or a car loan, and the girl oozed Panic Attack and ran for the hills. Elise tried desperately to assign the fear simply to Claire's age. Twenty-eight was still so young. Though she herself had had two daughters by the time she was twenty-eight, Elise realized that for this generation, twenty-eight was, technically, just barely out of adolescence. At least that's what they said these days. She could only imagine what her own mom would have thought about that — being a teenager while your best childbearing years were slipping away like broken yolk from a cracked egg.

Could be immaturity, could be some sort of unnamed trauma or a faulty gene, but sometimes Elise suspected her daughter's reluctance to grow up could simply be blamed on where she currently lived, which was to say, not in Missouri. Not only not in Missouri, but in California, of all places. California seemed to Elise to always be a great place for young people to go show off their bodies and abuse their hearts, but the Midwest was where *connection* was made. Where *commitment* happened. Ah, but she supposed that making this assumption about a place she'd never even visited was unfair. California could be perfectly respectable. How would she know?

Every so often Elise had the nagging feeling that it was more about the way Claire had been raised. Had Robert permanently bruised her youngest's heart? Was it beyond repair? Elise didn't even want to think about that. It was one thing to bear a child with a faulty gene; it was quite another to take a perfectly healthy gene and ruin it.

Besides, did it really matter now? The girl was nearly thirty. Her father was dead. And even though his death was new, his absence from Claire's life certainly wasn't. The two hadn't spoken in years, ever since that horrible night at the Chuck Wagon. If Claire was still hurting over that, she'd never said as much during one of their monthly check-in phone calls. Though Elise supposed she had taught the girls that being long-suffering was a virtue. Maybe it was her mistake.

Oh, how she didn't want to start counting mistakes. She was sitting on the mother of all mistakes.

Elise's knees shook and for a moment she wasn't sure if the bare-branched crab apple tree near the driveway was swaying or if it was her vision. Dear God, Claire's father was dead. The girl wasn't here for Christmas, or here for a visit. She was here for a funeral. Her father's funeral.

Claire arrived in a taxi, of all things, and Elise watched from the porch as her daughter flung crumpled bills over the seat at the driver's shoulder before tumbling out, carrying a tattered camouflage backpack over one shoulder. She was wearing huge sunglasses, even in the dim winter-afternoon light, and Elise could see how her youngest daughter might often be mistaken for a celebrity when she was home in Los Angeles. Her yellow-blond hair and sharp features were the spitting image of a younger

Robert, with the tininess of Elise's own side of the family, the McClure clan, making her look fragile and feminine. She was button-cute. Adorable. It could perhaps even be said that she was "the beautiful sister," but beautiful in a haphazard way, as if beauty meant nothing to her. An unfair beauty.

In her mind, Elise hopped off the porch step and raced down the gravel path to her daughter, wrapped her arms around Claire's slight shoulders, maybe even squealed a little and let a few tears squeeze out onto her cheek. How many years had it been since Claire had come home? Six? Seven? More than that, even? She didn't want to think about it.

But, for reasons even she couldn't understand, the idea of rushing into her daughter's arms never translated into the actual motion of doing so. Elise leaned forward on her toes with the desire to make it happen, but her arms stayed wrapped tightly around her torso, her hands clutching the sweater she'd draped across her shoulders when she heard the taxi's tires first crunch on the gravel around the bend on the Miller's Creek side, signaling an approach off the main highway to the farmhouse. She watched, coiled and motionless, her lips pulled into a tight line, her eyes squinting against the wind that had begun to blow, as her daughter hoisted the backpack higher on her shoulder and picked her way up the long walk, slow and steady as a well-coached bride, her lithe legs, tan and poking out from beneath a pair of cutoff shorts, pooling into a pair of natty fur boots.

"Jesus, Mom," Claire said a few feet before reaching Elise's perch on the porch, her nose wrinkled. "I forgot about the cow shit."

Elise allowed herself the tiniest grin. "We haven't had livestock here for years," she said, the same defensiveness in her voice that had always been there when Claire complained about country living, about the land that had sustained her family for generations. Which she did often. Other than Tilly, Claire had no use for animals. Or farming. Or living in a town that had only one grocery store and no gay bars.

Claire sniffed the air. "Then it must be the Hennessees'," she said, clomping up to the porch and stopping just in front of her mom. She let the backpack drop to the ground and tilted up her sunglasses-covered face.

This was the part Elise never quite knew what to do with. Claire had always been the demonstrative one, the one always clawing

25

at Elise's belly, always grabbing for her hands, wrapping her whole body around Elise's legs, her eyes needy as a beggar's. And a part of Elise ached to hug her daughter, her limbs absolutely twitching with longing to reach out and pull that child up onto the porch, bury her face in those blond waves. But Elise's own mother had so rarely touched Elise and her brothers, unless it was to set after them with a hastily torn branch or a wooden spoon. And Robert had never so much as patted the girls on the tops of their heads in approval. This just wasn't a huggy family, and that fact felt like a mountain between Elise and her daughter. One she regretted and wished she could go back and change, but it existed just the same. She could no more reach out to Claire than she could fly.

"Cliff Hennessee died three years ago," Elise said instead. "Marie moved up to Kansas City soon after. The young couple that bought their property farm corn. No cattle."

Claire shrugged, turning her head slowly, peering into the sky. "It's infused in the air, then."

Elise nodded. "Could be." But before she could decide what to say next, Claire wrapped herself around her mom, trapping

26

Elise's arms where they were, across her chest, mummy-like. Elise was startled, rigid under her daughter's grasp.

"God, Mom, I can't believe he's gone," Claire breathed into her neck. Not sadly. No tears that Elise could detect. No heaving sobs. Elise wouldn't expect there to be. From anyone.

"I know," she croaked, because she'd had the same thought earlier that day when she'd started to pour his thermos of coffee and had caught herself just as the first drop splashed against the glass inside. Involuntarily, her eyes closed, and once again she felt herself swirling and whirling as if swept inside the bitter, cracking wind, the click of the crab apple branches against one another perhaps instead the sound of her bones breaking, splintering into dust. As if Claire would soon be clutching the sweater and nothing more, her fur boots covered with pieces of her mother.

They stayed like that until the cab had backed down the long driveway and headed toward the Miller's Creek turnoff, leaving nothing but the sound of crunching gravel in its wake, and then Claire abruptly let go. Involuntarily, Elise's hand reached for the wall to steady herself. Her sweater dipped off of her right shoulder and hung loosely across her back.

"It's so damn cold here," Claire said. "And it really does smell like cow shit. Why do people live on farms anyway? Let's go in." But Elise caught a hint of hesitation on her daughter's part — was that a deep breath filling the tiny woman's chest? — just before Claire bent to pick up the backpack. She wondered what memories might flood Claire as she walked into the house for the first time in so long. Was she afraid?

Maybe not. Maybe the hesitation was on Elise's part. Once Claire crossed the threshold of the old farmhouse, would it be just like it had always been? Was Elise counting on that too much? Was she really expecting to see Claire prancing around on a stick pony and stealing bites of divinity out of the bowl Elise had set on one of the end tables this morning? Surely she wasn't expecting something so ridiculously impossible. Robert was gone. And, the way he'd gone, he'd taken so much of her with him. She was ripped with guilt over it, but she simply had to put what had happened out of her mind and get a grip.

"I want a shower," Claire was saying as she jerked open the storm door and disappeared into the entryway. "Longest flight of my life. You know how long a flight from

28

LAX to Kansas City is?" She turned, mugged wickedly at Elise. "Of course you don't. You don't ever leave cow town." She yanked off her sunglasses, her icy blue eyes red-rimmed and bloodshot in the gloom of the front room. Elise really needed to put some brighter lightbulbs in the floor lamp. "Smart woman," Claire added. "A lot of crying babies on that flight. You mind if I shower?"

And with that, Claire had gone, eaten by the shadowy hallways of her childhood home. The storm door had squeaked shut, and Elise was still standing on the other side of it, staring in, bewildered, one arm bare and goose-pimply in the wind. She blinked, shrugged the sweater back up onto her shoulder, and turned to stare out at the road.

Julia would be arriving from Kansas City soon. Maya would be here within hours. All three girls, home together at last. After all that had happened between them. After all that had happened with the whole family. After what had happened with Robert. After what had happened the night of his death that they didn't know about, could never know about. The very thought chilled Elise. Her teeth chattered.

A hawk swooped down across the road,

lighting on top of the orchard gate on the other side. It sat there, silent and stately, not even so much as a muscle twitch as the breeze ruffled its feathers.

The wind pushed an old tire swing lazily back and forth on its rope, and for a crazy second Elise was sure she heard Claire call out to her. Not the mature Claire wearing the oversized Nike sweatshirt and barking about cow shit and long flights and crying babies. The young Claire, her untamed hair springing out from her temples, the gap between her front teeth large enough to push a quarter through.

Mom, she heard. *Watch me, Mom! Look what I can do!*

And Elise's heart caught as she saw that little girl stand atop the tire and shimmy up the rope to the limb above without so much as a pause to breathe.

You be careful, Claire! she heard herself calling back. *You break your arm and your father will have both of our hides.*

A giggle. A leaf dislodged and falling to the ground. A call of *I did it!* And Elise's relief, despite her repeated worried glances over her shoulder to see if her husband had been watching out the front room window.

Yes, you did it, she thought to herself. Claire had always done it, everything she ever put her mind to.

The wind shifted and the empty swing turned a lazy circle, and just like that the little girl was gone. Just like that, the squeals and giggles and monkey-like springing from branch to branch and the pulling of the ticks and the Popsicles were gone. Elise found it almost impossible to believe that the woman with the camouflage backpack was the same girl, even as she knew she'd watched the transformation happen, bit by bit, argument by argument, year by year, until the years, and the child, simply . . . went away.

Maybe it wasn't California that caused her youngest daughter to be so unattached in life. Maybe it wasn't that she was still an adolescent like all those TV psychologists with their ill-formed theories said.

Maybe it was only a matter of Elise not praising Claire for climbing from swing to branch, not telling Claire that a free spirit such as hers was a gift. Not building up her daughters enough, so worried was she about Robert's reaction to anything and everything they did. Maybe it was a matter of not stepping in enough. Or of stepping in too much. Of trapping that free spirit so it more closely matched his ideal. Maybe she had done it, by virtue of not being the mom her daughter needed.

The hawk had soundlessly taken off, and as the wind clacked the branches of the crab apple tree together once again, Elise turned to the front door, wiping a tear from her cheek. Memories would do her no good now. She had a funeral to get ready for.

More important, she had a Christmas to celebrate with her daughters.

Two

Elise was elbow-deep in the linen closet pulling out fresh towels to leave in all the bedrooms when she heard gravel grinding under tires again.

She quickly tugged out an armload of towels, wishing she'd made the extra effort to buy new ones. Maybe crimson and ever-green ones, or towels with little Santas or snowmen or colorful gifts embroidered in festive thread along their hems. A part of her — the irrational, unreasonable part that kept creeping up on her with no warning — worried that not having special Christmas towels would ruin everything. That she would never pull off the beautiful Christmas she wanted with her old yellow and brown towels. But the reasonable part of her, the determined-to-make-this-work part, over-rode her shaking hands, and she shut the linen closet door with her hip, concentrating on the sound of the car as it got closer and closer to the house.

She hurried down the hall, stopping only long enough to drop three towels on Julia's bed — one for each member of Julia's family — and then rushed upstairs to drop off a few in Maya's room, as muffled *whumps* of car doors slamming in the driveway drifted up to her. She realized she had given Maya her best towels, and paused to fold back the corner of the top one pristinely. Maya would appreciate details such as best towels and folded corners. Actually, Maya would *need* those details.

Claire had showered and retreated back to her bedroom to rest and freshen up before her sisters arrived, leaving Elise to wonder what else she'd forgotten besides the towels.

The back door creaked open downstairs. "Hello?" a voice called. "Mom?"

"I'm here! Yes! Hello!" Elise yelled back, heading down the steps toward the kitchen. She entered just in time to see her oldest daughter, Julia, primly set an expensive-looking suitcase on the tile just inside the back door and reach with one hand to pull off a crocheted hat. "You're here!" Elise cried, breathing heavily, excitedly. Now that two of them had arrived, it was starting to feel real — Christmas, Robert's death.

Julia ran her fingertips through her short hair, fluffing it back into place, and then folded up the hat and stowed it in her coat pocket. "Sorry if we're late. Eli had some . . . issues . . ." She shook her head. "Car sickness," she added, but something about the way her usually rich and commanding voice petered out over the word made it sound untrue.

"You're not late at all," Elise said. "Claire's here, but Maya's not yet." She stood awkwardly, gazing at Julia, so tall and lean, her posture not just straight and stiff, but . . . *important.* She might have described her firstborn as "handsome," with her grandpa Mick's sturdy chin and her aunt Nannie's wide forehead. Some days, even when Julia was a child, Elise felt as if she could look at the girl all day long. But standing around doing nothing but gawking at things was not something Elise did often. Instead, she moved toward her daughter, arms outstretched to take her coat. Julia slipped out of it and smoothed the sleeves of her turtleneck, glancing out the back door. "Where are Tai and Eli?" Elise asked.

"Oh. Well," Julia said, pulling out a chair at the table, "Eli's out there checking things over." She gestured toward the door through which she'd just entered. It had once led to

35

a high concrete-slab porch, one where all the cousins would sit, dangle their legs over the edge, and take turns cranking the ice cream barrel. Years ago, Robert had enclosed it, turned it into a sunporch that was more greenhouse. It was stuffy and moist inside, and filled with ferns and palms and — as of yesterday morning, between phone calls and cookies and arrangements with the funeral home — pots and pots of poinsettias decorated with tiny felt cardinals and golden bows. "And Tai stayed behind," Julia continued. "His research project is at a kind of critical stage and . . ." She trailed off, waving her hand dismissively, sinking into the chair and resting her elbows on the kitchen table. Her shoulders appeared abnormally hunched to Elise, and she had the thought that her usually poised daughter looked preoccupied. Maybe even a bit wilted.

"Research?" Elise said, carrying Julia's coat into the front room and hanging it in the closet by the front door, just as she'd done a million times over the girls' lifetimes. Was it her imagination or did the coat, for just the slightest second, turn lavender and sparkly? Was that a little heart appliqué she saw adorning the back of it, and the shadow of a rip in one sleeve where a nail caught it on the monkey bars at school? She shook her head to clear it, wrestled the coat (*Hunter green, Elise. Lands' End. Not a child's coat, for God's sake.*) onto a hanger, and stuffed it in the closet. "He's working during Christmas break?" She shuffled back into the kitchen.

Julia shrugged her wide shoulders, staring out onto the sunporch, and once again Elise thought she saw distraction in her daughter's face. "Life of a professor. It's not a big deal, really. He never knew Dad, and it's just a couple of days."

Elise felt a knot form in her throat and she had to turn away. She had thought everyone would come. She hadn't planned for families to be apart during the holidays.

She walked over to the sink and stretched up on her toes to peer out the window. There, standing with his arms crossed over his chest, staring out at the pasture, was Julia's only son, Eli. "Goodness, he's grown so much just since I saw him last," Elise said.

"Tell me about it," Julia answered, deadpan. "More than you know."

Elise took in the boy's mop of dark hair with the cowlick sticking up in back, his long, knock-kneed legs. "He looks like a little man out there. Just almost exactly like . . ."

Robert.

Elise had fallen for Robert Yancey when he was not much older than her grandson was now.

Quarterback. Glee Club. Youth minister at the little Baptist church on the south side of town — the one Elise's father had always called "the Jesus-save-me hand-raisers." He had dimples. He smelled like fresh-cut mint. He drove a slick car and listened to country music and spit tobacco into paper cups.

He had a hard side, one that was reminiscent of her grandpa Mick, and as the son of a hog farmer himself, he knew farming. Elise found him irresistible, and one year after they met, they were married in that Jesus-save-me-hand-raisers church, Elise in a plain white satin gown feeling queasy and frightened and excited and breathless and in love.

"Like what?" Julia asked, snapping Elise back into reality.

"What?"

"You said he looks almost exactly like . . ."

"Oh," Elise said in a small, faraway voice, touching her collarbone with her fingers lightly, not noticing the concern etching itself on her daughter's face. "Like your father." She offered Julia a feeble smile.

Julia looked out the back door again. "I suppose I can see a resemblance," she said. "I never really thought about it. People always say he looks like me."

"Of course. I'm probably just imagining things," Elise said. "I'm sure I'm seeing the resemblance to you. That makes sense."

But the boy did look like his grandfather. As Eli shifted his weight, dropping his messenger bag on the grass next to his feet and then sinking, cross-legged, onto the ground beside it, Elise was sure she'd sped back in time fifty years and was seeing her Robert going through those same motions.

But Robert was gone, and Elise knew that. She tore her eyes away from Eli, and stared instead over his head at the derelict chicken coop, so long out of use that one wall looked like it might cave in if so much as a leaf fell on it. She'd often thought about fixing it up, having chickens again, seeing if a tidy coop would bring back some of the magic she'd felt as a child on McClure Farm, but looking at that wall made her feel so tired inside, as if she hadn't slept in decades. Maybe she hadn't.

McClure Farm had been in Elise's family for three generations, and had always been an extended-family affair. Every Midwest McClure lived there at one time or another, and it was once a writhing, buzzing hub of auntie and uncle business, cousin encounters, and backbreaking chores, with Elise's grandmother McClure overseeing it all with her tough stare and hard, calloused hands. There was always enough bacon for everyone, always fresh-baked biscuits on the stove, always babies squalling and crawling after grasshoppers through elbow-high patches of clover. But make no mistake — there was also always work to be done.

And, God, that farm — that vibrant, living farm that she'd grown up on — had been gone for so long. Robert had retired, had let everything go to weed, and as with everything else that he'd ruined over the years, she'd simply let it happen, no matter how much it meant to her. How many years had she been pining to get the farm back in running order? How many years had she been miserable? Enough to let the wall of the chicken coop, where she'd spent so many summer mornings gathering the breakfast eggs, a bandanna over her nose and mouth, fall into ruin. Had that been Robert's fault? Or hers? She was having a hard time deciding what was whose fault these days.

"So I was telling Tai that you'll probably want to come stay with us sometimes. He's

40

okay with it," Julia was saying.

Maybe a Barnevelder, Elise thought. Weren't those the ones that laid the dark brown eggs? Or was she thinking of a Jersey Giant? Now, those were some hardy chickens. No matter, but something fancy would be nice. Maybe one of those chickens with the poufy feathers around their heads. What were they called again? Those would delight the grandkids.

"Mom."

Elise startled, whirled so that the small of her back was pressed to the sink.

Julia's eyes were as wide and steady as ever.

"I'm sorry, I was thinking about the chickens," Elise said, trying to sound nonchalant.

"What chickens?"

Elise paused, gathered her thoughts. What chickens, indeed? They were only in her mind and she knew that. Of course she did. She waved her hand. "Nothing. Never mind. I've been distracted lately."

Julia leaned back in her chair, her eyes so enormous that Elise wondered how anyone could not feel her stare from a hundred yards away. Something about that gaze had always made Elise feel small and lacking, even when it was prodding at her from inside a bassinet. "Well, of course you are, Mom. That's why Tai and I think you need to spend some time with us. You don't need all this space to yourself. We can talk about options."

"It's really not that much space."

"It's a hundred acres. All that area behind the tree line? The pond? The fields? You and Dad together were barely able to take care of it as it was. How can you keep up with all of that by yourself?"

Elise set her cup down and pressed her fingers to her temple. "I don't know, Julia. The man's only been dead for a day. I have plans, but no time. There's never time. I don't need people telling me what to do and how to do it. I got enough of that from him." She winced when she heard her own voice, realized the harshness of it. Julia's mouth was frozen open in surprise, and immediately Elise wanted to stuff the words back into her mouth. This visit was supposed to be different, was supposed to be light and loving. She was supposed to be bonding with her daughters, now that she could. She was not going to lose her control.

But . . . she only just needed a few minutes to think about hens. Get her thoughts straight.

"Queenie!" she heard from behind her,

and let out a gust of air as Claire shuffled into the room, yawning and looking puffy with sleep.

Julia's mouth clamped shut and she visibly straightened her spine. "Hello," she said, her voice not altogether warm but not icy, either. Just hesitant.

"God, you look old. Where's your kid?"

"Thank you. So sweet of you to point that out. And *Eli* is outside."

Claire padded to the storm door, her furry boots replaced by woolen socks, and peered outside. "Shit, he got big."

"That's because he's fourteen now."

Claire turned, her face bemused. "It's been that long?"

Julia offered her a condescending smile. "Time flies."

"He just had a birthday a few months ago, you know," Elise said, ladling some steaming wine into three mugs and bringing them to the table. Claire pulled out a chair and plopped into it. Elise settled into her seat at the head of the table.

"That so?" Claire blew across the top of her mug as if she were blowing the heat off a cup of cocoa.

Elise nodded, the conversation deadended, and she wished that she could think of something new to say. Something not

43

volatile. Thing was, she wasn't sure what was not volatile between her daughters anymore. She wondered if they knew anything about chickens.

"And did Maya come to the birthday party?" Claire asked.

"She lives in Chicago," Julia said, as if they didn't already all know this. As if they didn't already have her flight schedule memorized. The very moment she would arrive at the house hung over them like doom. As chilly as things were between Julia and Claire, it was nothing compared to the fracture between Maya and Claire. That fracture was a canyon.

"I just thought . . . ," Claire said, but she sipped her wine rather than continue.

"No, I haven't seen her since before Will was born."

"That would be because she ran away before Will was born."

Julia shot Claire a look. "She didn't run away. Bradley got a job."

"More like Bradley got a sexual harassment suit from whoever he was really boning."

Elise stared, her eyes moving between her two daughters. "Now, nobody knows exactly what —"

"I know exactly what, Mom. Don't get

me started on what." Claire's eyes never left her sister's face, even as she tipped the mug to her lips and sipped.

Julia stood abruptly, her chair rustling against a potted poinsettia. *Maybe I went a little too far with the poinsettias,* Elise thought, and wondered if she could move them around during the night a little, see if she could make it seem less like she was trying too hard when the girls woke up in the morning.

"I really don't want to have this conversation right now," Julia said. She scooped another ladleful of wine into her cup. "My father is dead."

Claire laughed, a single bark. "What a coincidence! So is mine! Or is his death all about you, Queenie? You being the Sister in Charge and all."

But before she could continue, the storm door opened, letting in a whoosh of stale green air, and Eli tromped in on untied high-top-sneakered feet. He tossed his mess of dyed blue-black hair (*quite festive, actually,* Elise thought), revealing one dark, brooding eye that so closely matched his mom's, Elise felt as if she'd been transported back to the 1970s when she looked at him.

Mom, she could hear tiny Julia saying,

those wide eyes brimming with tears, *Daddy won't let me bring in Mr. Claws. It's freezing out there. And he's sick. The coyotes will get him.*

Julia, Elise heard herself say back, *he's an old barn cat. You can't get too attached to those. You know that.* Though Elise had later gone into the barn and cried her eyes out, stroking the cat's fur, covering him with an old quilt, and wishing that just once her husband had let their oldest daughter be led by her heart. Oh, how Elise hated to see those eyes, as impossibly deep as cave pools, spill over once again.

"Eli!" Elise cried, holding out her arms in a weak invitation and taking a few steps forward, but not enough to fully close the gap between them. She hadn't seen her oldest grandchild in what seemed like ages, hadn't held him since he was a little boy. Perhaps it was the hug from Claire, or the emotional drain of losing Robert, or the spirit of Christmas that made her reach for him. All she knew was she wanted to fill her arms with him. Wanted to feel him, young and vibrant and so utterly alive. Wanted to smell his scalp, see if it smelled like Julia's used to when she was his age. And she didn't know exactly how to make that happen.

The boy simply shifted his weight, gazing at the floor, his messenger bag strap looped over one arm, the bag resting on top of his shoe. "Hi," he said, more to the tile than to her, and Elise felt her hands lower slowly, like a white flag of surrender.

"It's so good to see you, honey," she said, and he responded with a soft grunt that might have been a word, but Elise couldn't tell. He swayed uncomfortably, and Elise picked something imaginary off the front of her shirt. "Well . . . ," she said, trailing off, trying to decide what to say next that might break through the invisible barrier that seemed to always spring up between Yancey family members, and bring her grandson into her arms.

But Eli spoke first. "Car's here," he said in a new man-voice, changing the subject and shattering Elise's hopes of a tender reunion moment. She noticed that the hems of his jeans were filthy and had holes, that his T-shirt was threadbare, his chin dotted with pimples, his mouth an uneven scowl.

He had been the baby who was always in a clean bib. The one in tiny designer overalls and expensive baby shoes chewing on the edges of black-and-white flash cards with images of boats and balls and shapes on them. Bred to be as well kept and as brilliant as his mother and father. Now he was a slob. What had happened? Was it simply that he'd become an indifferent teenager, or was there something more?

"Hey, sport," Claire said, ignoring his news. She reached up and tousled his hair; he ducked away from her hand.

"Hey," he responded, and crossed his arms.

"You remember me?"

He shook his head. Elise caught Julia rolling her eyes from across the room, the unspoken question — *why would he?* — floating uncomfortably over the kitchen.

"Ah, well." Claire's smile stuck in place, but her voice got a little tinier, and she seemed unsure how to go on from there.

"Eli," Julia said, "why don't you go out and see if Aunt Maya needs help with her bags?"

"She won't."

"Go see."

"I don't need to."

"I'm asking you to go out anyway." Julia took two steps toward her son and crossed her arms over her chest to match his posture. There was an edge in each of their voices, and both Claire and Elise froze, embarrassed and confused by whatever was passing between the two of them. "Go help your aunt with her bags."

"Mom! God! She's not alone! Uncle Bradley is with her."

All three women stared at one another.

"Fabulous." Claire sighed and pushed away from the table. "My room is calling." She patted Eli's shoulder on her way by, though this time he didn't duck away from her hand. "Thanks for the warning, man."

They could hear the front door bang open and the pounding of Maya's children's feet across the wooden floor in the front room, followed by jubilant cries of "Look! Presents under the tree!"

Claire stopped when she reached Julia, pulled up on her tiptoes, wrapped her arms around her sister, and gave her a quick peck on the cheek. "It really is good to see you, Queenie," she said. "Relax a little. This is gonna be . . ." She shrugged, then sauntered away. "Great! It's gonna be just fucking great!" Her voice echoed from down the hall as she headed toward her room.

Elise felt the corners of her mouth twitch into a nervous grin.

It was going to be . . . something, all right.

THREE

Maya's four-year-old son, Will, was lying on his belly on the floor under the Christmas tree, coloring, as Elise peeked into the den after washing and putting away the dinner dishes. Gray evening light pressed into the corners of the room, and the boy looked cozy and sleepy in his footed pj's, his legs bent upward behind him, lazily kicking the bottom branches of the tree. A soft *clink* sounded with every kick as two ornaments butted against one another.

Nearby, seven-year-old Molly played with Elise's granny's porcelain Nativity set as if the pieces were dolls in a dollhouse. Her tiny, lispy voice singsonged as she moved baby Jesus up onto the thatched roof of the barn, a cow sitting sentry by his side.

Elise smiled. They were good kids. Well behaved. It broke Elise's heart to think of their upbringing being anything like their mom's, filled with difficulty and heartbreak.

But she supposed it probably was. After all that had happened, it was impossible to pretend that things were good between Maya and Bradley. Not that marital problems couldn't be fixed. But there were marital problems, and there were Maya and Bradley, tempestuous as the day was long, beginning the moment they met. Rather than "love at first sight" it seemed to be "distrust at first sight" with the two of them. Elise wasn't sure if she even knew the full extent of what had happened between them, only that it had been big and shattering and had somehow involved Claire.

Of all the unanticipated things that had happened over the past two days, Elise was most surprised to see Bradley standing in her kitchen now. She'd expected Maya, of course, and even the kids, but it was rare that the whole family traveled together. Bradley usually had "business" somewhere. What "business" meant for Bradley depended on whom you asked. And you didn't want to ask Claire.

The family had been too tired from travel to do much talking during dinner. Claire had eaten in silence and then ducked back to her room, Julia and Eli had made small talk, then bundled up and taken a walk to the creek, coming back after everyone had gotten up from the table and slipping into their room silently. Bradley had taken his laptop to the den, and Maya had dumped the kids immediately in the bathtub. Elise had heard them singing and playing while she'd cleared the table.

Which left her the chance for only the most minimal chat with her middle daughter.

How was the flight?

Okay, I suppose. Bradley slept, so it was just me and the kids. Hint of bitterness there.

Been a long time since you were down this way. Bet a lot's changed.

Mmm — yeah, I barely recognized the strip.

We got a Target.

I saw that.

There was nodding of heads, and Maya drank her mug of wine in two long gulps. Elise had stared at her daughter's feet, wondering how someone could travel all day in five-inch heels, and more important, why one would do such a thing.

Though she supposed she knew why. Maya's life would always be about trying too hard. To be beautiful. To be poised. To be thin. To be smart. To be . . . everything Bradley wanted. Why someone would want to try so hard to please such a man was beyond Elise, but she supposed nobody could make sense of how and who they loved. Love just happened, even when it was bad for you. If anyone could understand that, it was Elise.

Everyone but the kids seemed to be turning in early. Nobody was in the kitchen, and the back of the house was still silent. Elise pulled her coat off the hook by the back door and stuffed her feet into the rubber boots she left there year-round, then slipped out through the sunporch. She needed something to do. Something to take the edge off her worries. Something to make the memory of what had happened with Robert go away.

The frozen grass crunched under her shoes as she headed for the little garden shed behind the honeysuckle bushes. In years past, the shed was home to powders and sprays, pesticides and plant food and trowels and hoes and muddied gloves, and its door was constantly open. Seemed like, especially during the summers, Elise was always in the shed, fumbling around for the tool she needed or the right spray or a bucket or watering can. But, like everything else on the farm, in recent years she'd just gotten too tired for the garden, and had barely been inside the shed, much less had a yearning to restock it.

She pushed the door open and, by feel, poured three big scoops from the birdseed barrel into a bucket. She couldn't do anything about the chickens, but she could at the very least feed the wild birds. A walk with a purpose just might do the trick to ease her mind.

She decided to go to the tree line on the north side of the pasture first. Plenty of birdhouses and feeders out there, from back when Robert and the girls went through their woodworking phase. It had been years since she'd checked on those houses, which the girls had nailed, crooked and loose, to the trunks of the trees. Elise wondered if they were even still there, or if time, weather, and the squirrels had destroyed them by now.

Robert had always been good with his hands. Could fix anything, but also had a gentle touch, almost like an artist's. It was one of the things that had attracted her to him. In her mind's eye, she could still see the cowlicked young man standing sheepishly before her, holding out an oiled jewelry box.

Beautiful box for the beautifullest girl in school, he'd said.

"Beautifullest" isn't a word, she'd replied with a giggle, pressing her toes into the

ground to make the wooden swing she was sitting on stop moving.

They oughta invent it, though, he'd said. *Just for you.*

He'd hand-carved that box. Etched an intricate little hummingbird right into the top of it, surrounded by vines and roses and tiny hearts. It looked as if it had taken hours. Hours that he could have spent working on his father's farm or on his forward pass or on his car. But he'd used that time making a box for her. That was probably the moment that Elise first realized that he really did love her. It was the moment she realized it would be safe to marry Robert Yancey.

The memory nearly buckled her legs right in the middle of the old pasture, and she had to stop and put down the bucket of seed, lean over with her hands on her knees.

"Dear God," she moaned, puffs of steam circling her face with each ragged breath. "Dear God, he's really gone." And this time her knees did buckle, as the image of his face filled her mind. The cute boy with the dimples; the red-faced, hard man who called her useless and berated her and never once remembered a Mother's Day; the betrayed man, dead in his recliner at age sixty-seven. It seemed as if they could not possibly all be the same person. Who had he really been? And how did she not know?

She slumped back onto her bottom in the cold grass and gulped as much air as she could squeeze into her lungs. Still, it felt like only teaspoonfuls. The sky swam, gray and burdened with coming snow, and she was sure she saw a birdhouse nailed to a tree just about ten feet in front of her, but damned if she could take a single step toward it . . . or even push herself back up onto her feet.

Maybe it would be better to just freeze here. Maybe that would be easier. After all these years of stoically withstanding that which was so hard, maybe she could just, for once, go with the path of least resistance. Die in the fields, as her own daddy had done.

"Mom?" she heard distantly, but she was still too busy trying to steady her breathing to process exactly where it was coming from. She thought there were maybe some footsteps approaching along with the voice, but in her mind she wasn't sure if they were human footsteps or maybe the footsteps of Lucifer, Uncle Ed's nasty old bull that had scared her so as a child. Wait, no. It couldn't be Lucifer. They'd butchered him decades ago. They'd eaten him, Elise feeling halfway afraid to ingest his meat, for fear it would make her mean, too. *Think, Elise, think. You're really losing it now.*

Then she heard the voice again. "Mom?" And this time it made sense to her — the voice of her middle child, Maya.

With great effort, Elise pushed herself back up to standing. Still the world spun, but at least she could give the impression of having things under control.

Maya caught up to her, running clunkily through the pasture in her high-heeled boots.

"Mom! You okay? Did you fall?"

Elise nodded wearily. "Fine. I was just . . ." She trailed off, unsure how to finish the sentence. Distantly, she felt cold, and she wasn't sure if the words would form even if she willed them to. She took a deep breath, squeezed her eyes shut. "Just feeding the birds," she finally managed.

Maya squinted at the seed bucket at Elise's feet. "At night? On the ground?"

And the question was so ridiculous that things began to snap back into place for Elise. Come back to reality. The sky slowed and then stopped tilting, her lungs opened, her thoughts cleared. She waved her hand dismissively toward the ground. "Old hoof divot," she said. "I thought maybe I'd rolled my ankle in it, but I'm fine." She held one foot up and rotated it for proof.

Maya eyed her, unconvinced. Elise tried a tight laugh.

"Goodness, you girls are all watching me way too closely. It's your father who died, not me." Instantly, she felt guilty for saying it, but Maya looked unfazed. Elise picked up the bucket and tromped toward the tree line, Maya tripping after her in those ridiculous boots and a creamy white ski jacket. "Go back to the house. You're going to get that jacket dirty."

"It's last year's anyway," Maya responded, her breathing labored as she tried to keep up with her mother's stride. "It's the boots that are a problem. Why did I wear heels to the farm?"

"I was wondering the same thing. Really, you can go back now. I'm just going to see if any of your old feeders are still here. Give the birds some seed."

Maya's hand grazed Elise's arm lightly. "No, I want to spend time with you, Mom. Make sure you're okay. You are okay, right? You didn't look okay back there."

Elise stopped, put down the bucket again. "Well, of course I'm okay. Why wouldn't I be?"

Maya rolled her eyes. "You found him.

After. He couldn't have looked good."

Elise's heart threatened to skip a beat again. If only Maya knew the truth. But she pushed the thought away. What was done was done and there was no need to upset everyone. "He looked like himself," she said. "It wasn't gruesome, if that's what you're worried about. He might as well have been watching one of those silly college football games on TV. In fact, he had been, so that's exactly what it looked like." She picked up the bucket again and strode to the first feeder, filling it with fistfuls of seed.

"But he wasn't watching football, Mom. He was dead. Dead is dead. He couldn't have looked good."

"He looked . . ." *shocked, angry,* "peaceful."

Maya huffed impatiently, as if she was displeased at Elise's lack of proper grief. "You were married to the man for forty-seven years. You found him dead in his recliner. That can't have been the most peaceful experience of your life."

Elise whirled around, doing her best to look steady. In her mind she begged her daughter to stop talking about this. To stop making her see Robert's dead face behind her closed eyelids. To stop reminding her of that night, of what really happened. She

59

pasted on a smile. "Maya. He's gone. It's okay. We were prepared to one day say good-bye. Nothing lasts forever. You grew up on a farm. You know this. Things die."

Maya's shoulders slumped. "He wasn't a sick goose, for God's sake."

"I know that. You think I don't know that?" Elise ducked under a low-lying branch and found the second feeder. It was missing the pegs for the birds to stand on, so she just scattered some seed on the ground underneath instead, the seed rattling as it hit the layer of dead leaves below the tree. "I know you and your sisters are worried. But I'm fine. Really, I am. You make a life with someone, you prepare for this day. You'll see. Someday you and Bradley will be old and you'll start to prepare yourself for the possibility of his death." She tapped her finger on her temple. "Mentally."

Maya made a short snorting sound. "If we make it that long," she mumbled. "Which is doubtful."

Together, they wandered along the tree line, Elise peering into the thicket for the third feeder, which seemed to be gone. She felt better, almost as if she'd talked herself into feeling better by assuring Maya that she was much finer than she really was. The shaking in her knees was gone, and her lungs seemed to have opened up. She let her body go on outdoor autopilot, the tip of her nose numb from the wind, her hands red and chapped and gritty from running them through the seed, the crow's-feet at her temples collecting water from her eyes. This was what she knew best. As long as she could still do this, still work the farm as best she could, maybe she would be okay after all.

"Are there still problems?" she finally asked, glad for the change of subject.

Maya shrugged. Her pace was uneven; they were too near the creek and the heels of her boots kept sinking into the softer ground. Ruining them, surely. "I honestly just . . . I don't know. It's complicated."

"I was surprised to see him here."

"He refused to stay home alone with the kids. That's his new thing. There it is." Maya pointed to an old oak set a few trees back into the woods. Stuck to the side of it was the third feeder, looking as good as new. They walked over and began filling it, both of them taking turns with the fistfuls of seed. "I made this one," Maya said. "Dad yelled at me for wasting nails." She gave another of those sardonic snort-laughs, and Elise wondered if this, too, was part of Maya's Chicago Perfection Persona — the guttural, dysthymic chuckle. "He could be such an asshole. Is it a sin to say that?"

Elise blinked. "Your father? Or Bradley?"

And this time Maya really did laugh out loud, the laugh Elise remembered from her childhood — not that snorty laugh that sounded as if she were poking fun at a servant. "Both, I suppose."

There were just a few handfuls of seed left in the bucket now. They took turns sprinkling it along the ground, until finally the bucket was empty.

"Anyway, he refuses to stay home alone with the kids," Maya continued as they headed back toward the house. "Says he 'didn't go to graduate school to be a god-damn babysitter.' " She made air quotes with her fingers while she talked, her voice going low and taking on a buffoonish quality. "As if they aren't even his kids. I keep telling him it's not babysitting if they're your own children, but he doesn't listen. He's too self-absorbed to listen to anyone but himself. So he wouldn't stay with them, and I've been . . . under the weather, I guess . . . so I didn't want to travel all the way here with them by myself."

"You've been sick?"

"It's nothing. I'm taking care of it." Maya flicked her hand, then tucked it into her armpit. To Elise, she looked as if she were hugging herself, protecting herself, her dismissal flat and not believable. But before Elise could follow up, Maya continued. "And . . . so . . . Bradley is here. With . . ."

"With his family, where he belongs. It is Christmas."

"No, I was going to say 'with Claire.' "

Elise stopped walking. Of course she'd known this was going to come up, sooner rather than later. "Have you talked to her?"

Maya shook her head, her iron-straightened hair whipping around her face like filament. Elise noticed that despite the long day her daughter still had makeup in place. *My God, how exhausting that must be,* she thought. "She was still in her room. Though . . . you never know. Maybe he's seen her. Maybe he's in there with her right now."

"Oh, Maya," Elise said softly. "You don't still think . . ."

"Of course I do. I've never had any reason not to."

Elise grabbed her daughter's hand and began walking toward the house again. "She said it never happened. She swore to you. She's your sister. That's a reason not to, don't you think?"

"But he never denied it. And Claire has

63

sworn a lot of lies over the years."

Elise nodded patiently. "Always little lies. Nothing this big. Besides, even if she did, it's been so many years." She stepped over a large limb that had fallen off the plum tree during the last snow. It would make good firewood, but that had always been Robert's job. Elise wasn't even sure she'd be able to lift it by herself. But fortunately that was not something she needed to worry about right now. "You forgave Bradley."

This time Maya stopped abruptly, her hand leaving Elise's. Her cheeks were pink, whether with fury or cold Elise couldn't be sure. "Mom, I will never forgive her. You don't sleep with your sister's husband and just . . . expect forgiveness." She raised a manicured nail, pointed it at the house as if she were pointing to her sister. "Now, I will make nice for the next few days until we get Dad buried, but then she's back to not even existing in my world. Please don't ask me to accept her. Please. Queenie understands and you need to, too. Claire is not my sister. She lost that right eight years ago. She will never get it back."

"Maya, it's Christmas," Elise said, standing there, clutching the empty bucket in front of her.

"I know. I'm sorry. But it's not like we've

ever had a happy little family Christmas anyway," Maya answered. "I need to check on the kids." She turned on her heel and strutted off toward the house in those ridiculous boots, both arms crossed over her chest, her cocoa-colored hair fluttering beautifully against her jacket. Such perfection. Such torment. Elise could not see how you could separate the two when it came to that woman.

Elise considered calling after her, but decided against it. What would she say? Just as Maya had no proof that Claire had been lying, neither did Elise have any that Claire had been telling the truth. Would she like to say she absolutely disbelieved that her younger daughter would do anything so terrible to her older sister? Yes, of course. But eight years ago was such a tumultuous time for Claire. Especially that particular day eight years ago. That day was the worst. The last day Claire ever spoke to her father or her sisters, as far as Elise knew.

The day Maya found . . . Oh, poor Maya.

Elise had thought she would never live through the weeping and the screaming and the threats and the beseeching to take a side, any side, but she found that if she simply stuck with her usual silent poise, eventually everything would calm down.

She was hardly a pillar of strength at the time herself. She knew nothing about healthy marriages. And she felt like an utter failure over raising a daughter who would steal another daughter's new husband. It just didn't even seem possible. Surely there was a lesson she hadn't imparted, a moral she hadn't spoken.

Maya and Claire were at war. They vowed never to speak to each other again — Maya out of betrayal and Claire out of disbelief that her sister would distrust her so — and poor Julia, not sure whose side to take, vowed silence as well, just to stay out of it. She had marriage problems of her own to deal with, and a six-year-old little boy caught between two fighting parents like a pasture fence trembling with the effort to stay dug in during a tornado.

As far as Elise knew, that silence had mostly stuck. Claire packed a garbage bag full of clothes and slipped off to California. Bradley took a job in Chicago, where, cut off from family and everything familiar, Maya had no choice but to forgive him. And Julia lived her own separate hell up in Kansas City, leaving Elise to contend with Robert and all that achingly empty space in the house by herself.

And now they were all back. They were

under the same roof. They would be here for days.

And most important . . . their silence would be forced to be broken.

ATTEMPTS — I

The clock in his bedroom had the loudest tick he'd ever heard. Even if he'd wanted to sleep, there was no way he ever could. It was so quiet in the country — every little bump and noise and creak sounded like a bomb dropping.

Not that he really wanted to sleep here at all. He didn't even want to be here. He didn't have any great Christmas plans or anything, but just sitting at home watching old reruns of that Charlie Brown Christmas show alone would be better than this. This house was hot. And crowded. And he didn't know anyone, and they were all crammed around the kitchen table all the time and were all mad at each other. Stupid. Seriously, everyone tried to tell you that when you grew up, things got better, but as far as he could see, adults were no less likely to get dumb in an argument than kids were.

He turned over, his cot squeaking loudly

against the silent midnight, and stared out the window, the moon spotted by the filmy polka-dot curtain. He was pretty sure everyone else was asleep by now, but his eyes felt pried open by an unseen force. His mind felt electric, like it would never turn off. He could hear his mom's soft breathing over in her bed. She was turned away from him. The dotted moon-light fell across her like a second blanket.

After a while, he turned over again, and then again. And then, with a sigh, sat up and slipped out of his cot and padded down the hallway in his socks.

The hallway spilled into the front room, the room where his grandfather had died. Right there in the recliner. He reached out and slid his hand along the arm of the chair, touching the rough upholstery with his fingers. A death chair. The very thought excited him.

Slowly, carefully, without making any sound, he slid into the chair, easing back into it luxuriously. Every nerve in his body felt every bump of the fabric. It was like being on a drug — a death drug. It was the best thing he'd felt in a long time. Maybe for as long as he could remember.

He started to consider all the things he could do in this chair. All the things he could do, period. All the ways he could accomplish exactly what he wanted to accomplish. He pulled a pocketknife he'd found in the top drawer of the bedroom bureau, small but sharp, out of the waistband of his pajamas and unfolded it, taking in the gleam of the blade in the moonlit room.

But no sooner had he held the knife up than he heard a noise. He stiffened, every muscle tensing, ears straining to hear if it was just another pop of the house settling, or something more.

Creak, creak, creak.

Footsteps. It was definitely footsteps. Treading carefully down the hallway. Quickly, he closed the knife and stashed it back in his waistband. His heart pounded as he listened for more, sitting straight as a spike in the chair, hands clamped on the arms as if they would protect him.

Creak, creak, creak.

The steps moved closer and then turned toward the kitchen. He let out a shaky breath, as slowly as possible, and listened as the steps turned to the rustling of a coat and the whine of the back door opening onto the sunporch. And then a light click as it shut.

Gulping, trembling, he bolted out of the chair and, taking as much care as he could, raced back toward his room, plunging the knife under the cot mattress where he'd hidden it earlier in the afternoon.

His mom stirred and rolled over when he dove back onto his cot, but he simply flung the blanket over himself and closed his eyes, feigning sleep, feeling certain that his heartbeat could be heard across the room.

But the clock kept ticking. The night settled back around him. He calmed and even began to doze a little, the adrenaline rush subsiding and soothing his system. He began wondering who he'd heard. Who was wandering around outside this late at night? And why?

He tumbled into sleep. He didn't hear the second set of footsteps pass his bedroom and slip out the back door.

■ ■ ■ ■

DECEMBER 23

■ ■ ■ ■

"You can't take every
little threat seriously."

FOUR

Julia's hands shook as she fumbled in her coat pocket. She supposed she could blame the shakiness on the cold — it felt absolutely subarctic out here, especially when the wind zipped tiny pellets of ice around the garage corner and up against her face — but she knew her jitters had far more to do with the phone conversation she'd just had with her ex-husband.

Talking to Dusty always put Julia on edge, especially when his belligerent second wife, Shurn, listened in on the other line (okay, her name was technically Sharon, but the way she said it, with that masculine bravado, as if she was always talking around a mouthful of chaw, made Julia and Tai take to calling her "Shurn" behind her back instead). Why, in the name of God, had Dusty chosen such an uneducated, unrefined woman? Even after all these years, Julia still felt insulted that he would go from her, with her degree from Brown, a college professor, for God's sake, to . . . to that . . . *Shurn*.

But tonight's phone call had Julia particularly jumpy. This was no Who's Going to Take Eli to Practice sort of phone call. This was Important Stuff. This was capital-letters Co-Parenting. This was a cry for help to the one man who knew Eli as well as she did. And the one man who cared enough to respond.

Oh, not that Tai didn't care. Of course he did. But Eli was Tai's stepson, not his real son. He couldn't claim Eli's brown eyes or the way he walked on the outer edges of his feet or his natural propensity for algebra. He couldn't remember the day Eli was born. Plus, Tai never was all that into children. Always said he had enough children as it was, referring to his chemistry students. And Julia had been all right with that. She didn't need someone who was going to vie for Eli's affections, who would make things even more difficult between her and Dusty. Dusty had been a horrible husband. But he was a good father, and part of her reason for marrying Tai was that she knew he would never try to take that title away from Dusty.

But right now . . . Eli really could use as many fathers as he could get, and a part of

Julia wished Tai could see that.

Another gust of wind razed her face, and she turned toward the garage just as she finally wrapped her fingers around the cigarette pack she'd been hunting. She pulled it out and plucked a cigarette from it, tucking it into her mouth and digging back into her pocket for a light.

"That shit'll kill you." She turned, her heart leaping, to find Claire coming down the steps toward her. Claire sidled up next to her sister, her hands pressed deep into her coat pockets — a coat she'd borrowed from Elise — her face shadowed by the hood, which was ringed with woolly black fur. "I'm talking about standing out in the cold, not the smokes. I forgot how fucking freezing it was here."

Julia lit her cigarette and took a drag, closing her eyes and letting the nicotine give her limbs a relaxed buzz. She turned and leaned back against the garage door. "Want one?"

"Of course."

Julia held out the crumpled pack and shook it until a cigarette wiggled halfway out of the torn opening. Claire reached over and took it, then let Julia light it. She dragged, the cherry burning bright, and leaned against the door next to Julia.

"Why are you wearing shorts?" Julia asked, glancing at her sister.

"The question is, why aren't you?" Claire shot back. She blew out smoke and then added, "I haven't owned a pair of pants in three years."

Julia chuckled. "You have always been a strange nut, Claire." She flicked the dead ash off the end of her cigarette and rubbed it into the concrete with her boot. "You've seriously never had a need for a pair of pants in three years? Not one event?"

"Seriously no. And any event that would require them would not require me."

Julia tipped her face up to the sky. "Bet you own plenty of wet suits, though," she said.

"Only one, actually. For Casual Friday."

"I thought you were a waitress."

"Hey, I wear a uniform," Claire answered, feigning defensiveness.

"And I bet your surf board matches your wet suit," Julia teased.

Claire cocked an eyebrow. "What makes you think I own a surf board?"

Julia shrugged. "You're a Californian. You all own surf boards."

"Oh, that. And we all Rollerblade in bikinis and march in gay rights parades on the weekends too," Claire said, deadpan.

"And we all vote Democrat."

"Exactly."

They glanced at each other and snickered. "Okay," Claire said. "One surf board. For the weekends. But it doesn't match my wet suit. Not on purpose, anyway. I'm a terrible surfer."

"I knew it." Julia grinned.

"So why are you hiding out here in the cold?" Claire asked. "Dad is dead. It's not like he's going to bitch about the cigarettes anymore."

"Mmm. I promised Tai and Eli that I'd quit smoking."

"Ah. Hiding from the kid."

"Eli."

"What?"

"He's got a name. Not *kid*. Eli."

"Eli. Sheesh. Touchy about his name, Queenie."

Julia thought about it; Claire was right. She hadn't meant anything bad by calling him "kid." She knew no more about parenting, or children, than she did about the physics that Julia taught at the university every day. Just like Julia didn't know beans about surfing or rafting or whatever it was her sister did out there on the coast. "You're right," she said. "Sorry."

The two women dragged on their cigarettes again. "No problem," Claire finally said. "It's not like you accused me of sleeping with your husband or anything."

Over the whistling of the wind, Julia heard Claire chuckle from within the depths of her hood. And something about it made her chuckle too. Nervousness. There was still all this nervousness. First, Dad dying. Then having to be in this house with Mom and the sisters, and then, of all things, Bradley had to show up. And then the phone call to Dusty. She was lucky she wasn't cackling like a lunatic.

"So have you talked to Maya yet?" Julia asked.

"You mean has she given me a chance to talk to her? Nope. You saw how she was at breakfast. I'm like a ghost. She won't make eye contact."

Julia had seen it, actually. Had seen how Maya wouldn't even look in Claire's direction. How she'd suddenly found things to fiddle with on her kids — cutting their food into pieces, straightening their collars, folding napkins into their laps, topping off their milk — every time Claire had spoken. How she'd inched around her sister at the sink, the stove, the table. And how she'd kept her eyes solidly glued to Bradley the entire time, as if his every move were being recorded in her brain. God help him if his gaze should accidentally land near Claire. Julia hated to think what would happen then.

"You think she'll ever come around?" Julia asked. She took a long last drag on her cigarette and tamped it out on the heel of her boot, stowing the butt in her coat pocket and then scuffing her boot along the driveway a few times.

"Hell, no. I think she can't wait to get back to Chicago, away from me." Claire finished her cigarette too, but in Claire style, she flicked the butt end over glowing end onto the driveway, where it landed with a starburst of ashes in the gravel. She wrapped her arms around herself. "It's too damn cold out here even for a good smoke."

Julia looked down. "Of course you're cold. You're in cutoffs." She chuckled. "But your legs look fabulous."

Claire laughed, pointing the toe of one boot and swiveling her leg to show off her calf. "You think? I do run, you know. On the beach." Her voice was lavish, with a tinge of a purr to it.

"Well, la-ti-da," Julia teased, relishing the light moment with her sister. She vaguely remembered such moments from long ago. Too long ago. Moments when, to her delighted surprise, she and Claire connected.

Julia admired her littlest sister. Claire had something that she and Maya didn't. A certain playfulness. A laid-back attitude that Julia envied. Hell, she had the ability to move eighteen hundred miles away, alone, and never look back. She had the guts to do what she'd done at the Chuck Wagon eight years ago. The woman had balls. "Some of us don't have beaches to run on, Miss Hollywood."

"You have plenty of cow shit to dodge, though. Could improve your agility."

"I live in the suburbs now, thank you very much. We dodge minivans."

The two sisters stood by the garage door and laughed. Julia's fingers absently rubbed her coat pocket, feeling the bump of the cigarette pack inside, feeling an urgency that didn't really register anywhere else. Distantly she recalled the phone conversation with Dusty, and felt a pang in her gut that stripped away her smile.

Another squall of wind shrieked past them, almost through them, and they both tucked their chins down into the collars of their coats, squinting against the assault. Claire cussed and pushed away from the garage door and headed back up the steps toward the house, and Julia silently cursed the wind that had ruined whatever it was she and Claire had been experiencing just then. Eight years with no communication — surely there was something that would keep them talking. Hell, she'd talked to Dusty (and, in the background, Shurn) for thirty full minutes. Surely she could communicate with her sister for longer than the amount of time it took to burn one cigarette.

Desperate, without even thinking, she blurted, "Eli tried to commit suicide."

Claire stopped abruptly and turned. She flipped down the hood of her coat and Julia could see the shocked expression on her face. She suddenly felt embarrassed, exposed. She was the together sister. The brain. The professor. Admitting Eli's suicide attempt was like admitting failure. Up to this point, she'd barely admitted it to herself.

"Well, he didn't actually *try* try. But he was going to. I found . . . I found pills. He'd apparently been stealing and stockpiling from . . . God knows where."

"Oh, my God, Julia. Does Mom know this?"

Julia shook her head, simultaneously letting her now shaking hand snake back into her pocket and fish out the cigarettes again. She tapped one out and popped it into her mouth, then offered another one to Claire, who took it. "I haven't told anyone yet. Not even Tai. Just today I called Dusty. That's why I'm out here smoking these damn things. I needed . . . I don't know. To think. To relax."

"What did Dusty say?"

Julia shrugged. "He said a lot." Mainly that Julia was a horrible mother who was more worried about her career than her one and only son and how did she possibly think that the kid was going to grow up with no emotional problems the way she practically stole him from his father and tried to make the kid think that some . . . in his oh-so-eloquent Dusty-words . . . *some slant-eye science nerd* was his real daddy when he knew it wasn't the truth. Also that she was probably . . . how did he put it? . . . *one of them high-society rich suburban drug addicts who thinks prescription pills make them sexy and in style* and that was where Eli got the idea. Oh, and when she'd told him this had happened two months ago (it truly had taken her that long to get over the shock and the grief and work up the nerve to call him) and she hadn't taken Eli to a psychologist (Yet! Yet. She was going to. She was.), he'd really lit into her. She took a drag off her cigarette and blew the smoke out in a breathy burst. "He said he'll see me in court. He wants custody."

Claire's blue eyes swam over Julia's face. "No fucking way," she said, letting her cigarette burn down to the filter without bothering to drag on it at all. "Well, he can't. Surely he can't. I mean, the kid . . . Eli . . . is, like, fourteen. Dusty can't just rip him away from his mom after all these years."

Julia shrugged again, feeling shaky all over. The truth was, she wasn't sure Dusty didn't have a point about her. She wasn't sure she hadn't screwed Eli up. She wasn't sure Dusty wouldn't be successful in ripping Eli away. And she wasn't sure it wouldn't be best for her son if he did.

The numbing buzz of the nicotine combined with the horror of having revealed Eli's secret — to Claire, of all people! Not to her mom, her best friend, not even her husband, but to the sister who'd single-handedly wrecked her family eight years ago — was setting in.

"I don't know. Maybe he's right. I'm a bad mom, I don't even know my son, and he's suicidal and I suspected nothing. You know how I found the pills?"

Claire shook her head.

"I was looking for my car keys. I was yelling at him because I was late for my eight o'clock class and I couldn't find my damn car keys and was blaming him for it. I shook out his backpack and there they were." She took a deep breath, partly for effect, but also partly to steel herself for admitting the horrifying truth. "He told me later that he had been planning to do it in the school bathroom *that day.*"

Julia flashed back to the scene, of turning the whole house upside down looking for those keys. Screaming at Eli, pontificating about how she doesn't "just misplace things" and how he is always, *always* getting into her belongings without permission. God, she could lecture almost better than her father could. And the poor kid, still in his boxers with sleep-funk hair, his body peach-fuzzy and immature, stood in the kitchen doorway and watched her. Listened to her. Took the lecture. Just took it. Never argued. Never defended himself. *Why don't you fight back?* she'd felt like yelling at him, but she supposed she knew the answer. She'd been lecturing him for fourteen years; he'd probably learned that arguing only led to more lecturing.

And then she'd dumped out the backpack and found the plastic bag full of pills. And the whole world had seemed to stop. She'd even heard the kitchen clock ticking in the background. She wasn't sure if she'd breathed. She was afraid to look up, to let her eyes meet her son's eyes. Acknowledging what she'd just found would mean she would have to accept what it meant for her family.

She told Claire how she'd remembered about her class, and that her job was the only thing that made sense to her at that moment, so she had simply palmed the bag, stuffed it in her pocket, and barked out a gruff "You're late for school." She hadn't even talked to him about it until two days later over take-out Chinese, when he'd confessed to her what the pills were intended for, what he'd been planning.

And the keys had been in her laptop bag the whole time.

"Well, thank God you found them," Claire said. "The pills, I mean, not the keys. Has he . . . ?"

Julia shook her head again. "No, he hasn't tried anything else. But now that I know about it, he . . . you know, I realize he says it a lot. And has been for a long time. 'I hate my life. I'd be better off dead. I should be dead right now. Tomorrow I won't be here anymore.' That kind of thing."

"Jesus, why isn't he in a hospital right now? I mean, he's seeing a shrink, right?

87

You've got him on antidepressants? You've got to take that shit seriously, Queenie." Claire tossed her untouched cigarette out near the first one, where it smoldered in the wind until the tiny pellets of icy snow tamped it out.

"I do take it seriously," Julia snapped, taking one last, long, shaky drag off her cigarette and snuffing it out on the bottom of her shoe like the first. "But . . . how was I supposed to know what to do? I have my students, and Tai and . . . and then Dad died, and I . . . I don't know, I thought this might be my chance to reach him. Get us alone, just the two of us. Talk a little. Show him what my life was like growing up. Get him away from the pressures of school and . . ." She rubbed her face with her palms. "God, I don't know! It's just not as easy as that. Kids aren't as easy as that. You can't just put a bandage on this and wait for it to go away."

Claire was silent for a minute, then put up her hood as if in thought. "Is he going to be okay?"

"I think so. I hope so. I don't know."

"You want me to talk to him?"

Julia looked horror-stricken. "No. Absolutely not. I don't need him thinking I'm telling the whole world about this. He doesn't even know you." She let out a breathy laugh toward the sky. "I don't even know why I told you."

"Because I'm your sister?"

"Maybe. Or maybe because I figured you might know something about suicide."

Claire let out a dry, humorless laugh. "Can't say I do, Queenie. I'm fucked up in a lot of ways. But I like life. I'm all about the breathing."

Julia couldn't pinpoint why, but for some reason this surprised her. She'd always assumed Claire's life was miserable. That Claire was lonely and barely hanging on. Maybe that was what she'd needed to believe. "And please don't tell anyone else. I'm going to deal with this. I am."

Claire nodded slowly. "Okay. You got it. But if he starts eyeballing Dad's shotgun cabinet or something, I can't make any guarantees."

Julia's eyes widened. "Oh, God," she moaned. She leaned over and put her hands on her knees, hanging her head miserably.

Tentatively, Claire reached out and rested a hand on her sister's back. Distantly, Julia realized this was the first time her sister had touched her in . . . a decade, at least. After a second of thought, Claire started rubbing between Julia's shoulder blades, nervously, almost apologetically, and Julia leaned into it, surprised by how comforting it felt. "Hey. Queenie. Julia. He'll be okay."

The wind roared through again, and both of them stiffened against it, Claire squinching her eyes shut and Julia hunching her shoulders. Claire's curly hair seemed to stick straight out to the side. Finally, Julia straightened up and swiped her coat sleeve across her eyes. She took a deep, snotty breath. "I hope you're right, Claire."

"Can we go in now?" Claire asked, blinking against the sleet, which had begun to pelt them anew.

Julia felt her coat pocket again, considered another cigarette, knowing that if smoking was bad for her, smoking outside in a blizzard probably somehow made it even worse.

It was just . . . she didn't feel ready to face everyone inside again. Didn't want to wonder if anyone had overheard her conversation with Dusty. If anyone had picked up that something was off with Eli. Didn't want to turn her guilty face to them, dare them to figure out that something was going on.

Not to mention the Maya/Claire/Bradley drama. That had gotten old eight years ago. And after her conversation with Claire, Julia wasn't sure where her allegiance should lie. Claire had always maintained her innocence. But Maya was nothing if not resolute in her decisions. The girl could hold a damn grudge, that was for sure. Even if she was the one in the wrong.

Over the course of their sisterhood, Julia had always sided with Maya over Claire. Mostly because that was how it had always been: Maya and Julia versus Claire. Maya was smart, sharp, driven, just like Julia. They played the same games when they were little. They had similar aspirations. They protected each other from their father. They both wanted that protection.

But Claire. Artistic Claire. Head-in-the-clouds Claire, who couldn't care less if her jeans were ripped and who preferred her clothes to come from a thrift store. Claire, who jumped off the barn roof because she wanted to prove that girls could, who swam in the pond all alone at night, who always did exactly the opposite of what their mom told them to do. Claire, who never needed protection, because she always protected herself.

How was Julia to relate to that?

And why did she suddenly, now that she had a son she didn't understand, feel like Claire could understand him?

She took a deep breath, smiled, steeled herself. "Yeah, let's. It's cold out here."

"Mom's got more wine on the stove," Claire said, leading the way to the steps. She turned. "She seem okay to you?"

Julia blinked. "Mom? I guess. Her husband just died."

"I know," Claire said. "But this Christmas thing . . . seems like she's trying really hard, you know? All the wine, the cookies, the tree. Did you get a load of how many poinsettias are on the sunporch? The woman's gone Christmas crazy."

Julia shrugged. Her own house didn't look all that different from Elise's right now. Well, except that Tai would probably be working well into the night, like always, and wouldn't bother to look up out of his research notes and syllabi long enough to turn on the timer. Nothing uglier than unlit Christmas lights, in Julia's opinion, but Tai was oblivious to things like beauty.

"It's because of the grandkids," she said. "She probably didn't want them to spend the days before Christmas with the place all funeral-depressing. You know how proper Mom can be. Even in a tragedy."

Claire chewed her bottom lip. "I guess," she said. And she turned and led the way up the steps toward the sunporch, which enveloped them both with its sticky warmth, the heavy scent of poinsettias pounding into the backs of their throats like exclamation marks.

FIVE

Everyone was gathered in the kitchen by the time Julia and Claire ducked inside. Maya and Bradley were seated at the table, flanked by the kids, who had small piles of snack crackers scattered in front of them. Will was pushing crackers into his mouth, singing and chewing at the same time. Molly ate them daintily, swinging her legs under the table, every now and then pausing to glance up at the adults.

Elise was standing at the stove, stirring a pot of something Julia couldn't see from her vantage point, her back to the table. Eli was standing in the doorway, his arms crossed, his hair flopped over his forehead. Nobody was talking.

"Wow, so serious in here. Who died?" Claire joked, and when Maya rolled her eyes and sighed, she blushed deeply. "Joke. Just a joke," she said, but her voice was small, as if even she realized she'd crossed a line into poor form. She walked up behind Elise and draped an arm over her mom's shoulder. "Sorry, Mom. It was a bad joke."

Elise looked up, a forced smile on her face. "It's okay, Claire," she said, and continued stirring whatever was steaming in the pot.

Julia shrugged out of her coat, careful not to spill the cigarette pack onto the floor, and hung it on the hook next to the back door. She rubbed her dry, reddened hands together and looked from face to face. Something was clearly up.

"What's going on?" she asked.

Bradley leaned to one side and pulled his BlackBerry out of his pocket, began tapping on it. Maya simply stared at the table, spinning a glass of water between her fingers and shaking her head disgustedly, a sardonic grin on her face as if her whole shitty life was one big poorly told joke and she'd just discovered the punch line.

Julia moved to the stove and ladled herself a cup of wine, peering into the saucepan that her mom was stirring. Apples in butter and sugar and cinnamon. Her grandmother's dumpling batter on the counter next to her. She was going to make Granny's version of apple dumplings, just as she'd done for them when they were children. The smell took Julia back.

Mom, that smells like Christmas, she heard her tiny self saying. *I could eat it every day.*

But if I made apple dumplings every day, they wouldn't be special on Christmas, she remembered her mom saying.

She also remembered her mom flicking worried glances over her shoulder at the front door. Elise had always waited until their father was at the lodge Christmas party to make the dumplings. *Our little secret,* she'd told the girls every year. *A girls-only secret.*

But somewhere along the line Julia had figured out the real secret: that her father didn't like anything that might "spoil those girls," that apple dumplings fell into the category of unacceptable indulgence, that Elise would have to deal with the repercussions of an unfair and unkind man if she dared to serve them some, even at Christmas. It didn't matter what her mother wanted for them — if he disagreed, they'd better comply. Or deal with the consequences.

"Done," Bradley said, jolting her out of her memory. He held up his BlackBerry and waved it in Maya's direction. "Not a problem." He offered her a sickly smile, but she only pulled a gooey chunk of snack cracker out of Molly's hair and went back to glaring at the table.

Julia took a sip of wine. "What's done?" she asked. She turned to Elise again. "Mom? What's going on? Why's everyone so quiet?"

Elise tapped the wooden spoon against the side of the saucepan and laid it carefully on the spoon rest on the counter next to the stove.

"It's the funeral," she said, wiping her hands on her apron.

"What about it?" Claire asked. She was still in her coat, the hood still up and framing her face, tufts of her wild hair sticking out.

"It's been moved."

"Oh," Julia said. "Okay. What time?"

Her mom took a breath and turned to face the kitchen, pressing her hands against the counter behind her. "Same time. On the twenty-seventh."

Julia gulped her wine in surprise, then let out a cough. "Twenty-seventh? Why?"

Elise shrugged. "Joe Dale had a family emergency up in Cameron. He can't be here to bury anyone until the twenty-seventh. Nothing to be done about it."

"What do you mean, 'nothing to be done'?" Julia said. "Can't someone else take his place? One of his sons?"

Elise knit her brow. "Robert was friends with Joe. He wouldn't want someone else to bury him. And Joe would want to be there."

"But, God, Mom, that's six days after he died," Claire said. "Won't he be all gross and bloated and rotting and shit?"

Will laughed and Molly stared wide-eyed. "For God's sake, Claire, a little filtering would go a long way," Maya muttered, covering Molly's ears with her hands. "Not to mention a little sensitivity. But I guess you never were very good at that." For the first time since arriving, Maya met Claire's eyes, her glare wicked.

"Maya . . . ," Julia said, though she didn't know what to say next. The last thing she needed was for one of her sisters to be on her case, especially given what she was already going through with Eli. Thinking of her son, she edged over next to him and put her arm around him. He ducked one of his shoulders toward the floor, causing her arm to slide off. She bit her lip, hoping nobody else saw that, trying not to take it personally. Trying not to notice that once again her son was too far away for her to reach, even when he was in the same room with her. Once again she had no idea how long it had been this way or how to even try to find him.

"It's a valid question," Claire said, her voice going high and squeaky just like it always did when she was maintaining her innocence. "How can they keep a body fresh for seven days before burying it? Won't it start to . . . decompose?"

"Grandpa's gonna be rotted? Like a zombie?" Will said around his crackers, and Maya shushed him.

"No. Aunt Claire is just being rude," she said, and again sent a glare across the room. "As usual. Can you at least try to have some respect for the children in the room?"

"Maya." This time it was Bradley's voice that cut through the air, soft and unsure, gently chastising.

Time ticked by, the only sound Elise's apple mixture bubbling in the pan, and for a moment Julia felt, actually felt, hate slither past her like a rolling fog. Were she still a child, she might have said, "Uuummm," like they always did when someone said or did something that might get them in trouble. That was what the room felt like — one big collective *uuummm*.

Then the silence was broken as Maya's chair scraped backward on the tile. "Of course," she muttered through gritted teeth. "I should have expected." She stood so abruptly that the chair knocked over another potted poinsettia behind it, the dirt spilling out onto the tile.

"Here we go," Claire mumbled, scratching her head. She continued in a loud, bored voice. "We are not sleeping together. I've never seen him naked. I don't want to have sex with your husband. I never did."

"Claire!" Elise hissed. "The children!"

"No, please, Mom. Let her make an ass of herself, just like always. If she says it enough times, maybe it will actually be true." Maya stormed around the table and crossed the room, her heels clacking on the floor like gavels. Even in the house, in the middle of the afternoon, Maya was dressed to the nines. Julia's heart dropped as Maya strode straight to Claire, stopping only inches from her face. Claire's expression looked mildly entertained, but Julia thought she could detect the slightest hint of fear behind her eyes. Surely Maya wouldn't start a physical altercation in front of her own children. "I don't have the energy to fight you. I will stay here until the twenty-seventh to say good-bye to my father out of respect to our mother. But make no mistake, I will not deal with you. I will go sleep in a hotel by myself if I have to." She smirked. "And wouldn't that make the two of you oh so happy?"

"Maya, don't . . . ," Elise said, holding her dripping spoon in the air above the pan. "Maybe we should all just take a deep breath."

At the same time, Julia heard Claire say in a low, dangerous voice, "For the last time, I did not sleep with your husband. I won't say it again."

"How about you don't say anything to me at all," Maya suggested, both of them completely ignoring that Elise had ever spoken.

"Why do you think I moved all the way to California?" Claire said. "You won, that's why! And if it weren't for Mom, I wouldn't be speaking to you right now. I'm certainly not here for Robert Yancey. That abusive old bastard can rot in a trash can in the back of Dale Funeral Home, for all I care."

Julia gasped, her heart sinking, sinking, sinking. Any hope that she might have had of this being a place where she could spin Eli some happy family memories was gone. Her son never knew his grandfather, and she had never told him about Robert. About the tension he brought to the family. God, why had she brought a suicidal kid into *this* house? Dusty was right — she was a horrible mom. He and Shurn, ignorant as they both were, could certainly do better than she ever had.

Maya had let Claire's outburst sink in, slowly nodding her head, as if to say, *See? See how right I am about her?* Finally, she spoke. "So classy. I will never understand what he saw in you."

Claire's only response was an elaborate eye roll. She stepped around Maya and took her cup to the table, sitting across from Will.

"I'm not feeling well. I'm going to lie down," Maya announced to nobody, then left the kitchen without waiting for a response, her hair swishing behind her like a great silky fan.

Bradley started to stand. "You need anything, Maya?" he called. "The doctor said you should —"

"No." Her voice, sharp, jabbing at him from the hallway, cut him off. He plopped back into his chair, looking scolded.

For the few silent, awkward moments after the slammed door upstairs punctuated Maya's departure, Julia sagged against the doorjamb, staring at the back of her son's head. He seemed to be standing still as a statue, the same creepy way he always had, as if his life were a video game or a reality TV show and he was just the spectator, interested and alert but not at all invested.

She longed to reach out to him, to grab

102

his shoulders from behind and shake him. *Damn it,* she wanted to snarl, *react! If nothing else, just show that you're living . . . that you haven't already committed . . . mental suicide.*

After a while, Elise tapped the spoon against the side of the pan and turned off the heat, which seemed to slowly bring the room back to life. Julia turned her head to see the dumpling batter bowl empty. Her mom put the lid on the pot and stepped away, letting the dumplings rise on top of the apple mixture. Distantly, she was aware of Will singing again and the murmuring between Bradley and Molly, who had finished her crackers and wanted to play outside.

Claire sat staring down into her empty mug, as motionless as Eli, and suddenly Julia was sure she'd done the right thing telling Claire about her son. In that moment, the two seemed connected on some level, even if neither of them knew it.

"Can you stay a few days longer?" Elise asked, and with a start Julia realized she was talking to her.

"Oh. Um, yeah. Shouldn't be a problem. Semester's finished anyway. Tai can manage on his own. It'll be fine."

"He can drive down for Christmas, of

course."

Julia nodded. "Yeah. Good idea. I'll ask him."

Elise raised her voice. "Claire? What about you?"

Julia thought she saw her sister's red-rimmed eyes redden even more as she thought it over. She cleared her throat, then nodded. "Believe it or not, there's even less for me in California right now than there is for me here."

Another awkward silence filled the air, the kids finishing their snacks and scooting off into the front room, where the television blared to life. Julia wondered what Claire had meant by there being less for her in California than in Missouri, and realized too late that she'd been so intent on telling Claire all of her problems, she'd never even asked Claire about her own life. What was it like for her in California? What had she been doing all these years? Was there anyone special in her life? Claire gazed through the back door blankly, and then got up and stood in front of it instead, hands on her hips, hair sticking out in sprigs and fits.

"Mom, what kind of fern is that?" she asked, but before Elise could answer, she'd pushed the door open and stepped out onto the porch, almost dreamily.

104

Elise started to follow her, but was interrupted by the doorbell. She visibly jumped, then looked from the porch to the front room, as if she couldn't quite figure out how to be in both places at once. The bell rang again, and Molly's voice singsonged, "Someone's at the door, Grandma! And she's got a present!" Elise gave one more look to Claire's back and then headed instead for the front room.

The motion made things seem more normal, more approachable, and Julia finally found the nerve to reach out to Eli's back. She touched his shoulder lightly and leaned forward to talk directly into his ear. She couldn't see his face; maybe it was better that way.

"Some crazy stuff, huh?"

He shrugged, wordless.

"Probably I should have warned you about Aunt Claire's and Aunt Maya's little feud."

Again with the shrugging.

"Want to go for a walk? I'll tell you all about it," she said. "It's a juicy story."

The boy still didn't move, but his voice (God, how Julia was having a hard time getting used to that man-voice of his) floated over his shoulder, icy and sharp as the sleet that had been pelting her face by the garage before. Maybe sharper, actually. "Dad called me. He's, like, blowing up my phone."

Julia sighed, defeated, her chin sinking to her breastbone. Of course she had expected Dusty to call Eli. He was exactly the kind of father who would. It was one of the things she would always love about Dusty, his desire to be connected to his son. But . . . she supposed she wished he would have waited until after the funeral, until after she got back to Kansas City, to make his presence known. It was just like Dusty to give her feelings, her needs, no thought whatsoever.

And why would he? she thought. His last words to her before hanging up had been: *I trusted you to not screw him up, Julia. And you did.*

"You told him," Eli said accusingly. "He wants me to come live with him."

Over my dead body, she wanted to proclaim, but aside from that being the poorest choice of words ever, at the moment she wasn't so sure it was true. She wasn't so sure Dusty wouldn't get hold of a sympathetic judge who would rip Eli away like an old infected bandage. "He's pretty mad at me," she confessed instead.

Eli finally turned to face her. "Why did

you tell him? You told me you'd keep it a secret."

And she had. Of all the rotten things she'd done as a mom, even she knew that assuring him secrecy was one of the rottenest. But she'd been out of options. Promising Eli that she would tell no one about his suicidal plans was the only way she could get him to open up to her, and she was so hungry for some connection with her son, and so at a loss for how to find it, that she'd said the words before she'd even thought them through.

"I had to tell him. He's your dad."

"I'm not going to live with him. I'll kill myself first," Eli shot back, and Julia felt as if she'd been punched in the chest. This was the first time he'd made the threat so directly, and they were some of the most frightening and hopeless words a mother could hear.

She knew she needed to do something, to say something, to call someone. This was it. He was making outward threats. It was time for intervention.

But she was home. On this godforsaken farm. She was burying her father in five days. It was Christmas, for God's sake.

And, she had to admit to herself, she was weak. She'd spent so much of her identity in the professor half of herself, she had no idea how to be the mom half. She didn't think she could live through it. She didn't want to have a son with problems. She wasn't equipped.

"Don't worry," she told Eli, because soothing was the only thing she could think of that she had left. Was the only thing she'd been good at. "I'll talk to Dusty again. I'll calm him down."

She gazed into her son's deep brown eyes, mostly buried under all that hair, and for the briefest second she thought she saw her baby in those eyes. The smiling, jolly little boy who loved to kick soccer balls at the park and who thought stars were the coolest thing ever. But then she noticed the crease between his eyebrows, the unhappy droop to the outer corners of his eyes, and the baby vanished. This was her son. Her hurting child. And she couldn't fix him. Couldn't reassure him with a clucking tone.

He glared at her for what felt like forever, parted his lips as if to say something, then seemed to think it pointless and simply walked out of the kitchen, his threat lingering, ugly, beating in the room like a living thing.

She was only vaguely aware of Bradley at the table, tapping on his BlackBerry. And then of him leaving the room without a single word. Probably to check on Maya. She'd said she wasn't feeling well, after all.

It wasn't until much later, when her heart stopped banging so painfully against her ribs, that she realized.

Bradley had not gone to check on his wife as she'd thought. He had not even gone upstairs.

He had followed Claire to the sunporch.

Six

Evening approached in slow motion. Behind the closed door to Maya's room, it remained dark and quiet. The kids bustled around the kitchen with Elise, who had come away from the front door holding a casserole and saying something about the whole lot of them joining a slew of neighbors at Sharp's for a dinner in Robert's honor.

"What a thoughtful invitation," she'd said. "I'd never known he had such friends."

Julia had been shocked, quite honestly, to hear that her father had any friends at all. How could the same man who once yanked her pigtail so hard he came away with a fist-ful of hair be someone others thought of as decent? Not for the first time, Julia found herself wondering what kind of double life the man had lived — the abusive and ugly man at home, and the presentable one away. Surely he had lived that double life. Surely her mom had not been seduced by the man they'd all lived with. He must have shown her a different side of himself as well, at least in the beginning. To think otherwise was just . . . depressing.

Claire had come inside only long enough to grab Elise's coat again, and had disappeared out the front door, her tan legs gleaming against the whiteness outside. She said nothing about where she was going — just left with a determined stride, and it was obvious that Bradley was not with her. Later, Julia would peer out the back door to find him sitting on the steps of the sunporch, all but camouflaged by that blasted jungle of poinsettia plants, a bottle of booze she'd not seen him procure squeezed between his thighs.

The house ticked and creaked as dusk raced toward them, the children's voices floating, the silence of dysfunction enveloping them all. Eli, stretched out across his cot in Julia's bedroom like a mummy. Maya, silent and brooding behind a darkened door. Claire, outside in the whipping wind. Bradley, getting drunk alone in a cloud of humid plant stench.

It all made Julia feel so bleak, so empty, that she suddenly felt that if she didn't speak to someone soon, she might break.

Sitting on the hearth in the den, staring at

the Christmas tree, which was all but bowled over by handfuls of garish tinsel — what on earth had possessed her mother to pile all that tinsel on there? — Julia pulled out her cell phone and dialed home.

"You're there." Tai.

A sigh, heavy with relief, shuddered through Julia's body. Just hearing her husband's voice made her feel better, feel grounded.

"I'm here."

"And the others?"

"They're here too. Everyone. Maya brought the whole gang."

"Aw, Doc, I should've come."

Julia smiled at Tai's use of their shared nickname. They'd begun calling each other "Doc" years ago, when they graduated within one week of each other, both with their doctorates. For a while, just the word *doc* would spawn luxurious afternoons of excited sex between them — they were so turned on by themselves. But eventually it became just a nickname, something private and intimate between the two of them. He hadn't called her Doc in ages.

"I do wish you were here with us."

"But the project."

She nodded, even though she knew he couldn't see her. She was well aware of how important his research project was to him. He'd been working on it for years, and it was nearing completion. To ask a scientist to step away from a project this close to the finish line would have been almost cruel. He'd have come for Robert's funeral if that was what she'd wanted, but he'd have been little consolation anyway. His mind would have been with his students, his research.

But, still. To hold his hand. To lean back against him and feel him stroke her hair.

"It's okay, Tai. It's not a big deal. But there's been a change. I've got to stay until the twenty-seventh."

There was a pause. "Through Christmas?"

"I know. But we were going low-key this year anyway." He didn't comment. "It's just a date on the calendar. There's been a hiccup in the funeral plans."

A burst of air into the phone. "Okay. You're right. It's just a date. We'll have Christmas on the twenty-eighth."

"I'm sorry. You can come down here for Christmas."

"No, no, it's okay. I'll just work. How's Eli? Loving the rural life?"

Julia took a deep breath, peering toward the bedroom where she knew her son was still lying down. Chewed the side of her thumb, which smelled like smoke, filling her with a wave of guilt. She'd promised them both that she would quit smoking. As far as either of them knew, she had. Tai claimed that a scientist such as herself had no business partaking in any activity that had already been proven to shorten the human life span, unless said scientist was studying cures for said life-span shortening. Eli, on the other hand, just claimed it stank.

"About that," she said. "Listen, Tai, I had to call Dusty."

"Lovely. And what did the ex have to say today?"

"I told him about . . . about something I caught Eli with a couple of months ago."

"Caught him with? You caught him with something?"

Julia massaged her forehead, realizing she was too close to tears to ward them off. "Pills," she said, feeling her mouth move around the word, as revolting as vomit. "He was . . . he was threatening suicide."

She heard another burst of air from the other end of the phone, and she knew her husband well enough to know that he'd just made the noise that said he didn't believe it for a second. A *pshaw* noise. It was all a jest. She wished she could be as sure as he was.

"That kid," he said. "And so Dusty is

making a big deal of this."

Annoyance tinged the edges of Julia's brain. It was a big deal, wasn't it? "Yes, of course he is. He's threatening court."

A chuckle. "Let him threaten."

"It's not that simple, Tai."

"Of course it is. Dusty is no more the superior parent now than he was when you won custody of Eli twelve years ago. Under our roof, Eli has two educated, employed parents, a new home in a gated community, friends, every educational resource at his disposal. . . ."

So why does he want to die? Julia had to keep herself from asking. *If his life's so great, why does he want to leave it? And why can't I ask him? And would he even tell me? And if he won't, is that the answer in itself?*

"I suppose you're right," she said instead, because to articulate all the confusion looping through her mind would just exhaust her. Even thinking it exhausted her.

"I know I'm right. Don't let that asshole get into your head, Julia. He's been doing it since you were sixteen years old."

"I know." The fire crackled; her back felt as if it were glowing with heat.

"Listen, we can talk about this later if you want. I'm going to the school today," he said. "Got some paperwork I might as well

115

catch up on."

"Of course."

"You going to be okay? I can come down."

"No, I'll be fine."

"Good, because I really do think I'm about at the finish line with this project. A few days alone might do it for me."

"That's wonderful, Tai."

A pause, a metal lid clanging in the kitchen, a screen door creaking open and then clapping shut. "Tai?"

"Yeah?"

"You really think he's not going to do it?"

"Not when he figures out how expensive taking you to court will be. Besides, even if he does do it, you'll win. Dusty is no threat."

"No, I mean . . ." Julia swallowed, craned her neck to see if anyone was in the den, listening. She swiveled on the hearth, the bricks catching the corners of her denim pockets and making scraping noises, until she faced the fire. She gazed into the flames, feeling fluid and boneless. Like she'd been holding herself erect for decades and all she needed was to curl up for a good, long rest. "Do you really think Eli was bluffing? About the suicide?"

"Doc. He's fine. He's a teenager. They all say that kind of shit. You can't take every little threat seriously. You know that. You

116

work with teenagers every day. We both do. We know how they are."

But we're not their parents, Julia didn't say to him. *The stakes aren't as high for us when it's them. Even the students you really love are someone else's child.*

He went on. "Remember that freshman in your physics class last year? The one who said if she didn't get an A she would jump off the Paseo Bridge? Bluff. And that weirdo in one of your first classes who threatened to find our house and burn it down? Bluff. See? They all say stuff like that. We probably did too, and we just can't remember it."

She didn't want to, but at the moment what choice did she have but to let her husband's words soothe her? That was why she'd called him, after all, wasn't it? A part of her had known he would undersell the story, and after her phone call with Dusty and her conversation with Claire, that was exactly what she needed — someone to tell her that everything would be okay. That it wasn't a big deal. That Eli's threat was normal behavior and she could relax.

So she closed her eyes and leaned into the phone, into Tai's words. Let the fire lick her cheeks and hold her up.

"You want me to talk to him?" Tai said,

though she could hear weariness in his voice and papers rattling in the background.

"No. He's taking a nap. We've got some sort of dinner thing to go to this evening, so I'm letting him rest."

"How does he seem to you?"

She gnawed at her thumb again. "He's . . . you know, we're here for a funeral . . . and Dusty called him, which he didn't like."

"So, petulant as always."

"I suppose so."

"See? Nothing to worry about. He's acting like himself."

"I suppose so."

There was more rattling of papers, and what Julia recognized as the scraping of Tai's desk drawer sliding open and then shut again. She heard a jingle of car keys. "You sure you don't want me to come down?"

For one maddening minute, Julia wanted more than anything to say yes. Her mouth even opened, her lips ready to form the word. But she knew she couldn't bring Tai into this already heated situation. Tai's aloofness would only bring more awkwardness to the dinner table. And he had his work. He needed to do his work. If she stood between him and his work, his mood would be more than aloof. It would be agitated and snippy too. And, really, what could he do here?

"I'm positive. Stay there. Get lots done. We'll be okay. We've got a few days. Maybe I'll teach him to skate down at the creek or take some hikes with him or something."

"See? That's the winning spirit. Show him you've got things under control. Let him know these kinds of threats won't work, that life goes on." The jangling car keys got louder. "I've got to get, then, before Art leaves for the night. As you know, willing grad student helpers are only willing until the parties start."

"Yeah, of course." Julia said, purposely lightening her voice. Making herself sound bright and cheery. So stupid. Why was it never okay for her to lose face? Was she that much like Maya? "Love you."

"Yeah, love you too, Doc."

And he was gone.

Julia stood and twisted her back one way and then the other, feeling her skin stretch tight with heat. In some ways, she felt, she had it all. More than either of her sisters. Why was she wallowing like a spoiled child?

She gazed at the tree for a long moment, taking in her elongated reflection on a blue ornament. She saw no misery there. She only saw . . . herself.

"And a shitload of tinsel," she said aloud,

and pulled down two big handfuls before heading to the bedroom, where she could lie down for a few minutes alongside her son before dinner.

SEVEN

Sharp's had been around forever. Julia remembered it from her childhood, back when the city was more of an energetic town and there were precious few restaurants to be had. Not that her family frequented restaurants anyway. This deep in the country, you ate the food from your own land. Vegetables, grown and canned, pickled, boiled into preserves, frozen. Cattle, butchered and stored in town in a smelly meat locker. Fish pulled from the pond behind the tree line. Even honey harvested from the white beehive boxes that lined the perimeter of the soy field.

Julia was married before she'd tasted her first commercially canned green bean, her first jar of store-bought jelly, her first carton of ice cream bought from a supermarket. It had taken a long time to get used to the texture of preserved foods, the taste of the can.

121

But on the few occasions that the family had gone out, it was almost always to Sharp's. Robert had liked the fried okra there, and it was one vegetable they didn't grow in their own garden, so he felt justified buying it. Of course, Robert felt justified doing most anything he wanted to do. It was only Elise and the girls whose wants he denied.

Stepping in through the front door, Julia noticed that little had changed since her childhood. The same dirty black-and-white tile held the same scuff marks, and the same jukebox sat dusty and mute in the corner. The place still smelled of old frying oil, and the chairs were still sticky against the backs of her arms.

She half expected to see her father, flannel sleeves rolled to the elbows, frowning and chewing methodically, holding a fork in one fist and a knife in the other, at one end of the table. Silent to everyone, and everyone wanting it that way, because when he spoke at the dinner table it was only because someone had tested his last nerve, and it was frightening and appetite-killing. She would never have thought it, but Sharp's really did make her think of her father. In some ways, she may have felt his absence there even more than she did his absence at home.

She tried to drum up a feeling of mourning, but nothing would come, other than a remote sort of grief, a loss that she couldn't quite feel because she'd spent so many years of her life pounding it away, pounding *him* away from her heart. You couldn't miss something you never had. She supposed she had grieved him little by little, year by year, many years ago, and now, where he should have existed in her heart, there was simply a void.

Julia couldn't be sure, but she was almost positive that she could remember a time, way back before her sisters were born, when Robert had occasionally smiled. When he hadn't worn that angry vein in his forehead all the time. When her parents seemed flirty, happy. Could it have been the pressures of the family and the farm that made him who he was? Julia hated to think so, and she hated to have those fond memories, even foggily, because it was just so much easier to feel nothing but distance.

They trailed into the restaurant, one by one, and Julia pretended not to notice that the dinner crowd had seemed to stop and clam up, as if witnessing something spectacular. She wondered if the small-town gossip train still rolled through this area, if she and her sisters were speculated about, reviled. She wondered if her father ever came into Sharp's alone and told stories of ungrateful children over sweaty glasses of stale beer. She wondered if what had happened at the Chuck Wagon was still legend to some folks. She didn't know why, but she thought it likely.

The waitress led them to a room in the back. This, Julia didn't remember, and the slightly modern decor of the add-on room was a physical reminder that time had apparently marched on, even at Sharp's, while she'd been away.

"This work?" the waitress asked, and Julia nodded, appraising the long table, already set. The waitress methodically placed a menu at every place setting while the rest of the family filed in and began claiming seats. "Real sorry about your dad," the waitress said on the way out, and again Julia just nodded. What was to be said? She was certain that the man the waitress was sorry to hear about couldn't have been the man who'd bellowed in the barn, his fists of rage frightening and painful against the sides of her skull.

It took some uncomfortable shifting, but eventually everyone got seated. Nobody seemed to want to say much to anybody else, and it was obvious that Maya and Bradley were shielding themselves with their kids — Molly at Maya's side and Will at Bradley's. Though they, for some reason, looked no more comfortable sitting next to each other than they might have if they'd been sitting next to one of the sisters.

In the end, they were able to artfully arrange themselves so the empty seats would fall like moats between enemies, and before long those empty seats were taken by friends of Robert's and Elise's that the sisters didn't recognize. The friends brought cards and breads wrapped in tinfoil and clucked their apologies to Elise and then fell into comfortable chitchat about the farm and bugs and rain.

Julia sat next to Eli, wishing she could fall into conversation with him, but the boy never talked, and she didn't know what to say to get him to open up. Just like always.

The salads came, and went. The crackers stuck in Julia's throat and the dressing tasted acidic as bile and she chugged water, but was overpowered by the sulfuric taste. She tried to shut out the lulled conversations around her.

Have you thought about what you'll do with the farm?

125

Well, I intend to live on it. It's been in my family for generations.

Oh, but, honey, how will you keep it up?

I haven't figured that out just yet. Seems like I've been working this land forever. I sure could use a rest sometimes. But my grandfather Mick gave everything for that plot of land. Wouldn't be right.

My Jeffrey could help you out, I suppose. I'm sure you could work out a deal of some sort.

Of course, of course.

I have a nephew, you know . . .

On and on it went, everyone expecting Elise to have all the answers. Hell, even Julia had expected her mom to have answers, and how could she possibly have them already? Good God, her husband had only been dead two days . . . When would she have had time to think through what she might do without him? Julia swallowed, and swallowed again as she fought her urge to turn to the neighbors and tell them to shut up, just shut up, and when the desire became too much, she turned to her son instead.

"So, what do you think of this place?" she asked. Her voice sounded high, strained, as if she were trying too hard. She wished she could make herself sound relaxed, in control, not like she was scared of her own kid.

Eli shrugged. "It's small."

"No, I mean the whole place. The farm. The town."

"It's a farm and a town." Brushed off again.

The waitress came, and began setting entrées down in front of everyone. Julia could hear Molly griping that the macaroni and cheese was "the wrong color" and Maya trying to soothe her in weary, staccato sentences. She set a huge fried catfish in front of Eli, and a grilled chicken breast, perfectly swimming in greasy french fries, in front of her.

"Thank you," she said to the waitress, and then pointed to Eli's plate with her fork after the waitress had gone. "You want me to bone that for you?"

He frowned, his cheeks blooming high with red patches. "No. I got it."

"Are you sure? You know how to bone a catfish? I can do it for you."

"God, why do you always have to act like that, Mom? I'm not an infant."

She knew that. Oh, boy, did she know that. The more she replayed palming that sack of pills in her kitchen, the more she knew that. *That's right,* she wanted to say to him. *When you were an infant, you were so*

127

much easier. I could ball you up tight in a blanket and move you where I wanted you to be. I could say exactly what you did to your body all the time. I could pull you out of the way of danger any time I saw it. When you were a baby, you were all mine.

And I ruined you.

She took a few bites of her chicken, trying to will Tai's words back into her mind — it was an idle threat, kids made them all the time, don't take it so seriously — but she had a tough time swallowing past the lump in her throat. What if Tai was wrong? Why did she feel like he *was* wrong? Despite herself, she kept feeling tears collecting in the corners of her eyes and had to blink rapidly to keep them from falling over onto her cheeks. She also had to pretend she didn't know they were there — every time she consciously acknowledged them, they got worse. She just wanted to go home. And not home to the farmhouse where all the ghosts lived, but home to Tai, and to an earlier time, when raising Eli was a no-brainer. Easy. As easy as raising an infant.

She felt a hand on her forearm, and looked up into the sagging eyes of the woman who sat next to her, a woman who'd introduced herself as Clem Hebert's wife.

"I lost my daddy when I was nineteen,"

she said around a wad of something green in her mouth. "So I understand how you're feeling right now."

Julia swallowed, forced a smile. "I'm just glad he didn't suffer," she said, because it seemed like the right thing to say. She had a list of those kinds of sayings: *It was the right time. I'm grateful I can be here for my mom. It is a trying time, of course.* And *I'm just glad he didn't suffer.* She'd even practiced them in the shower back home in Kansas City before leaving. She wanted to sound genuine to other mourners. She wanted to make it sound like the loss of Robert Yancey was deeply felt, deeply mourned. *He was a good man.* That was another one she'd practiced. But she reserved it for last, in case she got desperate, because the truth was he wasn't a good man. He was a difficult man. A mean man. A tempest of a man.

Clem Hebert's wife leaned forward, her freckles looming large in Julia's line of sight. "It's okay to let those tears loose, honey," she said, and Julia noticed Claire looking up and studying her from across the table.

By now the tears really were gone, the space filled by burning embarrassment. "I'm fine," she whispered, and took another bite of chicken.

Clem Hebert's wife's attention was diverted by a conversation about taxes, and Julia was never so thankful for the government than she was at that moment. Once again, she turned to her son.

"Since we're going to be here for a few days, what do you say we take some hikes into the fields tomorrow?"

He shrugged, but didn't say no, which, sadly, Julia had to take as a hopeful sign.

"We can go out to the pond, though it's probably too warm to do any skating."

He said nothing, just continued to dig through the mushed-up mess that was his catfish. He was stroking bones into the flesh with his clumsiness, and it took all Julia had to keep from exasperatedly snatching it away from him and doing it right.

"I can show you the tree I fell out of and broke my arm when I was a kid."

Still nothing.

Julia took a breath. "We can talk," she said, and popped another piece of chicken into her mouth as nonchalantly as she could. As if talking was something they did regularly.

"I said I'd go with you, okay?" he answered, then pushed his plate away. "Why do you have to be so pathetic about it? I'm going to the bathroom." He stood abruptly and strode through the restaurant so quickly that Julia barely had time to swallow her chicken.

"Eli," she tried, but her voice felt impossibly loud, almost a yelp, coming out of her mouth, and she looked around nervously. All of the soothing Tai had given her had drained completely away, and she was once again a jangle of nerves. She wiped her mouth on her napkin and scooted away from the table. "Excuse me," she said to nobody in particular, and followed the path Eli had taken, weaving past tables of locals, all fat and jovial in their plaid snap-front shirts and baseball caps.

Of course he'd already gone into the men's room by the time she got there, so Julia paced outside the squeaky wooden door waiting for him, chewing on the side of her thumb to keep herself from imagining her son killing himself in a public restroom. Every time the door squeaked open and someone other than Eli walked out, she had to bite her tongue to keep from asking if the young man inside was okay.

Finally, after what seemed like an impossibly long time, during which Julia had begun to imagine that he'd not gone to the restroom at all but had gone outside and found a bridge to fling himself off of instead, Eli emerged through the door, wiping his hands on the back of his pants. His eyes grew alarmed and then narrowed.

"Mom, God, what are you doing?"

"I was worried. I was checking on you. Are you sick? Is everything okay?" She reached over to put a hand on his forehead, because this was what worried moms did, right? But he ducked away from her touch, his glare disgusted.

"Mom, seriously. I don't want to bond. I don't want to talk. I don't want you cutting up my food and I don't want you following me to the bathroom or feeling my forehead. I just want you to leave me alone. You should be really good at that. You've been doing it my whole life."

Julia was stunned into motionless silence. She could do nothing but watch as her son turned and walked away from her, shaking his head as if she was despicable. Shaking his head just like her father had been known to do so many years ago.

So it really was about that. It was about her. She had ruined her son. She had caused her son to want to die, and then had failed to recognize it until it was almost too late.

Hell, what was she saying? He was so far away from her. She really was too late. Even if he lived . . . she'd lost him long ago.

Julia rushed into the ladies' room and

leaned over the sink. She turned on the crusted faucet for the noise. Her stomach rolled and rolled and she concentrated on the gushing water to keep from vomiting. She splashed a handful of water on her cheeks; then slowly, she looked up, met her own gaze in the mirror, only to find her father staring back at her.

You are one selfish shit, Julia, he was saying. *You know that? Demanding, selfish brat. I feel sorry for the man who marries you.*

As if on cue, her earlier conversation with Dusty pressed in on her, ringing in the back of her mind, his voice overtaking the voice of Robert Yancey.

It's not all about you all the time, Julia. You never seemed to get that. You have a kid to take care of. Our kid. My kid. You're supposed to be taking care of him. This is not taking care of him. But I bet your students are totally taken care of. It's always been like that. It's always been all about what Julia wants. All about your career. Never about your family. Never about me, never about Eli. Why do you think I left? And, look, now Eli wants to leave you too. How long till that Chinaman of yours takes off? Not that you would care. Because it's always about you.

Maybe they were right. She was a selfish, selfish woman. But she'd never meant to

133

be. Surely that counted for something. Surely intent had some amount of importance.

She ripped a paper towel out of the dispenser and ran it over her face, taking a few deep breaths to clear her mind. She couldn't do this now. Not while they were in public. She had to pull it together.

The door opened and Julia caught a familiar mess of wiry blond hair coming up behind her in the mirror.

"You okay?" Claire asked.

Julia nodded, wiped her face, gulping in a cleansing breath, all business. "Eli come back to the table?"

Claire smiled. "Yeah. He's got Bradley boning that fish for him. Looks a little tedious at this point."

"Well, at least he's eating." Julia turned the water back on, washed her hands to busy herself. Claire hung around awkwardly, looking as if she wanted to say something but didn't know what exactly it should be. Julia dried her hands and turned, leaned against the sink. "So did you and Bradley, um . . . talk? Earlier?"

Claire's face flushed, and once again Julia noticed how red her sister's eyes appeared to be. If she didn't know better, she'd almost think Claire had been crying recently. No. Not Claire. Claire didn't do that. Claire didn't show weakness. "Not really," she mumbled.

Julia let out an anguished sigh. "Sometimes I envy you, Claire. I used to think your life had to be lonely — no husband, no kids, no . . . ties. But now . . . I don't know. I love them, of course, but . . . it's just that sometimes family life is so hard, you know? Sometimes I think back to when I was young and free and I wish I'd appreciated it more."

And, oh, how she did. How she looked back on the freedom and ease of her life before Dusty had walked into it with that lazy, bowlegged stride of his and wanted it back with such an intensity it almost made her limbs ache. How she watched her students, arriving late, hungover, already making plans for the next night's party, and wanted to leave the classroom with them. Leave the stacks of paper and the battered laptop case and the . . . suicide worries . . . behind and dive into a bucket of Mexican beers, her only concern whether or not her bra matched her panties, just in case she might get laid. What happened to that life? Where did it go?

Claire disappeared into a stall, a cutting chuckle echoing off the tile walls, leaving

Julia at the sink alone once again. "Well," Claire said from inside the stall, "I'm maybe not as free and easy as you like to think, Queenie. I may have a little drama left behind in my own life." Her voice was tinged with sharp edges. "And it isn't easy, anyhow."

"What do you mean?"

But before Claire could answer, the restroom door whooshed open again, and Elise entered. "Oh, there you are," she said to Julia. "You left the table so quickly we thought something was wrong."

Julia wadded up the paper towel she was holding and tossed it in the trash bin. "I just needed some space," she said. "I'm going back now."

"Oh. Well, the others have gone. It's just us now. Well, and Bradley. Maya took the kids home. Maya doesn't seem like herself." She touched Julia on the elbow. "Do you think there's something else going on there?" she asked. "Between Maya and Bradley? I know Claire makes Maya tense, but —"

"I'm in here, Mom," Claire said over the stall door, and Julia could have sworn her mom blushed.

"Oh, okay," Elise called out, then continued in a loud whisper. "It just seems like

136

there's more going on between those two than . . . you know . . . the old thing with Claire."

The toilet flushed, and Claire stepped out, pulling the bottom of her sweatshirt over the top of her shorts. "You mean the *lie* about Claire."

"That's not what I meant. You know that."

Claire edged Julia out of the way at the sink and turned on the water. "Of course I know that, Mom, but nobody seems to say it but me. And to answer your question, even though I know you weren't asking me, I'd say yes, it's a fair bet there's something else going on between Maya and Bradley. It's a fair bet something else is going on between Bradley and someone with a boob job and a spray tan, if you know what I mean."

Julia stepped back to avoid water droplets slinging through the air as Claire flicked her hands over the sink. "Did he say something about it out on the sunporch this afternoo— ?" she said, but Claire shot her a look, causing the words to dry up in her throat. Clearly, her sister didn't want anyone to know that she'd been with Bradley on the sunporch earlier, and while Julia believed that was because Claire didn't want any more suspicion cast over her, a part of her — the same part that remained unconvinced about Claire's innocence years ago, the same part that saw too many unanswered questions, too many shifty behaviors to ignore — wondered if Claire was once again covering. She shifted gears. "Maya did say something about not feeling well earlier. I thought it was an excuse to leave the room, but maybe she's sick. Maybe that's what we're all picking up on and everything with Bradley is fine."

"Well, I hope it's not serious," Elise said, and pushed into the stall Claire had just come out of. "I'd hoped that the two of them had gotten over everything and moved on. The children really need a happy home."

Julia and Claire glanced at each other, and Julia guessed that both of them had the same thought on their minds: Where had their mom's concern about children needing happy homes been when their father was still alive?

There was a beat of uncomfortable silence, during which Julia tried not to look at Claire, tried not to catch her reflection in the mirror, tried not to listen to Elise's noises in the stall, tried not to think about her family. Tried to pretend that everything was normal — that they were gathered together to mourn the loss of her father and that nothing stood in the way of that. But it was impossible. She knew, as she always had known, that when it came to her family, there would always be more questions than answers, more discomfort than joy, more queasy silences than laughter.

Maybe that was why she'd emotionally bugged out on Eli so long ago. In her world, emotion was a complicated and fruitless monster.

She cleared her throat and edged around Claire as the toilet once again whooshed into life behind the metal stall door. She mumbled something about needing to get back to Eli and plunged out of the stuffy restroom and back into the garish colors and sounds of Sharp's.

At the table, Eli had eaten a good portion of his catfish and was sitting in his usual pose — arms crossed over his chest, chin pointed downward, tucked into himself, silent and brooding. Bradley was scooted sideways in his chair, one arm slung over the back of it, talking up the waitress, who was nodding and giggling like a crushy teenager. Julia could almost swear that Eli shook his head, ever so slightly, disgustedly, every time Bradley opened his mouth to speak.

Julia poked around on her plate a few

times, hoping to find her appetite, but there was nothing to be had. Her chicken still looked pale and fleshy. She tossed her napkin over it and pushed the plate away, just as Claire and Elise came back to the table and scooted in.

Claire's head was tilted down, but Julia could feel her sister's eyes pointed her direction. She was half afraid to meet them, though. Half afraid that she would see in them what might have been said in the restroom after she'd left. She just wanted some peace for a few moments.

". . . were only planning to be here until today," Bradley was saying, and the waitress nodded as if she'd never heard anything so riveting. Julia rolled her eyes. No wonder Maya was so insecure. The man didn't even attempt to hide his flirtatiousness. She tried to block him out, but his voice broke through again. ". . . only brought clothes for two days. Hopefully nothing tragic happens or I'll be out of underwear."

Just as the waitress threw her head back to laugh at his incredibly indecent "joke," Bradley sitting there smugly, that arrogant grin on his face, his eyes roving over to Claire and back to the waitress again, Julia saw it happen.

It was just the tiniest flinch, really. Could

have been mistaken for an involuntary spasm. But it was there.

Eli's elbow flicked sideways about three inches, knocking into the full soda the waitress had just set down on the edge of the table between him and Bradley. The cup teetered, swerved, and then tipped, soda and ice sloshing across the table and down the front of Bradley, landing with a liquid *thwack* in his lap. The glass shattered on the floor.

The whole room seemed to suck in its breath as Bradley jumped up, brushing at the front of his clothes frantically. Eli's face immediately turned shocked, contrite, as he said, "Sorry, Uncle Bradley. I didn't see it there." And as Bradley dabbed at his crotch with a handful of paper napkins, his face furious, Julia heard her son add in a low voice, "Wow, how ironic, huh?"

At that moment Julia and Claire locked eyes across the table. And they both grinned.

ATTEMPTS — II

What he liked best about the farm was the way the frozen grass crunched under his feet. Not that this was something special about the country — the grass in Kansas City crunched when it was frozen too. What was different about it on the farm was how loud it sounded, especially in the middle of the night, when it seemed like the whole world was asleep.

The last car had turned down the gravel road hours ago. The cousins, who were both all right, he supposed, but were kind of annoying in that I'm-a-little-kid-so-everyone-must-entertain-me-all-the-time sort of way, had been in bed for a long time. Grandmother Elise had finished washing dishes and shut up the house and turned off the lights. The creaking in her bedroom, just above the one he was sharing with his mom, had stopped and, unlike the night before, he had counted to one-thousand-Mississippi after he was sure everyone was asleep before he moved a muscle.

He'd crept through the house on ghost's feet, practically floating above the warped wood floors, and had, just like the night before, gone to the front room and sat in his grandfather Robert's recliner. The one he died in.

He had heard that people shit and piss themselves when they died, and he wondered, as he sank into the worn nubby fabric of the chair, if Grandfather Robert had done that. It didn't smell like he had. And he doubted that Grandmother Elise, who was kind of nutty, but not nutty enough to be gross, would have kept the chair in the house if he had. But it might have been a little bit cool if he had. If he'd been all shit and piss and bulging eyes and purple tongue and veins in his neck. That was the way he wanted to go — repulsive and shocking. Something people would talk about for a long time.

Just as he'd done the night before, he sank into the chair. But tonight he had more time. He'd left his pocketknife under his cot mattress. So he pulled up the footrest, positioned himself in what he guessed was the same pose his grandfather had been sitting in, and held his breath. Held it until his vision was grainy and his lungs burned. Held it until he felt so miserable he might have been having a heart attack and dying. Held it until he could feel his pulse in his stomach, imagined it getting slower and fainter. He stayed motionless. Still as a corpse. Not even an eyeball twitching. Soon his eyes were burning too, and one of them let a tear loose down his cheek. He wondered if Grandfather Robert had cried a little when he died. He'd never heard anything about people crying while they died, but it made sense that they might.

He held it, held it, held it.

And then let the air out in a rush that sank his belly and made the chair bounce a little and squeak on its hinges.

He was alive.

Damn it.

He sat there for a few more minutes, trying to soak up death in his grandfather's death chair, and then quietly eased the footrest down and slipped outside into the crystalline air.

It was freezing. His stocking feet made the frozen grass crunch. A dog barked off in a field somewhere. But otherwise there was nothing. Still as a morgue.

He wanted to walk farther tonight than he had during the day.

Earlier, he'd taken a walk, but had only gotten halfway through the old soy field before the cold seeped into the bones of his feet and made him hobble back home in defeat, shivering under his jacket violently. Tonight he wanted to get all the way through the soy field and to the pond on the other side of the tree line.

It wasn't fit for skating. His mom had said so herself. You could fall through the ice and get trapped beneath it. You'd freeze to death before the sheets on your cot had even lost all your body heat. You'd be a frozen brick on the bottom of the pond before anyone even noticed you were missing.

Quickly, so as not to lose himself halfway through the soy field again, he followed the old rows toward the tree line. Once inside, he could hear the wind shake the limbs of the trees, which sounded dry and brittle like bones. A perfect setting for a suicide.

Much better than the men's room at school, where he'd planned to take the pills his mom had confiscated, the one lousy day of his life that she decided to take an interest in what he was doing. And better, though maybe not as dramatic, as some of the other scenarios he'd imagined: A gun in the backseat of his stepfather's SUV. Stepping onto the tracks just as the Amtrak rumbled through. Hanging himself from the rod in his closet, although that one was getting a little overdone. Seemed like every time you got online these days, somebody was hanging themselves in their closets. Throwing himself out of the car on the highway. Plunging a knife under his ear in the locker room showers during a basketball game.

Drowning under ice could almost be made out to be an accident. Definitely not the same effect. But he'd be dead; what would he care, anyway?

Popping out on the other side of the trees, he stood staring at the pond. He'd made it. It was way bigger than he'd imagined. They wouldn't find him easily.

He didn't think about what he was doing. He didn't need to. He'd thought it through so many times already. His life sucked. It wasn't going to get any better. Mitch Munde wasn't going to stop calling him "faggot" and giving him titty twisters in the hallways and he wasn't going to get any better in phys ed and no girl was ever going to be interested in him. He wasn't going to suddenly wake up with no zits and his parents would never get back together and he would never stop feeling like such a little bitch for wishing they would. He was never going to come home to cookies and the smell of laundry day. His stepdad was never going to take him to an amusement park or a baseball game. And his mom was never going to put him before her all-important students.

And he was never going to get happy. He'd tried. Ever since sixth grade he'd tried. It wasn't happening. He just wanted to die and get it over with.

He paused only briefly to wonder if you shit and pissed yourself if you died underwater. He doubted it. Weird.

The wind ripped through him and he half hobbled down the short bank and stepped once, twice onto the creaking ice at the edge of the pond.

Don't think about it, he told himself. *Just do it. Walk fast to the middle and jump hard up and down. And when you hear the ice splinter . . . breathe.*

But just as he lifted his foot to take a second step, he heard a noise drifting in on the breeze from the edge of the tree line. He froze, listening.

It wasn't an animal. It wasn't the wind. It wasn't the cracking of the ice.

It was talking. He heard it plain as day, the lilting, the rising and falling of a woman's voice. The low rumble of a man's.

Slowly, he stepped back up onto the rocks at the edge of the pond and turned around, dropping his hands to the ground to give himself cover as he scanned the tree line with his eyes. His hands started to shake against the ground. His teeth chattered.

He peered into the trees, trying to make out shapes, straining to hear the voices again.

And then he saw them.

Sitting on the ground, wrapped in their coats, talking to each other in low, urgent voices.

Uncle Bradley.

And Aunt Claire.

■ ■ ■ ■

DECEMBER 24

■ ■ ■ ■

"Soon you'll only cry at night."

EIGHT

Maya awoke to the sound of her son's snore. The room was still dark, but she knew daybreak was coming, even if the sky never lightened up enough to actually look like day.

She knew dawn was approaching because she knew her son. He slept so deeply during the night, scarcely moving a muscle, sweat brimming his bangs as if sleeping soundly was hard work, but come daybreak when he began to float to the top of his dreams, he snored. Always had, ever since he was a baby and slept in her arms.

Molly was curled into a ball in the cot next to him, her thumb poked into her perfect pink O of a mouth. She still sucked it like a newborn, busily and greedily, and Maya had worried over children's advice books on how to make her stop. She didn't want the girl to grow up with crooked teeth. Girls with crooked teeth went through a lot of

151

hellish teasing. Maya didn't like to think about it, but she and her friends had doled out that hellish teasing to many an imperfect girl in their time.

Maya lay on her side and stared at her children. She knew them. Everything about them. There was rarely a surprise when it came to her babies.

Unlike the twitching, snoring form at her back. After nine years of marriage, she felt as if she scarcely knew him at all.

He liked brunettes. She knew that. He preferred trim figures, which, God knew, was not an easy feat after having two eight-pound children and nearing forty to boot. He liked year-round tan skin under cream and eggshell and bone colors in clean-line fabrics and designer labels. He liked a well-spoken woman, but preferred she save that skill for things like PTA committee planning and homeowners' association meetings. He had exacting standards on just what turned his head, and if she didn't keep up . . . well, he never exactly said what would happen if she didn't keep up, but she had her theories.

Of course one of her theories involved wiry blond hair and frumpy U of C sweatshirts and a filthy, opinionated mouth that would embarrass even the most clichéd construction worker, so go figure.

But Maya refused to think about Claire this morning. It was Christmas Eve, and she was sleeping in her satiny pajamas for the third night in a row, and everyone knew how satin could begin to smell after just a couple of days of sleep heat being trapped in it. She should have packed something more practical.

She would have to go shopping today. She couldn't sleep in those things another night. And she couldn't have her children waking up on Christmas morning to no Santa Claus. She knew it wasn't her mother's fault that the funeral got moved to after Christmas, but . . .

Well, Elise had seemed a little strange. Not that Maya could blame her. She supposed that when your husband died, you were going to have a few "off" days, no matter how much of a cruel shit he was when he was living. Maya had sympathy for her. She'd been off lately herself. Well, not so much "off" as scared for her life, but she was trying so hard not to dwell on that. Not over Christmas.

Maya sighed and pulled her trim body to a sitting position. She felt fat and bloated, eating the rich Missouri foods, drinking all that fattening Christmas wine and snacking on cookies, and with no morning Pilates workout. She really needed to stop napping and start hiking, but she still hadn't gained back all her strength — the treatments, the stress just seemed to sap her energy — plus there was something about being in the same house with Claire again that brought back all those horrid old memories and, quite flatly, wore her out.

The last time she'd seen her sister had been after she'd taken Bradley's car in for detailing as a surprise. They were newlyweds and were living that fabulous phase of life where there was so much promise and so few worries. No kids to grab the attention in the family. Just the two of them, and Maya loved how romantic they were — it was such a departure from the family she'd grown up in, the family Claire had still been growing up in, the poor thing.

They were living in an apartment just beyond the baseball diamond, maybe fifteen minutes from the farm. Saving money for their dream house. Making plans. Making love. Doing the things newlyweds do.

But the surprise had been on Maya, when she'd opened the ashtray and found a used condom nestled on a couple of wadded-up gum wrappers. Disgusted, she'd picked it up between her thumb and forefinger, her whole body going numb with disbelief. There was no way it could have been Bradley's. He loved her. He'd married her. He'd made promises to her.

She tried to come up with alternative explanations. Maybe it was a friend's. Maybe it had come with the car and they'd just never noticed. Maybe . . . But it was hopeless. Whose could it be if not Bradley's?

She'd cried. Right there in the parking lot of the U-Clean Car Wash, she'd sat on the curb next to the trash bins and bawled like a lost child. She felt everything slipping away from her, her whole life loosing itself from her grasp before she'd even had a good hold on it. She'd worked so hard to win Bradley. She was the most perfect she could possibly be, all for him. If he didn't love her, she was nothing. If he didn't want her, she might as well be dead.

After a long while, spent from the sobbing, she felt the overwhelming grief give way to a sort of maniacal anger. Her fists clenched and her fingers nearly ached with the desire to be washed of the scum that had been on the outside of that condom. Scum that belonged inside another woman. How dare he!

Nearly blind with rage, she dove back behind the steering wheel and tore out of the car wash parking lot and sped toward the baseball field and to the roundabout that took her down by the railroad tracks and would eventually lead her to the only place she could think to go.

And that was where she'd found her husband, locked in an embrace with a woman. All Maya could see over his shoulder was the shock of curly blond hair, the tanned hands gripping the backs of his arms. But that was all she needed to see. She could recognize her sister from a mile away.

They denied it. Of course they did. Well, Claire did. Bradley never really said one way or another. Just stuck with some bullshit story about how it wasn't his condom and he had no idea how it'd gotten into his car's ashtray. As if some random stranger just went around breaking into people's cars to hide their used condoms. As if she would believe that.

"Do you love her? Are you in love with her?" Maya had asked him time and time again.

"This isn't necessary," he would always answer, or, "She told you it wasn't hers. I told you it wasn't mine. Why don't you drop it?" or, simply, "Maya, I told you on the day I married you that I loved you."

It didn't exactly take an expert to recognize that none of those answers was the "no" she'd been looking for.

So whether or not Claire was innocent, as she maintained, in Maya's eyes she was guilty. Because whatever had transpired between them — and make no mistake, something had! — it had made Bradley fall in love with Claire. And as far as Maya was concerned, Bradley having sex with Claire was hurtful and destructive, but Bradley loving Claire was unforgivable.

She'd made a vow that she would never forgive her sister for what had happened. Had pushed Bradley into taking a job in another city. And had been thrilled when he got one in Chicago. Far away from her sister, who was nothing and at the same time everything that Bradley wanted in a woman.

And now she was back home at the farm where her marriage had taken such a dark and harrowing turn, a single floor's distance from the woman who'd destroyed it. And how ironic was it that her life had recently taken an even darker and more harrowing turn, and no matter how far and how fast she tried to run, she could never get away from this new development.

Will's snores got louder, and Maya

thought she heard, in the distance, the drone of a chain saw, which meant somewhere out there people were up and at 'em. She slid out of bed, careful not to wake Bradley and the kids, and padded to the bathroom for her shower. Her hair needed straightening, her eyes were in desperate want of some firming cream, and how she was going to live for three more days without her teeth whitener she had no idea.

All she knew was it was Christmas Eve and she had to get up and moving. She had shopping to do.

Maya showered, dressed, and was in the process of throwing together a sour cream coffee cake when Julia shuffled in, rubbing the sleep out of her eyes.

"You're up early," Julia said on a yawn.

"Is it? I can't find a working clock anywhere in this place."

Julia plunked into a chair at the table. "It's about six now. Looks like you've been up for a while."

"Is that all? Feels later. I couldn't sleep," Maya said, spooning batter into a pan.

"Too quiet? I forgot how quiet it is here."

"Too loud in my head," Maya answered. She fussed with the oven control, turning it to the preheat setting.

Julia seemed to not really know what to

158

say, and for a beat the only sound in the kitchen was Maya's fingernails against the plastic of the buttons on the oven as she beeped it awake.

"Is that a coffee cake? Where'd you get the recipe?" Julia finally asked.

"Know it by heart. I made it every Sunday morning when Bradley and I were first married. It was his favorite. I saw last night that Mom had some extra apples in a bushel downstairs and decided to throw one together. It's been a long time." She seemed to get lost in thought, then visibly shake it off. "Wait till you smell it. It'll make the whole house smell incredible. Great way to wake up."

Julia let out a breath. "Good. I can have a smoke." She dug a pack of cigarettes out of her pajama pocket and lit one, leaning over to crack a window just a bit and angling her chair so her cigarette smoldered in the direction of the window. "It's cold out by the garage. Too cold for first thing in the morning."

Maya regarded her sister for a minute. Queenie, they'd all called her, because she was so put-together, so regal, so in control, in charge, like a little queen. She even had the strong jaw, the long face, the sharp cheekbones that suggested royalty. How

Maya had envied her sister. Smart, educated, driven. Married the perfect guy right out of high school, and when he turned out to be not perfect at all, had simply shrugged him off and kept walking, like leaving a discarded and outgrown piece of clothing at her feet on the floor.

But something about Julia seemed different now. Was Maya imagining that? Being hopeful, maybe, that she was not the only sister struggling? No, there was definitely something off about Julia. She seemed nervous and unsure. Awkward around her own son, who, by the way, was the most angry and sullen teen Maya had ever seen. And now Queenie was a smoker too? When had that happened?

The oven beeped and Maya bent to slide the coffee cake inside, then set the timer. She turned, brushed her hands off, and slipped out of her mom's apron. She opened the refrigerator and pulled out a carton of orange juice, got two glasses from the cupboard, then set them on the table and filled them, sliding one toward Julia and sitting down in front of the other one.

"Smoking gives you wrinkles," she said, trying to sound light, but hearing in her own voice a tinge of judgment instead. Why did she always have to do that — sound so shrewy? No wonder Bradley constantly had his eye on other women. No wonder she was losing him, had lost him.

Julia took a drag, blew it out toward the window. "Don't bother. I have the entire lecture memorized. I live with it. Wrinkles, heart attack, cancer, death, blah blah blah."

Maya stiffened at the word *cancer,* but forced herself to shrug it off. "I wasn't going to lecture. But when did you start doing that?"

"What? Smoking? The day I found our father's stash in the barn." Julia laughed. "Do you really not remember the first time he caught me? Spanked the shit out of me. I could barely walk afterwards."

No, Maya didn't remember. How could one spanking possibly stand out from all the rest? How could one lecture, one vile name-calling, one drunken beating possibly be memorable?

Well, there were memories. The day he got rid of Claire's horse and she'd been so heartbroken she'd lain in bed sick for days. The day he knocked Julia's head against the car window and a crack had snaked down the glass. The day he kicked Grandmother Ruby out of the house and told her to never come back, to never visit again. Those days, Maya was not likely to ever forget.

"Became a game after that," Julia said. "I'd only take one or two per pack, would smoke them in little bits, to make them last longer. Would hide the butts, throw them in the pond, usually. See how many I could get away with before he'd notice. I think he always suspected, but he was never quite sure. It was the one thing I had the upper hand on with him." She sighed. "Until I was in high school and could keep my own in Dusty's car. So, yeah, I guess forever. But Tai and Eli are always after me about it. I'm trying, but this week is not a good week to quit."

Maya chuckled. "It actually may be a good week to start."

"You want one?"

Maya shook her head, rubbing the pads of her fingers along her cheeks. "No. I was serious about the wrinkles." Again, the word *cancer* echoed in her mind, and she moved her fingers down into her armpit protectively.

A sweet apple scent began to waft out of the oven. Maya stood and filled the coffeemaker, which gurgled into life. Nothing smelled better with a sour cream apple coffee cake than a fresh pot of coffee.

"You know," Julia said, finishing her cigarette and walking over to the sink to run water over the burning filter, "you are probably the only person in the world who gets up at five a.m. on Christmas Eve to make coffee cake in high heels."

Maya bristled. "I doubt it," she said. "There's nothing wrong with looking good."

"I suppose," Julia said, but Maya could have sworn the words were laced with an accusation she couldn't quite put her finger on. That was the other thing that had been sticking in Maya's craw about Julia — the one other thing that had changed about her. She no longer felt like an ally.

"So what's up with you and Claire?" Maya asked, rounding on Julia suddenly.

"What do you mean?"

"Come on, Queenie. You were all about Claire being the worst sister on earth for sleeping with Bradley, and now you're buddy-buddy with her. What's changed?"

"Maya, I honestly don't know what you're talking about. Claire is my sister, and our father just died. It's been a long time."

Maya squinted her eyes. "You used to be on my side," she said.

Julia threw her hands in the air. "There is no side! Whatever happened or didn't happen . . . it was years ago, Maya! Don't you think it's time you let it go?"

Maya's eyes darkened. "I will never let it go."

"Well, that's probably not very wise. You think smoking will kill you? Try holding grudges. Try stress. Try isolation. It's time to let it go." She turned off the water and tossed the soaked butt into the trash, then walked back over to the window and shut it. "Look at what stress and isolation has done to Mom," she said, lowering her voice. She sat in her chair again and took a drink of the orange juice, her serious gaze never leaving Maya. "She's cracked up. Loopy. And she seems . . . secretive. Like she's hiding something and it's eating her up inside."

"She's fine. She's grieving."

"Haven't you noticed she's not said one word about him?" Julia asked. "Not a single thing. And she hasn't shed a tear. Hasn't even acted all that sad."

"Well, who has? Who would?" Maya said, and then felt her face flush with the ugliness of those words. But it was true. Nobody in the house seemed to really be what could be called grieving. Everyone seemed to be there mainly out of duty. Everyone seemed to be bumping around in their own little bubble, occasionally merging with another bubble and then separating again. Everyone seemed to be looking forward to getting this

164

burial over with. It wasn't the way she'd wanted her family to turn out, but it wasn't entirely her fault that they had turned out that way. In fact, it wasn't her fault at all. If anyone wanted to lay blame, they could begin with the man in the casket and work their way to the slut with the curly blond hair.

There was a moment of uncomfortable silence between them. The coffeemaker finished brewing with one final growl and the oven ticked as it puffed heat around the rising cake inside. Finally, Julia leaned forward, her voice so low Maya had to lean forward too, just to hear her. "Are you sad about him being gone?" she asked.

And despite herself, despite her desire to maintain her poise throughout this whole nasty nightmare, Maya couldn't help but shake her head. "Not at all." She pressed her lips together nervously, feeling the nude lip gloss she'd smeared on after her shower slip against itself. "When I told my therapist that my father had died, she was surprised to hear that he'd still been alive. I never ever talked about him. Isn't that weird? You'd think he'd have come up in therapy of all places. God, you'd think he'd have come up a lot. I think I wanted to forget that he still existed. It's been a lot of years since I've felt comfortable here."

"Only the good die young," Julia said.

"Maybe Mom isn't loopy or secretive or whatever. Maybe she's relieved. And who would blame her, you know?"

"Not me."

"Me either."

"And not Claire."

"God, do we have to keep bringing her up?" Maya angrily took a sip of her juice, feeling tense, wiry, as if she wanted to go lie down again, though she'd been awake for only a little over an hour. Normally she'd hit the treadmill at a time like this, do some sit-ups. But it had been weeks since she'd been up to her morning workout, and would be more weeks until she was up to it again. If ever. She shook the thought away. She would get back to the treadmill. She would return to sit-ups. She had to believe that.

"I didn't mean anything by it," Julia shot back. "Lighten up, would you? Jeez."

"You don't understand."

Julia sat back and crossed her legs. "Well, you're right about that."

The two sisters glared at each other, and Maya was struck with an overwhelming sensation of being all alone in the world. Her father gone, her mom — yes, Julia was right — possibly barely hanging on to reality, one sister her betrayer and the other her betrayer's champion, her husband . . . just . . . ugh. She didn't want to think about it. She didn't want to think about any of it. She wanted to sleep.

But before either of them could speak again, Will burst into the room, the way he burst into every room, with energy to spare.

"Mom! I dreamed I eated a dinosaur and I waked up really hungried," he said, and something about the sound of his voice calmed Maya. Maybe she wasn't alone in the world at all. Maybe these two children she and Bradley had created would be her champions. Even if it was wrong to want your children to be your champions, the thought soothed her.

"Was it a French Toastasaurus?" she said, opening her arms wide, inviting him, playing along with their script. This was the way they started every morning, coming up with dinosaur names derived from breakfast foods — French Toastasaurus, Pancakagon, Muffineratops. He scrambled up into her lap, giggling, his neck still damp from sleep, and snuggled his whole body up against her. How much longer would she have this with him? How long until little boys decided that mommies were uncool or embarrassing? How many days until French Toastasaurus would get an eye roll and a frustrated grunt? She nestled her nose in his hair and took a deep breath. She was sure she could be blindfolded and would be able to pick her son out of a crowd by the smell of his scalp. "Well, you're in luck, then," she said against his head. "We're eating cake for breakfast this morning, and it's almost done cooking."

Will turned his head to look up at Maya, his mouth open in a huge smile that made her grin no matter what else was going on in the house and her world. Such a precious boy. She never wanted to leave him. She hoped she wouldn't have to. "Chocolate?"

She shook her head. "No. Apple."

"But I'll bet Santa will leave you some chocolate tonight," Julia said.

Will turned back around in his mom's lap and laid his head against her chest. "Molly said Santa won't come because we don't live here," he said sadly.

Maya manipulated her arms to turn him around again. "Well," she said, "Molly doesn't know everything, and I'll bet she's wrong about this."

"You think?"

"I think."

"Can I have chocolate milk with my cake?"

"Yep."

"Can I build a fort under the Christmas tree?"

"Don't knock it down." Maya kissed him on his forehead and watched as he slithered out of her lap and scampered off into the den. "I'll call you when the cake is done," she said.

After he left, the kitchen felt empty, as if Julia wasn't even sitting there. As if maybe Maya wasn't even sitting there herself. Something about Will's absence made his presence seem all the more real, and all the more fleeting, and it was all Maya could do to keep from crying. She wanted so badly to capture her children and keep them at this age forever. She wanted to watch them grow, but if her fears came true and she couldn't do that, she wanted them to stay forever this way so that she wouldn't miss a thing.

"Santa?" Julia whispered across the table. "How are you going to manage that?"

"I'm going shopping later. Bradley will just have to stay with the kids for a few minutes whether he likes it or not. You want to come?"

"Yeah, sure," Julia said. "After the cake. It smells amazing."

Maya grinned. "I told you so," she sing-songed, and she and her sister both giggled

169

as they listened to the lilting voice of Molly, who had apparently joined her brother under the Christmas tree. "The secret is in the heels."

Apples and cinnamon once again wafted through the house. One of the kids had turned on the Christmas tree lights, which blinked against the walls between the two rooms. Outside, the sky had turned white and begun to shed fat, wet flakes onto the ground. The poinsettias were gay and colorful in every corner, and if Maya closed her eyes and concentrated really hard . . . it felt like Christmas. A real Christmas.

A happy one.

Please, God, she silently prayed. *Let it last.*

And, despite herself, she hoped the prayer would be answered.

NINE

By the time they left the house, it had turned into a family affair. Elise had jumped at the chance to run into town, going on and on about having forgotten the candy canes in a way that made Maya uncomfortable once again. Death of a husband or not, the woman was such a far cry from the stoic, stern mother who had forced them to so delicately toe the line that she was almost like a different person.

And then Julia went and invited Claire, proving to Maya once and for all that she was no longer on her side, and Maya didn't care one whit what Julia said about there not being sides — Julia just didn't understand. She didn't know how it hurt to even catch the tiniest glimpse of that stupid blond hair. She didn't understand the full force of what she was expecting Maya to forget. And at what a bad time.

But it was Christmas Eve. And she needed

pajamas. And the kids needed gifts. And she wasn't going to screw up what could end up being her last Christmas just because of one lousy person. She gritted her teeth and dug her French-tipped nails into her palms. It would not be her last Christmas. She had to stop thinking that way.

The four of them climbed into Julia's SUV and headed toward town, to the big-box store, the only sounds inside the car their blowing and gasping breath against the cold and the squeak of the windshield wipers fighting the snow, which was coming down hard.

Maya remembered when she was a child and always prayed for a white Christmas. She liked the way the world seemed muted beneath the blanket of white. She loved the way it felt insulated and small and as if she could hide in plain sight. Hide from her dad, who always seemed to have the weight of the world on his shoulders, and who always seemed to be looking for someone to dump it on. The feeling was liberating and empowering and it was during those moments, and those moments alone, that Maya felt like she could do anything. Like she could be somebody.

She never felt that way at any other time of her life. She mostly wandered and waded through her days feeling ugly and stupid and insecure and as if she had to grasp onto things with a grip that might break her knuckles in order to keep them. She often raged against the unfairness of it all, how everything seemed to come so easily for everyone else.

She hoped Bradley would be a decent father for once and take the children outside. Let them play in the snow. Let them hide in plain sight. Let them feel big. Maybe instead of buying a carload of junk for them, she should have stayed home and taken them out instead. Maybe that would have been the best gift she could have given them: the gift of confidence.

The drive was slow and uncomfortable. Maya could feel Claire's presence behind her, could feel the unspoken accusations from her mom and Julia, a noxious cloud floating above her. She knew they wanted her to speak, to make nice. *It's Christmas Eve,* she could practically hear them thinking. *It's a time for peace.*

But they didn't know. They hadn't held a nasty used condom in their hands. They didn't see their husband wrapped around another woman. They didn't stand in front of the love of their life and watch him crumble away from them.

They didn't see newly wed Bradley break down into frame-racking tears, his back hunched dejectedly.

They hadn't been working for ten years to forget the image.

You did it, didn't you? You screwed my sister, you asshole! she heard herself saying, standing, shaking, in front of him in the living room of their new apartment, the memory as clear as if it had happened just yesterday, not ten years ago. Saw herself fling a book at him, saw him bring a knee up to cover himself, but the tears were not coverable. The tears had been there for her to see. *Why don't you just admit it!*

He shook his head. *Maya, please, you don't know what you're —*

I know enough! I can see it on you! I can practically smell it on you! Her own tears were hot and furious. She picked up another book, feeling as if she could throw it clear through a wall. Was that how her dad had felt every day? Like he wanted to throw something through a wall? Had she inherited his rage?

She winged the book at his feet this time, wanting only to see him jump, to see herself make him move, but she missed by miles, and as if she had flung all of herself with that book, she suddenly felt so weak, so tired it was as if she had no muscles left. Her fight was gone. Her anger replaced by a bone-dissolving sadness. *God, Bradley,* she'd cried into her palms as she sank to her knees and then to her butt on their dirty apartment floor. *We've only been married for two months. How could you?*

And when he didn't answer, only stared at his feet, she looked up at him, squinting through her burning eyes, and leveled the one accusation she wished she'd never allowed out of her mouth. *You love her, don't you?*

At first she thought he wouldn't answer her at all, and that silence would really be all the answer she needed. All of her effort hadn't been enough to keep the man she loved; her sister had him, and she hadn't even ever needed to try. But eventually he did speak, shuffling miserably on the hardwood of their apartment bedroom.

Maya, he'd said, and she could hear the reluctance in his voice. Eventually, she would take that reluctance and hold on to it like something dear. If he didn't want to hurt her, maybe that meant that she hadn't lost him entirely. Maybe it meant he still loved her a little. *I can't help the way I feel. I've . . . I've tried.*

He had kept talking, Maya remembered

as Julia's SUV curved around the baseball diamond and pointed toward the main drag, but what he'd said had bounced off of her like hail. Things about working it out. About being committed to the marriage. About moving away — away from the family, away from his dead-end job, away from Claire. And she had at first raged against this. Demanded better for herself than to be second fiddle to another woman. Beaten her breast and railed that she deserved a marriage where the love was effortless.

But in the end, she'd just been so tired. Too worn down to fight him. Too committed to the dream of not just a marriage, but a marriage with *this man,* having children with *this man,* too unsure of her desirability to break free. She'd stayed because it was convenient. And it was hers. She would just have to work for it. Work harder than she ever had before. Work harder than she knew she could.

Work harder than Claire.

When they'd moved to Chicago, Maya felt as though a veil was lifted from her face. And when, a year later, she'd discovered she was pregnant, she felt as though she could, for the first time ever, see her life clearly. Bradley was not a philanderer. He wasn't out screwing every flirt in a push-up bra. He had fallen in love with one woman. He hadn't even meant to. He'd tried not to. And that woman was very far away.

Well . . . at least that was what she had thought back then.

God, but that was a long time ago. So much had happened since then. So much had happened just recently.

And then to come back home . . . it almost felt as if God was trying to tell her something. As if God was trying to tell her to let Claire have him.

"What do the kids want this year?" Elise asked, breaking the silence, and jarring Maya out of her memory.

She shrugged. "They're not picky. Anything that takes batteries or comes in boxes with a thousand tiny pieces."

Julia chuckled. "I remember Eli's building-block stage. Stepping on one of those with bare feet in the middle of the night can make a grown man cry. Believe me, I've seen it."

"Molly's into dolls. The smaller the accessories, the better. Will, on the other hand, is happy with a box. Sometimes I wish I could just skip the toys and buy him the cardboard boxes."

"Well, I remember some other little girl who loved her dolls and all their little brushes and shoes," Elise said from the backseat. "I guess it's true about the apple and the tree."

"You did love girly-girl stuff, Maya," Julia teased. "You were forever doing those beauty salons in the bathroom, remember?"

Maya grinned. She'd forgotten about that. "Do you remember the time I used food coloring for your makeup? You looked like a clown for a solid week."

"Oh, Lord, I remember that," Elise interjected. "You ruined a set of towels that day."

Julia giggled again. "And I had to go to school looking like that. I was so mad at you."

"You think you were mad? Remember when she got the roller brush stuck in my hair so bad Mom had to cut it out?" Claire called from the backseat, and everyone in the car howled with laughter, even Maya, who was lost in the memory of little Claire running through the pasture, the roller brush bobbing out from her head at an odd angle, Elise chasing after her with a pair of scissors, Julia yelling at her mom that they were not supposed to run with scissors, Maya hiding behind the back porch, trembling with fear, sure she would be whipped but good when they finally got that hairbrush loose.

"I damn near killed myself running after you that day. I was sure I was going to slip on a cow pie and end my life right then and there," Elise was saying.

Julia sounded breathless with laughter. "And you kept yelling at me over your shoulder, 'Shut up, Queenie! Mind your business! You want me to come after you next?' "

Suddenly the SUV hit a slick patch and slid, the back tire coming inches from catching the ledge of a ditch. All four women screamed, Maya grabbing for the handle above her window and clutching it with both hands, as Julia turned and turned the steering wheel trying to get the SUV back under control. They fishtailed, then overcompensated and fishtailed the other way, and back to the middle again before coming to a stop diagonally across both lanes of the road.

For a moment there was only breathing to be heard. Maya's heart pounded in her chest, her fingers tingling with adrenaline and her death grip on the handle. Thank God it was Christmas Eve day in a small town in a blizzard, she thought. Back home, that little mistake would have taken out half a dozen parked cars and a few moving ones. And perhaps a pedestrian or two.

Nobody said anything, until the faraway telltale scraping of a plow came toward them.

"Shit, that was close," Julia finally breathed. She let off the brake and straightened out the SUV, creeping along in the direction they'd been going before they fishtailed.

They went just long enough to get some distance, and Claire added in a low voice, "Good thing you weren't carrying scissors, Mom, or we'd all been goners," and just like that they were all giggling again.

In some ways this was the most normal Maya had felt in . . . years maybe. These were the moments she longed for — the captured bits of time where things were so normal they were magical. Only now, after all that had happened, those were the moments that ultimately felt the bleakest to her. The normal moments, the trivial ones, would be the ones that would be missed the most if things took a turn for the worse.

The thought dried up the laughter in her throat like salt on a slug, and by the time Julia had maneuvered into a parking space, Maya felt downright shitty again.

"Well, I'm sure you all remember what Dad did when he came home and found that big chunk out of Claire's hair," she spat bitterly.

"Maya, don't," Elise said.

"Yeah, this is fun. Let's not think about that kind of stuff right now. Not with him gone and . . . C'mon, it's Christmas," Julia added.

But Maya couldn't help it. How could they? She really wished she knew this trick that everyone else seemed to have mastered, the one where they could just shrug off bitterness and grief and filter their memories until all that came out in the end was shiny.

How could they recall the hilarious scene of Julia chasing Elise chasing Claire through the pasture without remembering the thunder of their dad's voice when he came home? The way he'd thrashed all three girls like rag dolls, spanking their bottoms so hard their cries of pain came out soundless. The way he'd taken all of their hairbrushes and toothbrushes and creams and tossed them into the trash barrel and burned them. The way they'd had to go to school with ratted hair and smelly breath for a full two weeks before he relented and let Elise buy them new things. It felt like a horror movie to Maya sometimes . . . and whenever it dawned on her that the horror movie was her life, it seemed all the more horrible. And she didn't care how funny the rest of the story was, it would never be funny enough to wash away the horrible part. Never.

"You're right," she said through tight lips, and tried to stretch them into what she hoped looked like a friendly smile. "We've got shopping to do."

She shouldered the passenger door open and plunged out into the parking lot, which had gotten covered over with heavy flakes. Her sisters and mom followed her, the four of them trekking through the falling snow, zipping their coats up to their chins, holding their hoods over their heads, squinting against the wind.

Maya felt like she was encased in a blizzard — the one pelting her face and the one pelting her on the inside. She couldn't help but watch Claire's long, beautiful legs high-step across the lot, bronze against the white, like a supermodel's. And she couldn't help the feeling of coldness that swept through her. Perfect. Her sister was perfect. Without even trying.

And she never would be.

And a shopping trip wouldn't make her that way.

But it was all she had, so she slipped and slid over the snowy lot in her impractical heels and skinny jeans and plunged through the automatic front doors of the store.

Good God, she thought as she shook the snow from her body onto the swampy mat in the entryway of the store. What craziness awaited her here?

After a few moments of stomping and brushing and making the necessary *brrr* noises that accompany the shedding of snow, the women turned and surveyed the store. Maya hadn't been in one of these types of stores in years. She was actually kind of nervous about it. What if she looked stupid? To look stupid in a place like this? Hello, insult, meet injury.

She did what she always did when she felt self-conscious. She lifted her chin, swished her hair over one shoulder and then the other — this snow was not helping the frizz in her hair at all, by the way — pooched her lips in as hoity a look as she could muster, and plowed forward, as if she knew exactly what she was doing. She bought up cheap plastic junk in big-box stores every day, by God, or at least she looked like she did.

She pulled a folded piece of notebook paper out of her coat pocket and smoothed it open. "I've got a list," she said. "Mostly toys and candy. I shouldn't be too long."

But Claire had already started off down the main aisle, ducking into a rack of workout clothes, and Julia had become engrossed by a bargain bin filled with tacky seasonal socks just a few steps away. Elise blinked and absently brushed her bangs away from her face, distractedly looking over Maya's shoulder at the list.

"We'll all just meet back here, then, in about an hour?" she said, but Claire was long gone. "I'll go with you," Elise continued, placing her hand between Maya's shoulder blades. "I want to get some things for the kids, too."

"You've already got things for them under the tree, Mom."

Elise waved Maya off. "Those were bought in a hurry. Besides, it's not every day I get to have all of my grandkids in one house for Christmas."

True, Maya thought. It wasn't every day her mother had all her grandkids in one house for . . . anything. She felt a tiny twinge of guilt. She knew that was partly her fault. If she'd just forgiven Claire, who knew what the family might be like today? But she brushed away the thought like the snowflakes she'd just shed. She didn't have the luxury of thinking about history right now. She barely had the luxury of thinking about the future.

The women spread out, the sheer space of

the store bringing relief. It was easy to be alone there. It was easy to lose the others and have some space to think. To be silent and not feel as if that was a bad thing or as if someone would read something into it.

Maya stormed the place as if she knew it by heart, because that was what she did best. The action made her feel better, made her feel in control. Elise trailed behind her pushing a shopping cart, which Maya filled without even really trying. A football here, a board game there, a scooter, a bottle of fancy bubble bath, slippers with cute little character faces on the toes. Candy canes and chocolates and rolls and rolls of wrapping paper. A little doll. A pack of cars. Cheap shit that she knew her kids would delight over in the morning, but would never look at again once they were back in their bedrooms in Chicago, but that didn't matter. What mattered was Christmas. You never knew which Christmas would be your last one.

Why couldn't she get rid of those dismal thoughts? She had promised herself that she would leave them behind in Chicago. They weren't healthy. They weren't going to help matters at all.

But little lipsticks and building blocks and a pair of flimsy pajamas that didn't smell like sleep crotch would help. Those things would help tremendously.

She knew that Bradley would balk when he saw all the things she'd bought. He'd complain about how they were never going to be able to get them back to Chicago. He'd question what would happen to the closetful of Christmas gifts that awaited the kids at home. He'd say they would get spoiled with this kind of behavior, and that would lead her to remember her dad and how he was always so damned worried that any measure of happiness would spoil his daughters, so he spent his every miserable day making sure they were decidedly unhappy, and she'd have to take painkillers and go to bed with a warm washcloth to cover her eyes like she'd taken to doing so often lately. But it would be worth it to see the looks on her kids' faces tomorrow morning when they saw that Santa had arrived after all. That hope and magic still existed, by God.

She was so busy shopping, so engrossed at a turning rack full of faux-leather wallets (finding something for Bradley in this place was going to be no easy task; she might as well get him something practical, if not ugly), she didn't even notice that her mother had gone missing.

186

"What do you think of this one?" she asked, holding out a black tri-fold that wasn't too obviously plastic. When she got no answer, she turned, but found only the cart behind her. "Mom?" she called. No answer. "Mom?"

She gave another look to the wallet, and then dropped it into the cart. She shrugged and moved behind it to push it, though she hadn't pushed a cart in ages. Not even at the grocery store, where she always just carried a basket over her arm to pick up necessities. Her housekeeper, Tildy, did all the hard grocery shopping for her. Especially since the treatments had begun.

She moved on, casting glances down every aisle that she passed, looking for Elise, while at the same time continuing her shopping. It was odd that her mom had just disappeared, but she wasn't too worried — the woman wasn't six years old, for Christ's sake.

But it wasn't long before she was done and ready to go. She'd run across Julia, who had a cart full of things for her son as well, and then Claire, who carried two pair of yoga pants awkwardly over her arm as if so much fabric was weighing her down.

"You seen Mom?" Maya asked, rolling up to each of them, and each, in turn, shook her head. "She just took off," Maya mused, standing on her tiptoes to scan over the tops of the clothing racks for the sight of her mother's silver hair. She was starting to grow alarmed.

"Well, she couldn't have gone anywhere," Julia said. "I drove."

"Unless she got it in her head to walk somewhere," Claire said. "You know, she's been a little . . ."

"Scattered, yes, suicidal, no," Maya snapped. "She wouldn't just take off walking down the highway in a snowstorm. That's ridiculous."

Claire backed up a few steps, offense registering on her face. "Sorry. It was just a thought."

"Well, it wasn't a helpful one," Maya said.

Claire pressed her lips together tightly, then nodded once and said, to Julia, "I'm going to go try these on." Julia nodded back, wordless, and stared at the ground.

"That was mean," Julia mumbled after Claire got out of earshot. "She didn't do anything."

Maya sighed. "Yes, I know. I'm a horrible sister. But can we concentrate on the more pressing issue at hand? Where has our mother disappeared to?"

"Let's check the seasonal section. Maybe

she went . . . for more poinsettias."

The two sisters locked eyes and snickered. The last thing their mom needed was more poinsettias. The laughter took the edge off and they pushed their carts, side by side, to the aisles where Christmas trees and ornaments were already being replaced by Valentine's Day candies.

They split up, each of them going up and down aisles and then meeting in the middle. No Elise.

"Electronics?" Maya suggested, and they repeated the process there. And then in sporting goods. And then in grocery.

And finally, just as Maya began to get a lump in her throat, imagining that maybe Claire had been right all along, she turned down an aisle in pharmacy and there was her mom, standing behind a cart loaded with pack upon pack of tinsel, clutching an armful of aftershaves to her chest.

"Mom?" Maya said, then called to the next aisle, "Found her!"

Elise didn't look up, or even budge. She seemed deep in thought.

"Mom?" Maya asked again, and put her hand on her mom's shoulder. "Where were you?" Though one look in Elise's cart answered that question. They must have just missed her in the seasonal aisle. But, dear

God, why did anyone need that much tinsel? The tree was already overloaded with the tacky stuff as it was. "Mom? You okay?" Movement caught her eye, and Maya looked up to see Julia turning her cart down the aisle to join them, her eyebrows creased with worry.

Elise seemed to startle, but her face relaxed when she saw Maya. "Oh, I'm sorry, honey. I guess I got wrapped up in trying to decide which aftershave to get your father this year. You know how picky he can be. Which one says 'I'm sorry' the most?"

Maya swallowed against the lump in her throat. They'd all mentioned it — even Bradley had said something when they were alone in the bedroom the night before. Elise was acting unusual, and Maya wasn't sure she could attribute all of it to losing a husband. Was it normal to forget he'd died before he was even buried? "What do you mean, 'I'm sorry'?"

"Mom," Julia said, stepping around her cart. "He's gone. Remember? He died three days ago."

Elise blinked, seemed to take in Julia's words one syllable at a time, her mouth moving slightly as if she were repeating the words to herself. Finally, after a spell, she nodded and, one by one, placed the aftershaves back on the shelf. She let out a breath of air that might have been meant to be a laugh, but was a little too confused-sounding to actually be mirthful. "Of course. What was I thinking?" She gazed at her daughters, standing side by side with matching concerned expressions on their faces. "This is going to take some getting used to, I suppose."

Maya felt a quiver in her chest like her heart was breaking, and put her hand on her mom's shoulder. "But you will," she said, and inside she felt crushed, like her insides were wearing down. She'd never have guessed that anyone would miss her father, much less the woman whose life he made miserable, and the knowledge that you weren't safe from love even in an abusive relationship was almost the bleakest thing Maya could imagine. She suddenly felt very tired, like she'd pushed herself too hard. Her body needed rest. Bradley was right — the doctors had been clear about the importance of rest right now.

Julia reached over and tugged on her mom's arm. "I think we're ready to go," she said, giving Maya a look, and Maya sprang into motion, pushing her cart toward the checkout counter as Julia pushed her own cart with one hand, her other leading their

mom, both of them pretending the aban-
doned cart full of tinsel didn't even exist.

Ten

The best part about wrapping Christmas gifts, in Maya's estimation, was that you had an excuse to be undeniably alone. You could lock yourself in a room for hours, and the children would only grow happier as time passed, imagining that there must be a mountain of toys in the room with you to be taking so long to wrap.

At home, Maya would shut herself into the guest bedroom, pop a chick flick into the Blu-ray, and snack on gummy candies and microwave popcorn while spread out across the bed, slowly, slowly winding paper and tape around each gift. It was like a mini-vacation. A reward for all the hard work she'd put in shopping.

But that was before. That was when she felt like she would never run out of time with the kids.

That was before her doctor had said the word *cancer.*

Now every second away from the children felt like time falling through an hourglass.

But these were Santa gifts, so she waited until the kids were distracted in the kitchen with Elise, then quietly snuck downstairs to the basement and shut herself in her father's old workshop. She pulled the string to turn on the bare lightbulb that hung in the center of the room and looked around. It was dusty, as if it hadn't been touched in ages. She wondered when was the last time he'd been down there.

She used her palm to brush off the work-table, sawdust and cobwebs flinging into the air and drifting downward. The room smelled like him. She felt as if she could close her eyes and hear his saw running, hear him banging metal against metal or scraping sandpaper against something. She blinked, determined to keep her eyes open. She didn't want to remember him right now. Even the most innocuous memory would certainly be followed by a nightmarish one. And she had enough nightmares in her life as it was.

As if on cue, her side began to ache, high up next to her armpit. A light but nagging pain so un-pinpoint-able that she almost wondered if she was imagining it. Right where the lump had been cut out. Right where the radiation dot had been tattooed on her. So they could fix her. So they could make her live. After her first treatment, she'd joked that she was going to get a target tattooed there, just for a laugh, but now that she was in the thick of it, she just wanted the damn thing off of her, just wanted the ordeal to be over with. She wanted to be done. There was nothing funny about cancer, nothing funny about radiation. She couldn't help but think the permanent dot would be a cruel reminder of the scariest time of her life. And the most painful.

Absently, she rubbed the pain away, even though she was never sure if it was real pain and she was quite certain it wasn't something that could just be rubbed away like a sore muscle. It was habit.

Setting her bags on the floor next to the worktable, she pulled her cell phone out of her pocket and dialed her friend Carla, the one she'd met in the waiting room at the oncologist's office.

"Maya! Happy Christmas Eve!"

Maya smiled, closed her eyes, took in her friend's cool, deep voice. "Merry Christmas to you too!" she said, trying mightily to keep lightness in her voice. God, the workspace smelled like him. Why did she choose to wrap gifts in there? She rubbed her side again without even realizing it. "How's the family?"

"Oh, fantastic!" Carla answered. "Scotty and Phillip are having a blast with the cousins. John is in football heaven. And I just got a makeover."

"Makeover, huh? Sounds highbrow."

"Oh, it is. Going to be the new trend, I tell you. My little niece just painted my head to look like a Christmas ornament."

Carla laughed out loud, and Maya couldn't help it — Carla's laughter had always been contagious to her — so she laughed too. She pictured her friend's bald head glistening in red and green paint.

"Imagine what she'll do with you at Easter," Maya said.

"Well, I do have that Easter egg quality about me, don't I?" Carla said. "I think it's my stylish lack of hairdo," and they both laughed again. Though something about the laughter felt uncomfortable to Maya. Probably the gnawing knowledge that Carla might not even make it to Easter.

Maya had met Carla while trying, and failing, to be stoic in the oncologist's office months before.

Although she hadn't been searching for one, Maya had found a lump in her breast one morning in the shower, and her life had been a blur of doctor appointments and frightening words ever since: *biopsy, tumor, malignant, lumpectomy, radiation, oncologist. Cancer.*

She'd managed to keep a stiff upper lip when telling Bradley about the diagnosis, when laying out for him the treatment plan. She'd managed to get through all of it without so much as shedding a tear or wavering from her steadiness even the tiniest bit. She was a champ. The queen of positivity. She let only a few close friends know. She kept it a secret from her kids, her mother. No reason to worry everyone needlessly. Like with everything else, Maya would face this roadblock in her life with steadfastness and control.

But there had been something about sitting in an oncologist's office that was more than she could bear. An oncologist, for God's sake. A cancer doctor. You went to cancer doctors because you had cancer, and people died of cancer every single day and there was nothing to be done about it, and how would you know whether you would be a lucky one or the one your children don't even remember because you died so swiftly it was as if you'd never existed at all?

Carla had been sitting next to her, thumbing through a magazine, a pink bandanna tied around her head, little bits of fuzz standing up on the back of her neck.

"It gets easier," she said as Maya sniffled into a wadded tissue, trying her level best to be unnoticeable. "Soon you'll only cry at night."

Maya had looked over at the woman (no easy feat, by the way — Maya had never noticed it before, but looking directly into the face of someone who has clearly been battered by chemotherapy is never comfortable to do) and attempted a smile. But she found she couldn't say anything. She didn't want to be that woman with the bandanna wrapped around her head, and she couldn't think of how to talk to that woman without saying those words aloud.

But the woman had smiled, extended her hand. "Carla. IBC."

Maya found her voice. "IBC?"

"Inflammatory breast cancer. Kinda rare. Makes me special."

"Oh," Maya said. "I'm sorry. Um . . . something carcinoma in um . . ."

Carla nodded. "Ductal carcinoma in situ?"

Maya swabbed at her eyes again. "Yeah, that's it. And I'm Maya, by the way."

"Nice to meet you, Maya." She leaned toward Maya and lowered her voice. "The

198

first visit is always the hardest. You still think you're going to die every second of the day. Like, you might not even make it up the elevator to this office before you keel over, am I right?"

Tears threatened again. Maya shrugged hopelessly. The woman was right. Maya had had constant thoughts of dying since getting her diagnosis. She imagined herself collapsing midway through cooking dinner or while driving down the highway or while walking to the bathroom. Even though she knew it didn't work that way, that her thoughts were irrational and ridiculous, they still scared her so badly she'd begun being frightened to do anything. "I'm just afraid of leaving my kids behind."

"Me too. I have great kids. But . . ." Carla closed her magazine, looked toward the ceiling contemplatively. "But eventually you get used to that idea too. It's funny how the brain works, you know? It protects you."

Maya sniffled, her chin quivering dramatically, and swiped at her face with the tissue some more. "But I don't want to have to be protected," she said, and even she could hear the plaintive, childlike tone in her voice. She didn't like it, but understood that it was there, and having it there despite her dislike only served to fuel her tears. Is this what imminent death would reduce her to? A child?

Carla had put her magazine down on the empty chair on the other side of her and had reached over to pat Maya's shoulder. And for the next thirty minutes Maya had practically fallen into the other woman's eyes, dark green and glistening and hopeful, taking in her every word, trying to wrap herself in them like a blanket just out of the dryer. She wanted to have the same positivity that this woman had. She wanted it to be real, not just an act for Bradley. Not just another extension of her maddening need for perfection.

Over the course of the next few weeks, Maya and Carla became the best of friends. Maya found herself trying to time her appointments with Carla's so they would meet up in the waiting area, the two of them sometimes crying, sometimes laughing, Maya holding on to her new friend with a grip that practically begged for her not to go. Soon they began going back to Carla's house after their appointments, for coffee, for long chats about life and death and regret and dreaming. Their visits sometimes lasted long into the evening, the cute college girl at Will's preschool bringing Molly and Will home from school for extra cash.

Maya could hardly believe how much she already loved her new friend. How much she was rooting for her. How it hurt her to see Carla on her chemo days, when she was sick and exhausted and could barely keep down a sip of water.

And then when Maya had found out . . . well, when all the awfulness had hit, followed by the news of her father's death, she honestly didn't know how she would have made it through without Carla. Even though she knew there very well might be a day when she would have to make it through troubles without her. They both already knew the prayer that Carla would make it much longer was not much more than that: prayer.

"So what's Santa bringing to your stocking tonight?" Maya asked, easing back onto her father's workbench and shutting her eyes, pretending she was sitting across a kitchen table from Carla rather than miles away.

"World peace, I hope," Carla answered and they both laughed. They had been doing this for a couple of weeks now, coming up with lists of gifts they wanted more than to be cured of cancer. It helped keep things in perspective. "And yours?"

"Mmm . . ." Maya had to think for a

minute. She'd already used the expected — kids' health, happiness, long lives. "Clarity," she finally said. "Not for me. For my mom."

"She having a tough time?"

"A bit. I guess. She won't admit it. Today she was shopping for a gift for him, saying something about needing to apologize to him. As if she's the one who has anything to be sorry about."

Carla made a *tsk* noise into the phone. "It's got to be hard for her. They were married for a long time, right?"

"Unhappily. He was a horrible person. Forty-seven years."

"Well," Carla said, the phone clicking as she moved around, "death does something to horrible people, don't you think? Once they're gone, everyone remembers them as being really great. I think it's another one of those protective things that makes death easier, don't you? You know you'll be forgiven when you're gone."

Maya flashed to an image of her father digging his fingers painfully into her knees under the kitchen table because she wouldn't stay still. Remembered biting her bottom lip to keep from crying because she knew that crying would only make it worse for her. It was one memory of a million. Did she forgive that? "No," she said aloud.

"Not always. Though it is a nice thought to think that all of the times I've disappointed the kids or said something nasty to Bradley will just be swept under the rug after I'm gone."

"Many, many years from now."

"Of course. And you can spit on my grave if you wish, old lady." This had become another of their jokes of late — a threat that if one of them died, the survivor would spit on her grave for giving up the battle.

"I can hardly wait." There was a pause, and Maya heard little children talking in the background. She regretted taking Carla away from her family on what could very well be her last Christmas Eve with them. But her nerves were so much better already. She needed Carla as much as they did. Maybe more. Especially right now. As if she could read Maya's mind, Carla asked, "So what about Bradley? How's he been through all this?"

Maya groaned, leaned her head back against the concrete wall. Little strands of her hair adhered to the pocks in the concrete and tugged when she moved her head. "I can barely look at him. At them. It makes me feel physically sick. I want to strangle her. I want to smack him. I want to divorce him. I want to live forever with him. I want to forgive him. I want . . . God, I don't even know what I want."

"What does he want?"

"I haven't asked."

"What? You still haven't said anything to him about it?"

Maya felt pain in her chest so raw and open it felt like she was being ripped apart, her guts spilling onto her lap, hot and slick. All she could think about was the curly blond hair, the taut, tan dancer's legs, the lilting laugh and fake-ass smile that the bitch used every time Maya . . . "It's never been the right time. First Dad dies and now I'm here, with her, with him. All I can think about is my missed radiation appointment this week and I'm trying to give the kids a perfect Christmas and . . ."

"Whoa whoa whoa. A perfect Christmas? Who has one of those? My head is red and green right now."

"I know." Maya squeezed her eyes shut tight. "I know. But damn it, it's just . . . it's like there are two cancers eating me, you know? One on the inside and one on the outside and it's a race to see which one swallows me first." She felt a tear trickle out from under her closed eyelid and down one cheek and let it fall. She hadn't said it so plainly until now.

There was a pause. Maya could hear Carla whisper something to a kid. Then, "You have to concentrate on fighting the cancer that you can kill, Maya," she said. "Let the other one go. Listen, I'm sorry, but I've got to run. I am apparently late for a hot date with a cookie and some icing. Call me after the festivities, though?"

"Sure, yeah, of course," Maya said, and she bent to pick up a toy out of one of the bags at her feet to busy herself, even though she knew Carla couldn't see her, so the motion was pointless. "I've got to get all this wrapping done."

"Have a Merry Christmas," Carla said.

"You too. Enjoy your world peace. And your cookies."

"Especially the cookies."

Maya launched right into wrapping the presents after hanging up. She pulled toy after toy out of the bags at her feet, expertly scissoring off swatches of paper and folding them around the gifts. Each line was perfectly straight, each crease razor-sharp. She only wished she had a hot glue gun rather than tape to hold the edges down. It made for a much cleaner end product. But what she had would have to do. Life wasn't always clean and perfect, and besides, the gifts back home were practically works of art; people would cluck their tongues sadly over having to rip open such beauty, and . . .

Maya stopped, laid the scissors on the worktable in front of her. And . . . what? And what exactly would all that fucking perfection do for her?

She remembered the day that her perfect little world had come crashing down on her once again. The weather had really begun to turn, and so had Carla's health. The chemo had been making Carla so sick they'd taken to chatting in her bedroom, Maya sitting in a hard-backed wooden chair by Carla's bedside, her whole body filling with dread, not just at the idea of losing her friend but at the idea of losing herself. Even though she knew her prognosis was good — they didn't even expect to have to do chemo — it was hard to be rational about mortality when you had cancer in your body, and sometimes she felt like she was visiting Carla's deathbed and at the same time looking at her own short future. Sometimes it was more than she could bear. Yet she did it because she so loved her friend, and because she knew that Carla would never leave her side no matter what, and because she needed to do it. She needed to face that horribly ugly thing that visited her whenever she visited Carla.

Some of the visits went longer than usual. She'd had to call Molly and Will's babysitter and beg her to stay later just as Carla begged Maya to stay by her side until she slept. When Maya called, she would sometimes ask about Bradley, but he was always "at the office" or "at the gym" or somewhere other than at home with his children worrying about his sick wife.

At times Maya wondered what would happen if she did die. Would her children be raised by babysitters and nannies? Would they ever even see their father? Would they remember what it was like to have a mom? The thoughts agitated her so that she often had to take sleeping pills at night just to get away from them.

It was a rough period for Carla, and Maya had been by her side all the way through, but Carla had rallied and suddenly become more herself again, and Maya was glad that she'd spent that extra time with her friend. She'd come to know her almost as a sister.

Then she ran into Mrs. Winsloop at the grocery store. The old lady lived across the street from Maya's family, and Maya had always been fond of her. She quite often brought leftovers or desserts or breads that she'd baked to Mrs. Winsloop, and before Maya's diagnosis they'd often had coffee together.

"Well, there you are," Mrs. Winsloop called to her from across the produce aisle, clutching an avocado in one hand. "I haven't seen you in so long."

Maya smiled and rushed to her old friend's side. "I've been so busy," she said. "I'm so sorry I haven't been by lately."

Mrs. Winsloop patted her shoulder with one wrinkled, unsteady hand. "Of course you're busy. You're young." She said it in a positive way, not the way Maya had repeated it to herself on a loop ever since the diagnosis (*How could this be happening to me? I'm young!*). "I thought maybe you'd gotten a job and Bradley's sister was sitting with the kids. She seems so helpful for Bradley."

It was as if everything around them had stopped. Bradley's sister? Bradley didn't have a sister. Maya found herself answering on autopilot, her mouth moving around the words. "No, I've just had a few appointments to take care of." But the questions pushed forward around those words. "You talked to Bradley's sister?" she asked, her smile feeling frozen against her teeth.

Mrs. Winsloop nodded as she shook open a plastic bag to put the avocado in. "Oh, yes, I saw them together at the pharmacy, of all places. It's so wonderful to see how close they are. I've seen her a couple of times during the day, over there helping out. So nice."

Maya was stunned into silence. She honestly didn't know what to say. She realized, numbly, that she was still smiling and was even nodding, as if Mrs. Winsloop's words made total sense and she hadn't, instead, been hearing what she was pretty sure she'd been hearing.

"We're very lucky," she felt herself saying, and then felt herself saying other words to Mrs. Winsloop too, but the buzzing in her head made it impossible for her to hear herself. She was pretty sure she was saying something about needing to get home to the kids and exchanging promises to get together for coffee soon, very soon, and my how it was so lovely to run into each other and she hoped she stayed warm in the cold front that was on its way and all the shit people say to one another when they really just want to end a conversation and move on.

Maya stumbled away, pushing her cart in front of her, leaning on it. She felt her heels sliding on the floor behind her, and leaned harder into the cart, willing herself to stay steady. But everything felt so far away . . . the sounds, the food, the other shoppers.

She felt like she was wading through some-one else's life, through a nightmare-life.

Bradley didn't have a sister.

Bradley didn't have a sister.

Bradley didn't have a fucking sister.

The bastard was bringing some bitch into her house while she was out fighting for her life. He was probably screwing her in their bed. Mrs. Winsloop had seen them together at the pharmacy, for God's sake, most likely buying birth control or lubricant or some such disgusting shit. Out in the open like that! The humiliation was maybe worse than the heartache.

Halfway down the pasta aisle, Maya stopped cold. Her knees felt as though they might buckle, and she could feel bile rising in her throat. She was going to be sick or pass out or both. Her brain felt full, like it might explode from betrayal, and without giving it another thought, she kicked out of her new two-hundred-dollar wedge heels, turned, and sprinted for the parking lot, leaving her cart and shoes in the middle of the aisle, as if she'd simply evaporated on the spot.

Cutting the Christmas paper now, she remembered these things. She remembered how she'd told Bradley she was going to visit Carla and how, for a week, she'd sat in her car down the street from her own house and waited. How she'd followed him to his office and away from his office and all the places in between. How she'd seen him with her — his "sister" — and how she'd been shocked to find that it was Molly's dance teacher, Amberlee, and how Amberlee's shoulder-length, curly blond hair, tan legs, and bohemian style so reminded her of someone she knew. Bradley didn't have a sister, but Maya sure as hell did. Claire. And if her husband had admitted to being in love with Claire ten years ago, he certainly hadn't gotten past it like he'd promised he would. He was still in love with her. He was fucking another version of her while his wife was off getting cancer treatment. Amberlee looked just like Claire.

She noticed that her hands were shaking, her fingertips red and sore-looking. Chapped. She put down the scissors and closed her eyes and, as usual, she could practically see the cancer eating at her. Could feel it running through her veins, ugly and sinister. The lump was out, but the cancer didn't feel out. As long as she still had radiation treatments on the calendar — three more to go — it still felt as much a part of her as her broken heart. She wanted it gone. She wanted to kill it, as Carla had said. But, God, she felt so powerless. Without the doctors, without the lumpectomy or whatever you wanted to call it, without the radiation and the oncologist, would she have had a prayer of beating it? No, she guessed not. The feeling was so helpless it brought tears to her eyes. She couldn't kill this cancer. She couldn't do anything but beg and cry and pray and, of course, pay someone else to try their best to kill it.

But the other cancer that was eating her life . . . that one she had power over. That one she could unceremoniously remove. The real cancer was her marriage to an unfaithful man, and that was the one she had to let go of so she could concentrate on living.

Carla didn't understand. She didn't understand how Maya had shaped herself into everything Bradley could possibly want in life. She didn't understand how hard Maya had worked to forgive him, to believe in him, to be perfect for him. Perfect, goddamn it! *Think there's no such thing as a perfect Christmas?* she wanted to scream. *Try a perfect life! I used to think it was possible, but now . . .*

Well, now . . . what, exactly? What would she do?

Slowly she picked up her scissors and

went back to work, ignoring the shaking in
her hands. Carefully, she wrapped the toys,
her brow furrowing as she ran her finger
along each fold.

What would she do?

She would kill the cancer. The one she
could kill.

Attempts — III

He wasn't sure if he could do it on Christmas Eve. His mom ignored him half the time and pissed him off the other half, but he still loved her. And it's not like she would probably think any day would be a good day for her son to die, but Christmas Eve just seemed like a really shitty day. Colossally shitty, in fact.

The clock ticked. That thing was so loud. If he had to live in this place permanently, he would take a hammer to that clock.

Seemed like his aunt took forever putting out the Santa crap for his cousins. He could hear papers and plastic bags rustling for so long he came close to falling asleep twice. Both times he woke with a start, feeling as if he were rolling over the side of his cot and down a thirty-foot cliff. Both times he clutched his sheet between his knees and breathed deeply, trying to tamp down the anger that he felt toward his aunt for taking so long. He wanted to rush out to the den, fling the gifts under the tree, and tell her to go to bed. Who still believed in Santa anyway? He'd known the truth before he was five.

He'd figured it out at his dad's house. He'd arrived on Christmas morning, fresh and excited, clutching the new stuffed toy Santa had brought him at home. Some dog or elephant or something. He couldn't quite remember anymore. He'd turned the corner into his dad's living room and found gifts from Santa there too.

"Why did Santa come here, Dad?" he'd asked, genuinely perplexed.

"Because you were on the nice list. He always leaves gifts for kids on the nice list," his dad had said, sipping a cup of coffee and rubbing the five o'clock shadow on his chin.

"But he left me gifts at home. How come I get more?"

His dad had shrugged and said Santa was mysterious, but even at five he noticed the pointed look his stepmom had given his dad. Something that looked like irritation.

Later he'd heard his stepmom's voice in the kitchen, whispering, "I thought she said you could be Santa this year, since she got him that stupid bike last year."

"She did. She probably forgot. The woman never remembers anything that doesn't directly benefit her," his dad had said. The pieces had clicked into place in his little five-year-old mind. They were talking about his mom. They always whispered when they talked about her. But his mom hadn't gotten him a bike the year before; Santa had. And all at once it was clear: Santa wasn't real. He was just one more piece of Eli's life that was wrapped up in the custody agreement. The realization changed him in his own mind. He would never be anything but a Child of Divorce, in capital letters like a label.

His mom had tried to talk to him again tonight. Asked him all these lame questions about what he wanted for Christmas. As usual, she'd put no forethought into anything. Asking someone what they want for Christmas on Christmas Eve was basically the same as getting someone gift cards from a gas station on Christmas Day. It was the same message: You are not important enough to think about until I have to.

"I think you know what I want," he'd said as glumly as he could, and she'd flinched, folding her lips inward. She stayed silent for a while after that, sliding between the stiff, starchy sheets on her bed and turning out the lamp.

"You don't mean that," she finally said. "Tai said —"

He cut her off by making a noise in the back

216

of his throat. Like he gave a rat's ass what Tai had to say about anything. If his mom was in love with work, Tai was married to it, honeymooning with it, sleeping with it on a regular basis. Getting his rocks off on it.

He liked his stepdad enough, but it was sort of like liking the fern that hung behind the kitchen table. Tai was there, but not really there. Part of him was always lingering in his briefcase, in a stack of notes, in the creases of an impossibly thick book. They never hung out together. They never joked or played games. Basically, when his mom chose his "dad replacement," she chose another one of her: a paycheck that occasionally yelled at him.

"Well, if I had a Christmas wish," she'd said after a while, her voice floating through the dark, "it would be for you to feel better, Eli. To be happy."

"You might as well wish for something that could actually happen," he said, his tone thick with surliness, and then when she didn't answer he lay there feeling guilty but unsure what to say. Eventually he heard her breathing grow long and steady and he was stuck listening to his aunt's infernal rustling in the den.

Come on come on come on, he thought, almost like a prayer. *Be finished so I can . . .*

So he could what? He wasn't going to kill himself tonight. He'd already decided that. But he knew he'd never get to sleep if he didn't at least go out there, at least sit in the chair and fantasize about it.

It had snowed all day, just like a Bing-freaking-Crosby song, and it continued to snow through the evening. When he was a kid, he used to pray for white Christmases like this. He loved the way the snow fell all peaceful past his bedroom window back in Kansas City, how it covered the ground, a little bit at a time, how the snow made the street-lamps outside look like they were crowned with halos. But it rarely snowed on Christmas. It was a waste of time to wish for it.

Somehow he found it fitting that it had snowed this Christmas. Sort of like it was a sign that this should be his last Christmas. Somehow he knew it would be.

As the night wore on, the wind picked up, and he could hear the staticky sound of snow being blown up against the window next to his mom's bed. *Shusssh, shusssh, shusssh.* The sound mingled with his aunt's movements. But after a while he realized it had been a long time since he'd heard her movements at all. He'd been so hypnotized by the shushing wind.

He sat up on his cot, the sheet pooling

around his waist, and listened. All was quiet in the den. All was quiet everywhere. The house was asleep.

Slowly, carefully, he lifted one leg over the side of his cot, and then the other, then bent and retrieved his pocketknife, shivering, and tiptoed out the door and down the hall.

There it was. Big and brown and stately. It had seemed to grow since he first sat in it, had seemed to get bigger to hold his grand-father's memory. It almost seemed big enough to engulf him, to eat him up. He closed his eyes and imagined it growing foot-long fangs and, with a growl, biting him in half, blood spurting over the armrests, soaking into the seat of the chair, it all happening too fast for him to even scream.

When he opened his eyes he was embar-rassed. That was something he might have imagined when he was seven, a chair grow-ing teeth and eating him like a cartoon villain. He'd daydreamed about those kinds of things all the time when he was younger — inanimate objects coming alive and destroying him or buses losing control and smashing him flat and bloodless like he was made of clay or a truck full of knives stopping short in front of his mom's SUV and all the knives spilling out into his body — back when he was too young to put a label to his depression. Thinking those thoughts then just felt like imagination. Like stories. Now they felt childish. He could define his depression now. He could embrace it. His fantasies should be much more refined now.

He leaned his head back against the chair and thought about his dad.

He liked his dad. He'd often wished he lived with his dad. In fact, he'd asked his dad more than once if he could live there. Dusty always sighed deeply, shook his head, and answered, "Not right now, buddy. Your mom . . ." And he always just kind of trailed off that way. But he didn't need to finish. He'd said enough. His mom. His mom would have fought it. She would have been hurt. She would have made his dad's life miserable, and he definitely didn't want that to happen. His dad was a good guy.

So it was an ironic kick in the crotch that now his dad wanted him. Now, of all times. Now he was willing to make a stink, to face the shrew, to brave a court battle. Now, when it was too late. He would've gone to live with his dad, but it all seemed like a bunch of work for no reason now. He was too tired to contemplate moving out just to check out permanently. It seemed stupid.

For the first time, though, he was forced to think about his dad in the context of what he was about to do. The man would be devastated. And something about that felt like a big-

ger guilt blow than the thought of his mom being devastated. His dad had worked so hard
to create a good life. He'd married Sharon,
had been dad to his stepchildren, had blended
everyone together seamlessly as if they were
all real siblings. If he did this, he would be
leaving his dad alone with only stepchildren.
They would become his only kids. That hurt.

He sat up straighter, shook it off, squeezed
the folded knife in his palm. But it wouldn't
hurt for long. After he was dead, all the hurt
would stop. None of it would matter anymore.
Let his dad have his stepkids for real kids.
What difference would it make? It might help
him get over the pain a little.

He closed his eyes again, clearing his mind
of all thoughts about his parents, and took a
deep breath. Even deeper than the night
before. He held it, held it, held it, feeling his
eyes bulge against their lids, feeling tingling in
his toes, aching in his chest. He pressed his
lips together, hard, so not a single sip of air
could slip out, and pressed his back harder
against the back of the chair. His head started
to feel buzzy and he knew he would pass out
soon, and while he knew that his body would
involuntarily take a breath once he did so, he
felt excitement well up inside him at the
thought of coming so close to death that his
body would go on autopilot. For a few mo-

ments it would be like he was actually gone. He would be free.

But just as he began to have to fight the convulsing of his lungs begging for air, a door shut somewhere in the hallway where all the bedrooms were. He let out his breath as quietly as he could, inwardly cursing at having been interrupted when things were getting so good, and then held it again, this time straining to hear.

He heard feet padding down the hallway again, and fumbling by the kitchen coat hook. He heard the back door open and swing shut with a very soft click, and the faint sound of footsteps scuffing down the sunporch steps.

He held his breath some more, knowing what would follow, and it did. Another door clicking shut, heavier bumps and thumps coming down the hallway, and the kitchen door opening and shutting once again. Uncle Bradley, no doubt.

He grimaced. He didn't like the guy. There was something about him that just oozed houndishness, like he couldn't control himself, panting around that waitress, practically stroking off right there at the table. It was disgusting. Worse. It was wrong.

And when it came down to it, that's exactly what he was looking to escape right there. Not just his mom, who didn't care about anything that didn't come with a dollar sign attached to it . . . not just Mitch Munde and the idiots who called him names and punched him when he walked by . . . not just his stepdad who all but ignored that he existed. But all of it. Everyone and everything that stripped away his faith in humanity, his faith that it would get better. It wouldn't. Not as long as douche bags like his uncle wobbled around after big tits and tight asses with their dicks in their hands, not even caring who might get hurt in the process.

He knew that Aunt Claire and Uncle Bradley would be gone for a while. He was safe to try again. He pushed himself back against the chair, pulled open the pocketknife and held the blade dramatically against his throat, and then closed his eyes, gulping in a huge breath of air — maybe even bigger than before — and settling into his practice death once again.

But no sooner had he taken the breath than he heard a door open again and more footsteps pad down the hall. He let out the breath, feeling exasperated, and flicked the knife shut. It was like nobody ever slept in this godforsaken place.

But this time the padding had other sounds to it. A wet whimpering. Someone was crying.

The sound moved into the kitchen and seemed to stall for a long time at where he imagined the back door to be. But the back door never opened.

Probably he should leave. Sneak back to his cot. Slip in, go to sleep, try to get some rest before his cousins woke up screaming about Santa. But he didn't. He couldn't. He was still hoping for that breath. That fix. He wanted to pass out in his grandfather's death chair. If he couldn't smash through the ice and slip into a numb death, he could at least do that much, couldn't he?

So he stayed. And he listened. He listened as the crying got harder, as the whimpering turned into muffled little sobs. He listened as the paper towel holder rattled and then a nose was blown. As a chair scooted out and the sobs took on an echoey sound, as if the crier were facedown at the kitchen table. He listened and he let the sound of someone else's pain lull him, and he almost fell asleep to it, his head feeling too heavy for his neck, the buzzy feeling back in his mind. He pulled one leg up into the chair with him, and then the other.

He got so comfortable, in fact, he was still curled up in that position when the sobbing came into the room with him.

He sat up, startled, dropping his pocketknife down the front of his pajama bottoms, his heart racing.

Aunt Maya was looking right at him, a balled-up paper towel in midair in front of her face.

"Eli?" she asked, her voice husky and nasal. She peered at him through the darkness. "What are you doing in here?"

He wanted nothing more than for the chair to grow those teeth and swallow him up now. Now, of all times! Before it's too late! Just eat me in half, blood, guts, popping tendons, and breaking bones! Just do it!

But the chair remained a chair, and his aunt remained as still as furniture in front of him, her face shadowy and unrecognizable in the dark, and he said the only thing that came into his mind.

"Waiting for Santa Claus," he said. And he was glad for the dark so she couldn't see his burning cheeks. His embarrassment must have shown on his face. It almost hurt, it was so real.

She continued to stare at him, that paper towel ball still in front of her, for what seemed like forever. And then, just as it felt like she might never move again, just as he began to unfurl his legs and put weight on them to steal back to his room, she said, "Me too, buddy. But just between you and me . . . I don't think he's gonna come."

■ ■ ■ ■

DECEMBER 25
CHRISTMAS DAY

■ ■ ■ ■

"The same ugly tension, wrapped up in bright paper and tied with a bow."

ELEVEN

Elise had always been good at making the house feel Christmassy. Even when Robert was horrible. Even when they'd been up all night fighting the night before, Robert drunkenly slurring names at her back, Elise scurrying to put the girls' gifts under the tree and hoping Robert didn't notice that she'd bought them more than he'd agreed to.

Elise believed in Christmas. She believed in the magic of the season, even if she never really saw it for herself. She believed in George Bailey and that little girl Virginia and all that sappy black-and-white hopeful movie stuff. She believed that if she gave her girls a special enough Christmas, maybe they could come away feeling sappy and hopeful, too. Maybe they could forget how they were raised the other three hundred sixty-four days of the year.

But if every year Elise was hoping for a

good Christmas, this year she was practically bursting with glad tidings. Even if the house had been overdone just a tad, what with the yards of tinsel and forest of poinsettias. Even if the girls had arrived surly and distracted and still — still! — at one another's throat after all these years.

Even if her husband was dead.

Even if her guilty memory of the night he died ate away at her gut like drain declogger.

In the soft gray morning hours, while the snow and wind turned over to sleet ticking against the sides of the house, the Yancey Farm was calm.

Claire had come in hours before, shimmying out of her boots and carefully stowing them on the old towel her mom had placed by the back door earlier in the day to keep the kitchen floor from becoming a soppy mess. She'd brushed her hands through her hair, flinging bits of ice around the kitchen, where they would quickly evaporate. And then she'd slipped off to the bathroom to study her red, swollen face in the mirror once again, pondering how everyone in the house thought she was the cavalier one. How none of them could know how her heart was breaking over what had happened back in California just before she left and how confused and lonely she was and how guilty she felt because she knew her sister Maya would want — no, need — to know what had been going on all week. But Maya had shut her out so completely, how could she ever broach any subject with her?

In the end she had simply blown her nose and snuck down the hall into her bedroom, then fallen face-first onto her bed, still wearing the yoga pants she'd bought earlier in the day. She hadn't worn pants in years, and they felt oddly constricting against her legs, like casts. She couldn't help but think how appropriate that constriction felt in this, the house that had constricted her for the first eighteen years of her life.

The still night air pressed in on Bradley as he trundled through the back door, making few attempts at being quiet. He knocked his hiking boots against the bottom of the doorjamb two or three times each, and then squished his way back to his own bedroom, his boots leaving wet, snowy imprints behind on the hardwood floor. These, too, would evaporate before morning, and would be visible only when the light caught them just right, like the footsteps of a phantom. Bradley never worried about leaving a trail.

He'd gotten away with so much over the years, what was the purpose of getting all paranoid now? He'd gotten cocky.

He pushed open the door to the bedroom and paused in the doorway. He hated that they were all sleeping in the same room. Will snored, and Molly often got up in the middle of the night and stood by the bed, sleepily staring at her mother. It was creepy. Like something you'd see in one of those B horror movies made with camcorders.

Bradley had never been much of a kid person. For one thing, they wrecked a good woman's body. And not just with stretch marks — those could be ignored if you just turned the lights out. They ruined certain feelings of elasticity *down there,* in Bradley's opinion, and he hated how every young mom (including, but definitely not restricted to, his wife) that he'd ever slept with had turned into some sort of Puritan after the baby was born. What the heck did having a kid do to keep a woman from going down on a guy? That he could never figure out.

But more than that, Bradley just never really understood kids. Maybe not even when he was a kid himself. They always seemed to be thinking things he couldn't pick up on. They stared at him as if they were privy to private information. And they talked. A lot.

No, if Bradley had to do it all over again, he definitely wouldn't have had kids. He wasn't even sure he'd have married Maya, if truth be told. She was needy. And suspicious. And she tried too hard to be perfect all the time. All that perfection was annoying. He wanted her to be real. Genuine.

More like her sister.

He knew he looked like a real schmuck, the way he had been carrying on with Claire the past week. But he couldn't help it. Honest to God, and what Maya never knew, he was in love with Claire long before he was in love with Maya. He'd only asked Maya out on that first date all those years ago because he'd found out she was the sister of the sexy, adorable lifeguard that he'd been ogling all summer at the lake. He'd hoped things wouldn't work out with the short brunette who had those intense eyes and that rigid way of standing, and that his consolation prize would be to get with the blonde. God, when she uncrossed and then crossed her legs again up on that lifeguard stand, her swimsuit stretched so impossibly close to her skin . . . it still gave him a hard-on to think about it.

He'd tried to woo Claire while at the same

time making Maya think he was trying to woo her. He chased after Claire like a damned puppy, looking for every possible in, every possible second alone together. Every chance to touch her delicate wrist or wipe something from her tiny, upturned nose.

But Claire never seemed to even realize that he was there. Not really. Not as anything more than just a friend. Someone to talk to. *Bah.* He wasn't interested in talk. He wanted her. And her indifference to him only made him pursue her all the harder.

And then something happened. Maya started putting out. First, secretive hand jobs in the barn loft, her fingers cold and tense around his cock, such that it was almost painful. Then blow jobs in the woods by the pond, where he would sometimes peer through the trees over Maya's head to see if he could catch a glimpse of Claire swimming, imagining her wet body until he exploded in her sister's mouth, feeling guilty and ashamed and dirty.

Maya was good at reeling him in. She always had been. She'd give him a little to get what she wanted. She was always willing to do things that other girls wouldn't do: go to drag races or see action movies with those terrible actors or drive him from bar to bar, sipping water while he downed shot after shot and not even complain when he puked in her car. She was stiff and precise in a way that he found altogether unsexy, but she made him feel good about himself.

So when she'd promised him sex — the real thing, not the skin-ripping hand jobs she was famous for — he'd gone ahead and done it, knowing that what he was doing was unfair to her, yet being unable to help himself.

After a hurried fuck in the backseat of his car in a nightclub parking lot, he watched Maya's face, and the sadness in her eyes, the way she looked as if she knew she'd given up something precious to someone who didn't appreciate it, brought to his chest such a constriction that he realized that somewhere along the line he'd begun to love her too.

Not fall in love with her. Love her. There was a difference.

It wasn't the same gut-clenching, mind-bending adoration that he had for Claire, but it was real. He wanted to be around her. He wanted to impress her.

He proposed to Maya the following weekend, and he was happy, but he knew on the inside that if Claire should ever give so much as the slightest hint, he would not be able to hold on to that love he had for Maya. It just wasn't strong enough.

In the dark bedroom on Christmas Eve years later, he shimmied out of his boots and jeans and adjusted his boxers, then crept over to the bed, where Maya was already wrapped into a tight little cocoon in the bedsheets. He lay down next to her, feeling nowhere near the warmth that he'd felt from Claire just fifteen minutes before. All these years later . . . all that had happened over the past ten years . . . and he still couldn't be near Claire without wanting her.

Even though he'd promised Maya. Oh, God, he'd promised her so many things. Had he ever lived up to one of them? He wasn't sure.

And now she had cancer. Cancer, for fuck's sake. The thought of it made him feel numb. What if Maya were to die? He couldn't lose her. Even if he might not have married her over again, he didn't want her to die. He loved her. She was the mother of his children. And she was a damn good mother. She was a damn good wife. He hated that she was suffering. And he hated even more what he was doing to her while she was suffering. He'd been doing it for years, of course — a different woman, a different pair of legs or round butt or enormous breasts every so often, hiding from his wife as if she were the police. He thought maybe she suspected, but she had never said anything. She was that desperate to keep him, and he knew it.

What was worse was he wasn't even in love this time, unlike some of the times in the past. He'd always hated when he fell in love with one of the women he was screwing. It complicated things. It made him nauseous and worried and the breakup was always so messy that he would slink around his house for weeks waiting for the jilted woman to pop in and make a real mess out of his life.

So it was good that he wasn't in love this time, though a tad shocking. He'd thought he might be able to get there. Amberlee looked so much like Claire. But it wasn't the same. Amberlee had some of Maya's rigidity about her. And she was stupid. But he kept going back for more because the resemblance was uncanny. He'd noticed her right away, the very first time he'd had to pick up Molly from dance class and he'd walked into Move 'N Shake and his heart had caught in his chest thinking he'd just seen Claire. More than any of the others, if he just got Amberlee to shut up while they were in bed together, he could stare at her and imagine those uncrossing and crossing legs and it would almost seem real.

Maya would never understand that the affairs were his only way of being able to stay married to her. She would never understand that he needed them. That his heart needed them. She would think he was a bastard, for sure, because she'd given herself to him completely, and not once, not since that first fuck in the nightclub parking lot, had he ever appreciated it.

All he had in his defense was helplessness. Complete and utter helplessness.

He was a weak man. He knew it. And he hated himself for it. But he knew he'd never change. If he could give his wife one gift for Christmas, it would be to change. But he could only flip to his side, his back touching hers, and drift off to sleep, feeling every bit like he was damned no matter what he did.

Maya lay next to Bradley with her eyes open, her form so still she imagined she looked for all the world like she was asleep, or maybe dead. Her husband's back was still cold from the outside air and she wanted so badly to recoil from it. It felt like he'd brought his deception into bed with them, the cold just as horrible as the scent of another woman, the scent of her sister. But she feared that if she flinched or moved, he would discover that she was awake and then they'd have to talk.

She'd hardly been able to talk to him for weeks. Ever since she found out about him and Amberlee. She'd barely been able to look him in the face. The only reason she'd brought him here was because she couldn't bear the thought of leaving him at home to sleep with Amberlee in her house, worry-free. To screw her on the kitchen counter or in the bathtub where the children bathed. To let her try on Maya's lingerie, her stilet-tos. To wash Bradley's semen off of her legs in Maya's shower, using Maya's loofah, Maya's body wash. No way.

She would not let him abuse her that way.

But he'd only just continued the abuse, the deception, right here in her parents' house. On Christmas. When her father was lying dead in a coroner's refrigerator some-where, waiting to be buried. With their children right there in the house with them. And with her sister, for God's sake.

Oh, how she hated him. Hated touching his back with hers. Hated sitting at the same kitchen table with him. Hated sitting across the aisle from him on the airplane.

And she hated the very thought of dying and leaving him to care for her children, whom she loved so much. He didn't care about his children. He didn't care about his family. He didn't deserve them. Any of them.

After she'd left the gifts under the tree and filled the stockings, Maya had gone to bed, only to feel Bradley get up and dress himself a few moments later. She'd suspected he'd been sneaking out, but she had no proof since she was usually asleep. Maybe he'd forgotten about it being Christmas Eve. Maybe he hadn't even noticed that the lump next to him on the mattress was still tossing and turning, definitely not asleep at all. God, was she that insignificant to him? Maybe he thought she'd figure he was in the bathroom and would drift off without a care.

She'd slid out of bed and snuck through the house and, sure enough, not only was he missing but so were the boots that Claire had been using all week. It hardly took a rocket scientist to figure out what was going on.

And that was when it all rushed in on her. Everything that she'd been fearing and feeling and thinking and surmising and dreading over the past ten years — hell, maybe over her whole life! — had tumbled right into her lap. She had forced a man to love

240

her, she had forced herself to be blind to what was really there, and now she might be dying and it had become painfully obvious that he was only going through the motions. She was going to lose everything. And she was finally admitting to herself that there was nothing she could do about it.

She'd bawled until she was sick to her stomach, and then she'd begun to fear that Bradley and Claire would come back and she would still be sitting at the kitchen table, blubbering and weak. Giving them the upper hand.

No way.

Bradley would never have the upper hand again.

She'd scooted away from the table and had stood in the doorway to the den for a few moments, sickly admiring the way the lights on the blue spruce were twinkling off of the tinsel, making shimmery reflections on the walls.

It would get better, right? It had to. She had two children who wanted good lives, and damn it, they deserved good lives. Not a life where their mom was forever sobbing over their father's affairs. Not a life where their mom mattered that little. She had to live so that she could get them out of there. They didn't know it, but their lives were counting on it.

Sniffling, she'd left the den and made her way toward the bedroom, but was surprised when movement from her father's recliner had caught her peripheral vision. Her heart leapt a little, the irrational side of her sure that the spirit of her father had come back to add insult to injury just like some damned Dickens novel. Maybe to tell her that her husband was unfaithful because she was ugly. Because her hair was greasy and her face pimply and she was too short. Because she had a fat little stomach and spindly little legs. All the things he used to say to her growing up.

But it was her nephew, Eli, sitting in the chair. He looked startled . . . and somehow guilty.

"Eli? What are you doing in here?" she'd asked.

He'd paused, his eyes darting around nervously. "Waiting for Santa Claus," he'd said.

She'd doubted him, of course. Something about that kid wasn't right. He seemed so sullen and nervous all the time, like he was forever waiting for someone to jump out from behind the curtains and slash him to bits, and like he wouldn't be surprised when it happened because that was the way his

242

life always ended up.

Come to think of it, her sister Julia looked much the same way. Something was going on there, and Maya realized with a start that she'd never bothered to ask what it was.

"Me too, buddy," she'd said, "but just between you and me . . . I don't think he's gonna come."

Eli had sat stock-still in the chair, his deep brown eyes that so resembled Julia's peering out at her through the darkness. He looked like he wanted to say something but was afraid. A gust of wind whistled outside and blew against the front door on the other side of the room. Both Maya and Eli looked at it as it strained and creaked against the force of the wind.

Finally Eli spoke, his words fast and tumbling into one another. "They've been doing that every night," he said.

Maya's confusion was only brief. She knew exactly who he was talking about and what they'd been doing every night. She tried to smile knowingly, but she was embarrassed, and the corners of her mouth felt so very, very heavy.

"I saw them. Out by the pond," he added.

Maya physically recoiled. Out by the pond. Of course out by the pond. Where else? For a moment she felt as if she'd been transported back in time, traipsing through the burrs and ticks of the woods, brambles tearing at her ankles, and bursting out on the other side only to find Claire in Bradley's arms, his mouth brushing her lips. She willed away the images that flowed right behind it, the accusations and the tears and the way she'd collapsed on their apartment floor, devastated.

"Oh," she said, because she felt like she should say something, but her blood was running so cold through her veins that "Oh" was the only word that she could think of. The tears were threatening to start anew, and her impulse was to burst out the back door and run. Run past the chicken coop, the tractor shed. Run through the old garden where spiders and sweat bees had frightened her as a child. Run through the impossibly long soy field, past the beehives. Run into the tree line, in and through. Through and through and burst out the other side and catch them. Finally. Catch them finishing what she'd caught them starting ten years ago.

Catch her husband making love to her sister. See it and get it over with. Lose him in one fell swoop, which would have to feel better than losing him a little at a time like this.

But she wouldn't do it. Because she didn't really want to see, did she?

"You should get to bed," she finally choked out, and then left before her nephew could say anything else. Before he could see her life crumble.

For the first few hours of Christmas morning, Elise's home looked for all the world like a proper Christmas. The tree was lit, gifts billowing beneath, reaching in an arc across the floor. The poinsettias were blooming in the kitchen and on the sunporch. Stockings were bulging, laid out on the hearth, which still glowed from the embers of the evening's fire. Outside, the world was white and gleaming, silent, majestic. A pot of mulled wine still sat on the stove, cooling, fragrant. Cookies were arranged on a plate on the kitchen table, and a separate plate, which once held cookies and milk for Santa, sat next to it, empty save for a few crumbs to lend authenticity.

Had Elise been awake to see it, she would have been very happy. She would have felt like she'd finally gotten her beautiful Christmas.

Unfortunately, she, along with everyone else — finally! — had drifted into a dark and dreamless sleep, unable to shrug off the weight that she carried. Her unhappiness and her secrets were constant companions that took no day off, not even the most sacred day of the year.

Yes, had she been awake to see those few short predawn hours of Christmas, she might have felt as if she'd pulled this one off. But she wasn't awake. And all that awaited her under her tree when she did wake up was more of the same ugly tension, wrapped up in bright paper and tied with a bow.

TWELVE

Molly and Will bounded out of bed before dawn had really even been fully realized. Half of the windows were covered with drifted snow and stuck ice, which made it seem even darker and earlier than it was.

"Mom! Presents! Mom! Presents!" was screeched over and over again, as the kids tore through Maya's careful work under the tree, scavenging boxes and putting them into piles ready for opening. Maya opened her eyes at the first sound of bare feet running down the hardwood floor of the hallway, only to find herself face-to-face with Bradley, who was — no surprise here — still slumbering away as if he hadn't heard a thing. Bradley never woke with the kids. Not once had he ever.

Maya had one of those hazy morning moments where everything was all right and this was just any other Christmas. Her kids were happy, her husband was cozy and breathing softly against her, she had no worries, no adultery, no cancer, no dead father to bury. In that brief moment of confusion, she almost reached out and stroked the side of Bradley's face, the way she would have done when they were first married and the kids were babies. Back when it was only his transgression with Claire she had to forgive. *Merry Christmas,* she would have whispered in a flirty voice, running her fingertips softly down his jawline to wake him.

But before her fingers made it out of the blankets, she was slammed into reality. This was not their bedroom back home, and even if it had been, Maya would be thinking only about how he'd probably slept with Amberlee right in the very spot where she was lying and she would feel such loathing for him that she would have to use every reserve of strength and self-control she had to keep from waking him up with a punch to the throat.

She decided not to wake him at all. Let him miss opening gifts with the kids. Not like he was all that much into the family anyway. Not unless he was screwing one of the kids' teachers. Then he had a sudden interest in their extracurricular activities. Such as dance. God, she was an idiot to think he'd suddenly started volunteering to take Molly to dance just so she could rest after radiation treatments.

She pushed back the covers and sat on the edge of the bed, her feet searching for her slippers tucked under the bedskirt.

"Merry Christmas," she heard at her back, gruff, half-awake.

She glanced over her shoulder. Bradley was turning onto his back, flinging an arm over his eyes, sweat staining the armpit of his T-shirt.

"The kids are already up," she said by way of response.

"So I hear."

Maya stood and padded to the closet, where her terrycloth robe was hanging on the same hook on which she'd hung her robes throughout her entire childhood.

"Come here," Bradley said, his voice soft, sleepy.

She glanced over her shoulder as she pulled the robe off the hook. "What?"

He looked warm under the sheets, his chest comfortable and inviting. "I want to wish you a Merry Christmas," he said. He sounded sincere.

"The kids," she repeated.

"The kids are thrilled out there. They can wait. Come here." He held his arms out. In the old days, the days when Maya was working so hard to be everything to him, to be the only thing for him, she would have crawled back into bed and shrugged her way into those arms. She would have snuggled up against his side, resting her face on his chest, slinging one arm and one leg over him. If she worked it just right, moved her calf up and down one too many times, she could talk his morning erection into something workable and they would end up having sweaty, slow morning sex, which was always Maya's favorite. It always felt like she was laying claim to him for the whole day when that happened.

She knew that was what he was expecting. But then she remembered him being out with Claire last night, remembered Eli telling her that they'd been out together at night all week. How could he just expect to seduce her when he was out with her sister all night doing God-knew-what?

He is the real cancer . . . he is the real cancer . . .

Maya pursed her lips and cinched the belt of her robe tight. "I don't think so," she said, her voice clipped and as icy as the window behind him. She began heading for the door.

"Why not? Come on, Maya, what has gotten into you? It's Christmas."

She paused in the doorway, her fists clenched at her sides. As if he didn't know! Was he seriously that ignorant? Her nose still felt plugged up from all the crying she had done last night. Her eyelids were still fat and heavy. Her throat was raw and the side of her chest ached and her children — her poor children! — were out in the den hoping to unwrap a bunch of cheap plastic crap and were excited about it because they didn't know any goddamn better, but she did. She knew better and she had to bite her bottom lip to keep from telling him, right then and there, that this was over. That he was a cancer and she was going to fight him just as hard as she was fighting the breast cancer. That Carla had told her to concentrate on the cancer that she could make go away and, bad news, Bradley, that cancer is you. And that she was going to pull Molly out of dance like yesterday, but first she was going to make a public scene about it. First she was going to stand up in the waiting area of Move 'N Shake and tell all the moms to hold on to their husbands because apparently Amberlee wasn't satisfied with just getting her hands on your money. She was going to tell Amberlee that she knew everything, and that if she ever caught her blond, spindly ass near her house again, she would shoot her dead.

"The kids are waiting," was all she said, and she left the room.

THIRTEEN

Elise and Julia were already in the den by the time Maya got there. Elise sat on the hearth, a smile pasted so hard on her face it looked as if it might actually hurt. Her pink robe was pulled tight around her knees and she held a coffee cup between both hands.

Julia sat on the floor, shaking gifts and playing with the kids.

"Oh, this one sounds like it has a lot of parts," she cooed to Will, shaking a gift wrapped in Santa paper. His eyes grew wide as he heard the rustle of the pieces inside. "Maybe it's a robot."

He shook his head, laughed. "No, Aunt Dooleeuh. A robot would be really big."

"Not if you have to put it together yourself," she said. "Are you a good robot-builder?"

"He's better at destroying things," Molly said from within the tree branches. She grunted as she stretched for a just-out-of-

253

reach box.

"Nuh-uh, I am so a good builder," Will protested. He scurried under the tree with his sister, then backed out, dragging another box with him. He studied the tag, his forehead crinkling in concentration. "For you, Molly!" he said and pushed it in her direction, though she was still reaching for the elusive box up in the branches. To Julia, he said, "I know! It's a bunch of baby robots!"

"Awww," Julia said, cradling the box in her arms. "Aren't they cute?"

Will laughed again, a little maniacally, and Julia winced, remembering the days when Eli's laugh sounded similar. It seemed like so long ago. "Mom!" Will exclaimed when he saw Maya enter the room, and Julia turned to see her sister, who seemed to be making an effort to look cheerful but was failing. "We got presents! Santa came! Santa came!" He was jumping up and down on his knees. "Can we start opening them?"

"You want to wait for your daddy, honey," Elise said from her perch on the hearth.

Maya frowned. "No, it's okay," she said. "Sure. Open them."

She eased herself down onto the floor next to Julia. "What about Eli?"

Julia looked over her shoulder, as if she

could see down the hall and into their bedroom from where she was sitting. She shrugged. "You know teenagers. They'll sleep forever if you let them," she said, but she chewed on her lip nervously after saying it, her eyes glazing over just a little bit. Hopefully that was the only reason Eli hadn't joined them yet, but she doubted it.

As Will tore into his gifts, flinging wrapping paper carelessly over his shoulders, Julia slowly got up and moved down the hallway, where she pressed open the bedroom door just a crack, and peered in at her son, sleeping on his cot in the center of the room.

He looked so peaceful, his mop of hair fallen back off his forehead, his eyelids, fragile and veiny, jumping as he dreamed. His face was pale — the pimples wouldn't burst to the surface, angry and crimson, until he got up and began his day. It was as if you could see his disgust with life boiling through his very skin.

Why? she asked herself once again. Where had she gone wrong? And what would she do now? She tried hard to hang on to Tai's encouragement, but without him here to remind her, she felt so helpless and alone. How she wished she'd asked him to come after all. And how she wished even harder that she wouldn't have had to ask, that he'd just been there because it was where he wanted to be. She had often felt as if she had no business raising a child with her schedule and her lack of attention. Now, with the troubles Eli was having, the feeling was only stronger. Maybe Eli would be better off with Dusty and Shurn after all.

A squeal pealed out from the den, and Eli stirred. Quickly, Julia backed away from the doorway, pulling the door shut as she went. The last thing she needed was for him to wake up to find her staring at him. He so considered her the enemy as it was. He so felt like she was always up in his business. To find her gazing at him in his sleep would send him over the edge.

Instead, she moved back toward the ruckus, as Will went on and on about a gift he'd gotten, his voice excited and rambling. She remembered the days when Eli was like that. She'd often gotten annoyed by it. He had seemed so hyper. So ridiculously immature. He was a child. She should have let him be one.

Instead of going back to the den, she veered into the kitchen. Elise had already started some cinnamon rolls, and Julia could see a thick slab of bacon and two dozen eggs on the counter by the stove. Her mother would soon be cooking a huge Christmas Day breakfast, just as she'd always done. Only this year Robert wouldn't be stomping around, grumbling about this "fucking Christmas shit" putting him in the poorhouse. He wouldn't be sitting at the head of the table, taking away brand-new toys as punishment for the smallest of crimes. Julia remembered the year he'd taken away her Holly Hobby doll just moments after she'd gotten it, simply because she'd left one elbow on the table a fraction of a second too long. She never saw that doll again. She'd been heartbroken.

All of a sudden, Julia was so very tired. She wanted a cup of coffee, but there was a line. Bradley, pink-cheeked and stubbly, had just poured himself a cup and was turning to fill one for Claire, who was fresh out of the shower, her ringlets dripping onto her shoulders.

"Merry Christmas," Julia mumbled, pulling a mug out of the cabinet.

"Same to you," Bradley said. He held up the pot as a question.

"Please," Julia said, offering her mug so he could fill it. There was another squeal as Will opened another gift.

"Merry Christmas," Claire said, blowing over the top of her cup and taking a sip.

She winced, took another. "Eli still in bed?"

Julia nodded, rubbed her forehead.

Claire looked at her, concerned. "Everything okay?"

Julia wanted to smile, say yes, act as if everything was fine. But she was so tired. She wanted to get this week over with and go home. As if everything would be fine there. She knew better. She shrugged instead.

"Claire? Julia? Come on in," their mom called, and all three of them, even though she hadn't said Bradley's name at all, moved toward the den, all clutching their coffee mugs as if they were limping in on crutches. Elise was stooped, picking up an armful of gifts that were tucked between the tree and the desk.

Maya took one look at the group coming into the den and rolled her eyes. "Of course. Joined at the hip," she muttered. Julia's eyebrows shot up, but Claire and Bradley looked as if they hadn't heard.

The kids were just about done unwrapping their gifts, and had already dumped out their stockings into small piles in front of them: Hershey's Kisses rolled around on the floor and a giant chocolate Santa peeked halfway in, halfway out of its box, a bite taken from the hat. Molly was undressing a baby doll, singing to it sweetly, and Will was looking at the back of a box of little cars, sucking on a candy cane, finally silent.

As Bradley, Claire, and Julia searched for a place to settle, Elise passed around the gifts she'd been gathering.

"They're not much," she said apologetically. "I'm sorry, but there wasn't much time this year, with your father's death and . . ." She trailed off, her neck getting splotchy, then shook her head. "Open your gifts. It's Christmas. Not the time to talk about that kind of thing."

Candles. They had all gotten candles. Julia smiled, thanked her mom, but wondered how it had come to pass that her own mom didn't know her well enough to give her a personal gift. Candles. Something she got half a dozen of from her students. Something you got a sister-in-law or the Sunday school teacher. Her candle, which smelled like pomegranates and citrus, depressed her. No wonder she felt so alone all the time. While her friends had a mom to go to when intimate shit hit the fan, she had a mom who bought her . . . a candle.

The sisters smiled and thanked their mom, one by one, and at some point Bradley got up and left the room, then came back with a trash bag and the four of them

259

crawled around on their hands and knees, throwing away ripped gift wrap, careful not to accidentally toss a new toy. They drank their coffees and listened to the children play and pulled things out of boxes for the kids and helped install batteries, and for a few moments it might have begun to feel cozy, but then Claire spoke.

She cleared her throat, her eyes getting teary before she even said a word. "Maya," she said. Maya looked up at her sharply. She cleared her throat again. Bright red splotches appeared high up on her cheeks. "Bradley told me about —"

But before she could finish the sentence, Maya pointed a manicured finger at her. "Don't," she said. "Don't you dare sit here in this room with my children on Christmas morning and tell me something that my husband told you during one of your nightly . . . trysts . . . or whatever they are." Her finger was shaking as the rage coursed through her.

Claire held out a hand. "No, I wasn't . . . We're not . . . Oh, my God . . . See? I told you," she said, turning on Bradley. Though her voice remained steady, tears slipped down both cheeks, almost in tandem.

Bradley looked startled. "Maya," he said, "it's not . . ." But he never got the chance to finish, as Maya swept herself up, gathered her robe around her tightly, and left the room without another word.

The den practically ticked with silence in her wake. Even the kids were staring up at Bradley expectantly, their hands hovering in midair over their toys, their mouths open, their faces dotted with curiosity.

Julia let out a sigh. Claire swiped angrily at her cheeks, her lips pressed tightly against each other. Bradley rubbed his palm up and down over his hair. "Jesus," he muttered.

After what seemed like forever, the kids went back to playing, not asking a single question or saying a word, which left Elise wondering how often they'd witnessed similar scenes between their parents. How many times had Maya fled the room on a wave of harsh words? And what was wrong with her daughter that she seemed on such a seesaw of emotions these days? It couldn't be because of her father's death. She had never been a daddy's girl. Surely she wasn't going to start now that he was gone.

Molly had climbed back under the tree, and was worrying over the box tucked up on the branches again. Elise wondered what that gift was. At first she'd assumed it was one that Maya had left for her children last night, but she'd never said anything to them about it, and they'd been done opening gifts for a while now. Finally, Molly stretched and wrestled it out of the branches. A few strands of tinsel fell onto the floor. She pulled aside the bow and gazed at the tag under it.

"It says 'To Elise from Robert,' " she read. She looked up at Bradley. "Who is that?"

Elise's heart pounded. She had not gotten Robert anything. She never got him anything, and likewise, he never got her anything. Not in years. Robert didn't believe in gifts. He didn't believe in sentiment. Was this some sort of joke? Someone thinking it would be funny or amusing or poignant to make it look like her husband was sending her a gift from the beyond? After what had happened on the day he died? If so, it was a joke in the poorest taste.

Or had Robert really gotten her something this year, tucked it away in the back branches of the tree for a surprise? And what did that mean?

Bradley chuckled, gestured toward the hearth. "It's your grandma Elise, goof," he said.

"Oh." Molly laughed breathily, knee-walking toward Elise, and once again Elise felt sorry for the girl. She felt the tension. It was obvious from her laugh.

Swallowing back the strain that was creeping up her neck, Elise reached forward and took the gift from her granddaughter. "Thank you, honey," she said.

"Is it from Grandpa?" Molly asked, and Elise nodded. "How?"

"Well, he must have bought it and wrapped it up before he died," Elise said, rubbing her thumb along the side of the small gift. She couldn't for the life of her figure out why, but she felt a lump in her throat.

"Are you gonna open it?" Molly asked.

"Molly," Bradley warned right away.

Elise took a deep breath and let it out on a smile. "Sure I am," she said, and, knowing that all eyes were on her every move, she peeled back a corner of the paper, then more and more, and finally let the paper fall away.

It was a small white box, the type that would have jewelry in it.

She opened it, and pulled out the cotton. Inside was a necklace, gold, delicate, with a small heart pendant hanging from it. There was no note, no nothing. No explanation. Was this his attempt at an apology for the life he'd given her? Had he been planning to try to be a better husband before he'd died?

Elise swallowed and swallowed, holding up the necklace. She felt dizzy and sick to her stomach.

"Pretty," Molly breathed, touching the heart with the tip of her finger and making it spin.

Elise couldn't take it. She dropped the necklace back in the box and set it on the bricks of the hearth. "I'm going to make breakfast," she choked out, and stood on shaky legs, marching out as normally as she could and praying that she wouldn't pass out along the way.

FOURTEEN

Bacon and eggs. Cinnamon rolls. Skillet potatoes. Fresh-squeezed orange juice. French toast. Sausage links. Pies. Cakes. Pastries wrapped around fruit curd. Ham.

This was the same Christmas breakfast that had been made in the McClure Farm kitchen since Elise could remember. When she was growing up, it had been her job to collect the eggs early in the morning, some of them steaming in the basket as she raced through the cold yard back to the kitchen. She'd learned how to roll out cinnamon rolls from her mom, who had learned it from her mom. She'd watched as Aunt Nannie peeled potatoes, always wearing a red and green stocking cap, even though it was so warm in the kitchen the ladies would use dish towels to sop away sweat as they cooked.

When she was a child, there had been singing. Christmas carols and hymns, led by whoever had one in her heart and taken up by everyone who knew the lyrics. The kitchen was always a hub of activity — chopping and peeling and sizzling and shouted greetings and laughter and children racing through and good smells — the meal almost a gift in its own right.

She had tried her best to keep up the tradition as the farm deteriorated and the family dispersed. She had tried to make it her own tradition as the girls grew up.

But Robert had always resented the large meal. He'd felt it gluttonous, counter to biblical teachings about want. He'd always been hungover and sour, and he'd always punished the girls more freely during that meal than at any other, as if to make a point.

Her hands shook as she tried to crack the eggs into a bowl for the French toast. The image of that pendant flashed in the back of her mind over and over again. A heart. For God's sake, why? Why a heart, of all things? Why a gift at all? Her stomach lurched with guilt. What if he'd been ready to try anew? Would that have changed things the night he died?

She finally got all the eggs cracked and poured in a dollop of vanilla, a dash of cinnamon. She whisked, her arms stiff and tense as she felt anger rise up in her.

The man had beaten her. Hit her. With his fists. Broken ribs, twice. He'd berated her. A lifetime of being called worthless and lazy and stupid and ugly. He'd fought against her parenting sensibilities, and she'd gone along with him, always along with him, hoping her acquiescence would create harmony, hoping he would see she was on his side, and he never did see, it never did get any easier, and she'd ended up being a shitty mom in the process. Her girls, her poor girls. How she'd made them suffer his injustices. How she'd watched him punish them too harshly, abuse them as well. How she'd kept her mouth shut year after year after year until poor little Claire, with all her bravado, had finally done what she did that awful night at the Chuck Wagon. Oh, how Elise never blamed Claire for that night. How could she?

Who the hell did he think he was, to abuse her for decades, to change from the sweet, intense man who'd wooed her into a monster who'd made her cry out in fear and shame and sadness and bitterness and loneliness and hatred, only to leave her a gift after he'd died?

How dare he take her hatred away from her?

How dare he make her feel so guilty, as if

she didn't already feel guilty enough?

How dare he?

She finished beating the eggs and dropped the whisk into the sink, and suddenly it was as if someone had drained the very life out of all of her muscles. Her back to the cabinets, she sank to the floor slowly and rested her forehead on her knees as the bacon began to sizzle in the pan.

She sat there, images of her husband racing through her mind. His hands, big and brutal, lunging toward her. His eyes, cold and hard, mocking her.

His hands, shaking, clutching at his chest, reaching for her, for help. His eyes, the pleading in them, the pleading, oh, God, the pleading.

Around and around the images chased, until there was a beeping in her brain, incessant and loud. Bleating. Bleating. Voices, alarmed.

And then there were feet racing toward her and hands clutching at her robe, her shoulders, underneath her arms, lifting, lifting, scraping her back against the trim of the cabinets she was resting against.

"Mom!" someone was shouting. She looked up, thought she saw the face of one of her daughters — Which one was it? Was that Claire? — but the face was as if on the other side of a cloud. Was she in heaven? Had she been the one to die instead of Robert? No, couldn't be. Surely if she'd died, she'd have gone to hell after what she'd done.

But then things began to snap into place. The beeping, the cloud, they weren't in her head. They were real. Smoke. An alarm. Claire pulling her up, yelling something about getting outside for some fresh air.

"It's okay, it's okay," Claire kept saying. "Just a little grease fire. Bradley's got it."

And her son-in-law. She couldn't decide if he was misunderstood or a son of a bitch. Given her daughter Maya's reaction to him this morning, she guessed something really was wrong, but who would intervene in the plights of someone else's marriage? Who would she be to get involved, after the marriage she'd been through, after the way she'd let it end? Her son-in-law, ripping the old fire extinguisher out from under the sink and racing over to the stove with it. Blasting white foam all over the food. Ruining the eggs, the French toast batter, the cinnamon rolls.

The Christmas Day breakfast, which had been a tradition at McClure Farm since before Elise was born, was, for the first time ever, not going to happen.

This place was such a freak show.

Seriously, all the sneaking out at night and the crying and stomping off and the two aunts not speaking to each other and the uncle who skulked around like a thief. Makes a guy not want to even bother getting out of bed.

Not that he very often wanted to get out of bed anyway.

And then, of course, when he finally talked himself into getting up — it was Christmas Day, after all, and his mom had already been to his door once and was going to start flipping out if he didn't get up soon — and forced himself to go out to the den where everyone was, only the kids and Uncle Bradley were there. And then his grandmother had some sort of meltdown in the kitchen and nearly burned the whole place down.

By the time they'd gotten back in the house and all the smoke cleared out, everyone was in a bad mood and they all went their separate ways. Even his mom went to take a shower, and there he was, sitting by himself in the den, opening gifts with nobody to thank. Story of his freaking life.

He'd called his dad later in the day.

"Hey, buddy! I didn't think you'd call today. You were pretty mad last time we talked."

"Yeah. Sorry. I just wanted to say . . . you know . . . Merry Christmas and everything." That was a lie. He'd wanted to talk to his dad because he knew his dad would be there. Totally there. Not the there-in-body-but-in-mind-far-away kind of there that his mom always was. But *there* there.

His dad paused. "So how are you feeling today? Things better?"

He shifted uneasily on his cot. "I got some aftershave from Grandma Elise." He involuntarily palmed the side of his face. He hadn't even started shaving yet. He hadn't even begun to grow hair on his legs, much less on his face. All the other guys at school had. Just not him. Another way he was different. Another thing for them to jerk his chain about.

His dad laughed. "Well, you can save it," he said. "Hey, listen, Sharon and I have a few things over here for you. You think you might come by when you get back up to KC?"

He grunted. It was meant to sound like an affirmative. But he knew that he hoped to never make it back to KC. If he had his way, he wouldn't. But he couldn't tell his dad that.

"Tell your mom to call me, okay?"

"Yeah, sure, Dad."

There were some uncomfortable silences then, punctuated by even more uncomfortable small talk. His stepsister had gotten straight A's last semester. Sharon pulled a ligament in her knee. They'd made custard pies, extra nutmeg. Two of them, because they knew how much he loved them. But soon there was no more left to talk about, and his dad started to say, "Okay, well . . ." a lot, which was his way of saying he was out of small talk and ready to get off the phone.

"So have your mom call me, okay?" he repeated.

"Okay."

Another pause, then, "Are you sure you're doing okay, Eli?"

"I'm great, Dad," he lied. "I'm happy."

"Well, it doesn't sound like you're very happy. I used to have to peel you off the ceiling on Christmas morning."

"It's been a long day here. There was a fire in the kitchen and it kind of threw everyone's mood off."

"A fire? You sure you're okay? I can come get you."

"I'm good, Dad. It was bacon grease. No big

deal, really."

But it had been a big deal. Nobody seemed to want to be in the same room together anymore. Nobody wanted to speak. Even the cousins seemed subdued, playing with their new toys in the den or in their bedroom, quietly bickering every so often. It was as if everyone was trying not to wake someone, even though nobody was asleep. Maybe it was more like everyone was trying not to wake some . . . thing.

He didn't even need to wait for nightfall this time. His mom was on the phone with his stepdad, his aunts were God knew where, his grandmother was sitting on the floor by the Christmas tree, clutching some necklace and staring into the fire. His uncle had gone to the store with a grocery list. His cousins were, last he checked, taking turns diving into a drift of snow by the garage door. He was — typically, he noted — alone, even in a houseful of people.

He put on his shoes and a coat and headed outside. The snowfall had finally died off and the sun was shining. It was still cold as hell, but it was warm enough for some of the snow to begin melting. The result was a world glistening and gleaming so bright it made his eyes water to look around.

He took a walk this time. He felt like he had

all the time in the world.

He climbed over the pasture gate, the metal cold under his hands, and hopped down on the other side. Then he walked through the pasture, leaving a trail of footprints in the snow that snaked toward the creek where his grandmother and Aunt Maya had left birdseed a couple of days ago. He doubled back toward the barn, which was empty, save for a few bales of hay and some twine snaking haphazardly across the floor. A few barrels were lined up by one wall and he opened them. The first stank of mildew, but was empty. The second was about a quarter filled with what looked like moldy corn; a mouse scurried down into it as soon as he opened the cover.

He walked the entire length of the pasture, then ducked under the barbed-wire fence into the derelict garden, dead stalks barely poking out through the snow. From there, his pace grew less meandering, more steady, more determined.

He noticed a couple of trails of footprints in the snow. They were leading to and coming back from exactly where he was headed: the tree line and the pond beyond it. He knew exactly whose footprints they were, but why Aunt Claire and Uncle Bradley had kept trudging to the pond in the middle of the winter nights was beyond him. Maybe Aunt Maya was right. Maybe they were screwing each other's brains out. The thought grossed him out. He hoped he didn't stumble across any lovers' dens on his way to the pond.

To the pond. The very thought made his pulse quicken.

If Christmas Eve was a shitty day to commit suicide, Christmas Day was even shittier. He wasn't sure if he could do it, quite honestly. But he wasn't going to be offered solitary moments like this much more often, was he? In two days, they would go to his grandfather's funeral and then they would go back home, and if he was still alive at that point, he knew exactly what would happen to him. His mom would be all up in his grill, asking him those idiotic questions she was always asking now. Probably make him go to therapy. That was if his dad didn't make good on his promise and wrestle him away in a court battle. As bad as his mom would be, his dad would be worse. He'd never have a moment alone again. His dad wouldn't rest until he was cartoon-character A-OK.

Today might be his only day. The family was so fractured his absence wouldn't be noticed for a while. Maybe not until tomorrow.

Even if today was Christmas Day.

He plunged into the tree line, noting how much colder it was with the sun blocked by

275

the branches, even though there were no leaves on them. He shivered, zipped his coat higher. He wondered if he would be uncomfortable in the freezing water. If he'd shiver down under the ice. Or if he'd just go numb immediately. He hoped for numbness. He didn't want to suffer. He pretty much felt as if he'd done enough suffering for one lifetime, thank you very much.

For a brief moment, he wondered if his mom had ever walked through these trees. Surely she had, growing up on the farm. But she never talked about it. She never seemed to want to relive her childhood like so many of his friends' lame parents did.

But if this week had been any indication, was it any wonder why she wouldn't want to talk about her childhood? This place sucked. This family . . . it was the worst.

On some level, he felt sorry for his mom. She may have been a crappy mom who never seemed to really care about his life until she thought he might end it, but maybe she was that way for a reason. Maybe she was a crappy mom because she was raised by a crappy mom. Maybe all the fighting and the grudges had gotten to her, like . . . deep. Maybe she never had a chance.

He could see the pond ahead, through the trees. The ice was dull and covered with massive drifts of snow. But the center still looked wet, kind of slushy. It wasn't thick ice. He knew that. One good jump, or two, would probably do the trick.

He walked across the bank, toward the near end of the pond, where the biggest snowdrift was. He climbed to the top of it, remembering being a little kid and playing King of the Mountain with his stepsiblings. It had been fun. Addictive. They never even felt the cold. He wished life hadn't veered from that. He wished he could still be king of something.

He looked out across the ice, noting that the footsteps of his aunt and uncle that he'd been following stopped at the pond's edge and didn't seem to venture out onto the ice. Another good sign. They probably thought the ice too thin to stand on. Or lie on. Whichever they were doing.

He closed his eyes against the sun and held his arms out. *This is it,* he thought. *This is my last moment on earth.* He was happy to find that he felt somewhat peaceful, if not a little ramped up. Images flooded his mind, all of them bad. Unjust. Name-calling. Punches. Ignored pleas for attention. Hurt feelings. Embarrassment. Humiliation. Teachers who didn't give a shit. Evil bus drivers. He felt a tear slide down one cheek, leaving a warm line in its wake. He didn't care anymore about those people, about those things. This was his revenge. This was his justice. This was his peace.

Without opening his eyes, he took a step forward, down the drift and toward the ice. Then another and another until he was standing on the ice. Holding his arms straight out to his sides for balance, he walked, slowly, assuredly, toward the middle of the pond. The closer he got to the middle, the more he could hear the ice strain and creak under his weight. He liked the sound. His breathing began to quicken, and he wasn't sure, but he thought he might be hyperventilating a little. That was okay — all it would take was one or two breaths under water and it would be over.

"Hey!" he heard, and then a peal of laughter.

His eyes snapped open and he whipped around. He was almost to the middle of the pond, but back at the bank, climbing up the drift he'd just climbed off of, were his little cousins. They were giggling and pulling at each other, just as he'd done when playing King of the Mountain all those years ago. The ice creaked again under his feet, and he had a sudden realization that he couldn't do this right here, right now. Not with his little cousins watching. They would never get over the image of seeing their older cousin drown on Christmas Day. He couldn't do that to them.

"Hey!" he yelled, almost like an echo. But he was holding his palms out toward them, stop sign style. "Get off of there!"

But they weren't listening. They were too busy playing. Too busy being kids with nothing at all wrong in their world.

"Hey!" he yelled again, a little louder this time. "You guys, it's not safe!"

"Look out below!" Will called, bending low at the knees and then springing from the top of the drift to the ice below. Even from where he was standing, he could hear the dull crack of the ice under the little boy's feet.

"Will! Molly!" he cried, in a near panic this time, but they still weren't paying attention. Will had raced around to the back side of the drift to climb up again while Molly bent at the knees, readying her own jump. He began running toward them, no longer caring about shivering or hyperventilating or breathing under the ice. He could see the small cracks that spiderwebbed out from under his feet with every footfall, but still he kept running, full tilt, his hands out in front of him, his voice scratching out warnings. "The ice isn't thick enough! You could fall through! Will! Molly!"

Finally, he got their attention, and Molly froze, her knees still bent in jump preparation. She stopped and straightened as he reached the drift.

279

"What are you two doing out here?" he panted, pulling them off the mound of snow and onto the frozen bank. "The ice isn't safe."

"You were on it," Molly countered.

He took a few ragged, deep breaths, his hands shaking from adrenaline and fear. He started walking toward the tree line, ushering them with him. "I shouldn't have been," he answered. He looked over his shoulder at the ice, which from a distance looked pretty much exactly as it had looked when he'd arrived.

"I shouldn't have been," he repeated, and led the kids back to the house.

■ ■ ■ ■

December 26

■ ■ ■ ■

"Enough is too much."

FIFTEEN

Claire couldn't wait to get home. Even if it meant sitting on that long flight from Kansas City to L.A. between a set of colicky twin babies, she would welcome it.

She'd never heard of such a thing, burying a man nearly a week after his death. She couldn't help but get grossed out by the idea. The only images she could conjure all involved extensive skin decay and smells that made her sick to her stomach without even actually smelling them.

Dead people weren't like canned chili; they had a pretty short shelf life.

She supposed she understood why her mom was waiting so long to bury the old son of a bitch. When you had a personality like Robert Yancey's, and you found someone who actually wanted to befriend your mean ass, you waited around for that friend to be there when you died. Joe Dale was probably the only person who would show up to Robert's funeral for any reason other than to silently bid good riddance to bad rubbish.

But still. She didn't want to be here anymore. This place was toxic.

Not that she expected a reunion with her sisters to be something out of a Disney movie or anything. But . . . shit.

To be fair, it wasn't going spectacularly bad with Julia. Julia seemed to have left what happened ten years ago behind. Like maybe she wasn't wholeheartedly believing Maya's bullshit anymore. Like maybe she might be willing to give Claire the benefit of the doubt. Or like maybe she had her own shit to worry about. She had bigger problems taking up her attention, which was fine as far as Claire was concerned. She didn't need someone getting all up in her business.

Claire wasn't heartless. She was really worried about Julia's problems, actually. She wished Maya would get her head out of her ass long enough to see that Julia's problems were big too. She had a suicidal kid.

God, a suicidal kid. Claire had a hard time even wrapping her head around what that must feel like. Queenie, struggling. She never would have thought it possible.

Claire wondered what would happen if the

kid really did it. What would happen to Julia and to their family? She shuddered just thinking about it. She knew loss. Nobody else in the family would believe it, but Claire knew loss well. Her belly ached with loss every single stinking day.

As if on cue, she sat back on her bed and reached into the front pocket of her backpack again. For about the billionth time since she got here, she rummaged around until her hands landed on a small navy blue box, velvety and cool.

She pulled the box out and stared at it, afraid to open it. Afraid not to.

Afraid that no matter what she did, she would never make the hurt go away. Never.

She didn't open it. She didn't need to. She'd opened it enough times. She'd been gutted by what was inside over and over again.

She grunted and stuffed it into her backpack again, zipped it closed with ferocity. She couldn't do this. Not now. Not today. Not after that scene with Maya storming out of the den and then their mom getting that strange gift from their father. Not after her mom's breakdown in the kitchen that nearly burned down the house. Not after the silent, awkward makeshift breakfast — cold cereal and some fruit Claire had cut up on the fly after throwing away the burnt mess on the kitchen stove. Nobody had seemed into it anymore. If they ever had been. Why couldn't they just heave the old man into a landfill and call it done so they could all get out of here?

She slipped into her yoga pants with their weird clinginess. The bottoms were still wet from the night before when she'd walked to the pond.

Her pond, really. Had it ever been any-one's but hers?

She couldn't resist that pond. She'd been a swimmer her whole life, had always loved the way the water felt against her, like it was a part of her skin. An extension of herself. She'd lifeguarded at the lake, had been on the high school swim team, and had lived like an otter in the Yancey Farm pond since she was old enough to doggy-paddle. It was her sanctuary.

She'd met Bradley at the lake, in fact, when she was lifeguarding all those years ago. He'd hounded her, always sitting at the bottom of her chair, always asking her ques-tions, flirting with her. When his friends were around, he'd make crude jokes and sometimes she'd laugh. He was cute in the same way a puppy is cute. She'd played it up sometimes, puffed out her chest when she stood to stretch, spread her thighs luxuriously when she uncrossed her legs. She'd thought he noticed, but then he began dating her sister instead.

At first she was crushed, and remained aloof to him. Anyone who was into her uptight sister would never be a good match for her anyway. But then she noticed that he would follow her to the pond when Maya wasn't around. She would pull up onto the bank after a swim and see his shadow skittering in the woods.

"You can come out, you know," she'd called one day, lying on her back in the dirt, still breathing heavy from her backstroke, letting the sun soak into her bones.

He'd come slinking from the trees like a guilty child.

"Does my sister know you come down here to watch me swim?"

He shook his head. "She's on a run."

"Then why are you here?" She opened one eye, squinting against the sun, and turned her head so she could see him.

He swallowed, looking truly miserable, and then gazed at her with a look so intense it made her want to curl up and shield herself. "You're so beautiful," he answered.

"Don't be gross. You're dating Maya," she said matter-of-factly. "So you can forget it if you think you're going to get anywhere." And she meant it.

But he'd kept coming around anyway. Sometimes back into the trees with Maya, where they didn't think Claire could see what they were doing. Maya may not have known it, but Claire understood that he was watching her swim lazily back and forth the whole time. Sometimes he hung back in the trees on his own, just watching, always watching. And sometimes he would sit on the bank and ask her questions.

"Why do you come down here every day?"

"To get away. To swim. Why do you?"

"To watch you swim."

"You're disgusting."

"I can't help it. I'm in love with you."

"I should tell my sister." But she never would, because she knew that it would break Maya's heart. And she knew that nothing would ever come of his following her around. What harm was there in letting him watch? Plus, she sometimes enjoyed the company. He was her friend.

"What are you trying to get away from?" he would ask her.

"The same thing Maya is. Him."

"That bad, huh?"

"You have no idea."

"Tell me."

"Doesn't Maya?"

"Not really. I want to hear it from you."

So she did. Day after day she told Bradley about her father, about his abuse. Sometimes she cried. Sometimes she pulled her swimsuit strap up or down or to the side a few inches to show him a bruise. She told him about what Robert did to Maya. And somehow she felt like, by telling him, she made Bradley fall even more deeply in love with Maya, who experienced and felt and stowed away all the same injustices she did, but did so with a sturdy grace. While Claire whined and raged, Maya gutted it out and carved out a great life for herself.

In some ways Bradley was her best friend. The one she told everything. The one she trusted with her secrets. And in some ways the pond was their spot.

Even in the winter Claire loved the pond. She loved sliding across the thin layer of ice in her boots, tempting the ice to crack, wondering what it would be like to swim under that layer of protection, the ice between her and the air. And when the ice got thick, she loved putting on skates and twirling and jumping and daring herself to test gravity over and over again. She loved sitting on a blanket at its edge, just thinking. She loved imagining the fish underneath, staring up at her with their bug eyes, their mouths sucking, sucking, sucking.

When she'd come home for her father's funeral, all she'd wanted was that sanctuary. That place to go to think, even if it wasn't her father she was thinking about this time. It was truly the only reason she'd come back. Not to pay respects to him, nor to beat her head against the wall trying to connect with her sisters, not even for her mother. She'd come back for the space, the perspective.

The first night she'd gone out and sat on the bank, watching the moonlight shimmer over the ice, thinking about Michael, about the mess she'd left behind in California. She'd damn near frozen out there in her shorts, but she didn't care. The creaks and pops of the trees around her, the smell of the dirt under her, the feel of the blanket around her . . . It was as if she'd been transported back in time to her childhood. It was as if she'd gone back to the only place she'd felt comfortable and at home.

That was, until the day Maya caught them there, ten years ago.

Bradley and Maya had only been married a short time. Maya was so full of herself and her marriage Claire could hardly stand to be around her. It was as if Maya had landed some great coup or something. As if she and Bradley had invented marriage.

"You should really stop fooling around with all those boys, Claire," she'd say. "Pick one and get serious."

"I don't want to get serious. I'm having fun."

Maya would hold her hand out, spread her fingers wide, admiring her ring. "Marriage is where the real fun is, though. Having a man like Bradley living to please you is just . . ." She would sigh deep and dreamily, as if about to break out in song. "Bliss."

Meanwhile, Bradley was still showing up at the pond's edge. Practically the second their honeymoon flight had touched down in Kansas City, there he was, standing in the trees, watching Claire do the backstroke, his jaw slack. Was this bliss?

"Oh, Claire, you really don't know what you're missing, to have an amazing man adore you and only you."

The more Maya aggravated Claire, the more she played it up, pulling herself up out of the water sexily, arching her body as she floated on her back, drying herself off with her ass facing the woods, bending straight-legged and seductive until her fingers brushed her toes. She knew he was watching, and she knew he was loving it all.

And she knew what she was doing was wrong on some level, but she couldn't quite pinpoint why.

But then there was the argument about the car.

Claire had wanted to take it into town to pick up a new swimsuit. Hers had been looking a little threadbare. She'd asked her father, who promptly said no.

"I don't need to be letting no teenager take a ten-thousand-dollar piece of machinery out on the road to do God knows what."

"Dad, I'm eighteen. I'm not a little kid. And I've had my license for two years now. I'll be safe. And it's not God-knows-what. I just need to go shopping."

"I said no. I don't expect to have to say it again, damn it!"

But Claire had been relentless. Something about his refusal to hear her out made her all the more adamant that she needed that car. He was unfair and pigheaded and stupid and she was sick and tired of backing down to him.

She followed him into the house, where he shucked off his work gloves and started straight for the freezer, where he kept his bourbon.

"You're being unfair," she lobbied.

His eyes hardened on her and, not for the

first time, she felt real fear. This man was strong and lean-muscled. And mean. He could kill her if he wanted to, and she guessed he wanted to more often than she'd ever known. Still, she gathered herself tall and followed him as he walked toward the stairs, taking swigs of bourbon as he went.

"You're being unfair," she tried again, only louder. "You never listen to anything I say. You never listen to anything anyone says."

"Girl, I said no, now shut the hell up," he boomed, still walking, but Claire could see his shoulders tensing. She didn't care. She'd come too far to care. She was nobody's "girl" and she was fed up with cowering in the face of his abuse. She couldn't take it anymore.

"You shut the hell up!" she shouted to his back. "You are nothing but a hardheaded jerk! And nobody in this house loves you. Not one of us can even stand you. How does that make you feel, huh? Knowing that the only reason people stay around you is that they're afraid of you? Well, I'm not afraid of you. Not anymo—"

She didn't get to finish, as he reeled around so quickly she never even saw his hand coming. She felt it, though, as it landed across the side of her face so thunderingly hard it knocked her off her feet.

She skidded backward on her butt almost into the front room, her head buzzing with shock and surprise. It wasn't until minutes later that the sting would finally break through the numbness. It wasn't until half an hour later that the bruising would break through to the top of the skin, a dark mark across her cheekbone that would stay there for weeks.

She gaped at the retreating back of her father as he trudged up the stairs, as if laying out his daughter had no more slowed him down than stepping on an ant. Her mom appeared at the top of the stairs, peering down at Claire curiously, as if she couldn't quite figure out why Claire was on the floor.

"What's going on?" she asked.

Without a word, Robert reached out and shoved Elise forward, tipping her down the staircase. Her arms wheeled as she caught herself, just falling down a few steps, on her knees. A door slammed from within the shadows at the top of the steps and then it was just the two of them, mom and daughter, both breathing heavily and staring at each other in embarrassment and surprise.

After a few moments, Elise pulled herself to standing, one of her shins skinned and bleeding, and walked the final few steps down to where Claire lay.

"Are you okay?" she asked, her voice soft. She looked over her shoulder as she said it, almost as if she was afraid that he was there listening in.

Claire nodded. "I'm fine. But . . . I can't take it anymore, Mom. I can't do this anymore."

Elise nodded. "I know," was all she said.

Claire had gotten up and gone to her bedroom, pulled on her swimsuit, and headed straight to the pond, where her face was cooled by the water.

When she finally climbed out, Bradley was standing there, just like always, his wedding band catching the sun and glinting at her.

"What happened to your face?" he asked.

Her fingers automatically reached up and touched her cheekbone. She hadn't seen it yet, so she didn't know about the bruise, but it was very tender, so she guessed it was ugly.

"I . . . ," she said, but found that she couldn't finish the sentence. There were no words for the way she felt violated and humiliated. No way to express the desolation she felt, the desperation. She found herself instead racked with sobs. She stood, straight and miserable, her hands at her sides, her face scrunched up and ugly for all the world, for Bradley, to see. The pain that shot through her cheek as it scrunched up made her cry all the harder, and she found that she was at last able to talk, but none of the words were very decipherable or made sense.

Bradley had closed the space between them, his hands reaching out toward her, bent to look into her face, intent on understanding.

"He's . . . monster and . . . hits . . . my heart is . . . miserable . . . it's assault . . . fucking bastard . . ." Claire was saying, as Bradley rubbed his hands up and down her arms.

He had closed the space between them, his hands reaching down toward hers. He made quiet soothing noises, saying things like "Uh-huh" and "Of course" and "you're right" and "I don't blame you" at all the right times, and after a while, Claire's crying died down to a soft, miserable sniffling, and it was then that she noticed that she was standing very close to her new brother-in-law. Suddenly she felt very naked — too naked — in her threadbare swimsuit and suddenly his presence no longer seemed like something that couldn't hurt her sister.

As if he could feel her about to back away from him, Bradley suddenly pulled her into his chest, still making shushing noises, wrapping his arms around her and petting the back of her hair, trailing his fingers down her shoulder blades.

She pushed away from him just slightly and looked up, unsure how to handle whatever this was that was going on. "Um, I think —," she began, but was cut off when Bradley leaned down and kissed her, long and slow, his hands moving from her back to the sides of her face, which he held gently while he stroked her lips with his tongue.

This was wrong. Claire knew it was wrong. It felt wrong. As cute as she'd once thought he was and as okay as it felt for her to let him look when he wanted to look and as much as she thought that he could just remain her friend and letting him look would cause her sister no harm, she knew that this shouldn't be happening. And it felt good, kissing him. But she shouldn't be kissing her sister's husband just days after they got back from their honeymoon. *Push away,* her mind told her. *Push away and dive back into the pond. Let him leave gracefully.*

"What the fuck? You're the one?" resounded through the woods instead, and it was Bradley who pulled away first. Claire looked up just in time to see her sister racing back through the tree line toward the house.

Later, Claire would find out that Bradley had been sleeping with a woman from work. That Maya had found a condom in his ashtray that very day, and then she'd come home to find him kissing her sister, her former bridesmaid, on the banks of the pond. Of course she would put two and two together and assume that the condom belonged to Claire. But she'd put the wrong two together. Claire had tried to convince her, Bradley had tried to convince her, but Maya was so stubborn. She was dead wrong about what had happened between them, but never in ten years had she given Claire the chance to tell her that.

And now, with their father dead, that day of the slap, and the kiss, and later the scene at the Chuck Wagon, was all coming back to haunt her again. What Bradley had told her last night about Maya's cancer had made Claire sob just as hard as she had on that day. Her sister had cancer. She could die. And Claire would have wasted the last ten years of their lives in a feud with her. A feud over a fucking misunderstanding.

And now Maya wouldn't even stay in the same room with her long enough to let her apologize. To explain.

She rummaged through her backpack until she found her cell phone, still turned off from her flight six days ago. She thumbed it on and felt it vibrate with message alerts. She didn't need to look to know who those messages were from.

After avoiding Michael for weeks, suddenly all she could think was how badly she needed to hear his voice. She typed in his number and hit CALL.

"Merry Christmas to me," he said upon answering. "You called."

"A day late," she said, closing her eyes and squeezing out tears that instantly welled in their corners just from hearing his voice. God, she missed him so much.

"But you called."

"I don't know why, actually."

"Does that mean you're not calling to give me the gift I was hoping for?"

Claire glanced at the front pocket of her backpack again and tried to swallow. "No," she said, barely a whisper. "I'm sorry."

There was a long pause on his end. "Well," he said. "You called. That's a step in the right direction." And when she didn't respond, he added, "And might I remind you that it was the humanitarian acts of a certain doctor that allow you to step in any direction at all?"

Claire choked out a laugh. "That's desperate. You make it sound like I was carrying my foot into the ER in a grocery sack."

"That's how I remember it," he said. "I was a genius the way I reattached that foot. A superhero, really."

Claire tipped her face to the ceiling, the tears flowing even harder while she laughed. How did he do this? How could someone who made her so happy make her so sad at the same time? "You're going to love the cape and tights I bought you for Christmas."

"You got me a present?"

Claire blushed. "No, actually. I didn't."

"Ah. Well. One step forward, two steps back. How was the Midwest?"

"I'm still here, actually. And bad," Claire said. She swallowed against the pit in her stomach. "I miss you."

"Do you?" She could practically hear the smile in his voice. She didn't deserve someone as good, and as patient, as Michael. "Sounds like you got me a present after all, Claire Yancey. I love you."

Claire blanched. The "L" word. A conversation killer if there ever was one. She squeezed her eyes tight, hating herself as she let the words fall and die, unanswered. *I love you,* she said in her head, as she'd done so many times, trying out the words as if they were toxic, dangerous. *I love you, I love you, I love you.*

Instead, she said, "I've got to go."

"Call me again sometime," he said. So hopeful. So vulnerable. How did he do that? How did he still believe in her, in *them*?

" 'Bye." She hung up, unable even to commit to a phone call. If that wasn't fucked up, she had no idea what was.

Tomorrow. Tomorrow would be the funeral, and then this would all be over with. She could climb back on the plane and go home. Go sit on the beach. Go swim in privacy. Try to forget that she had a sister. Try to pretend she didn't care.

With another grunt, she flopped back onto the bed and once more unzipped the front pocket of her backpack and reached inside. Her hands wrapped around the small velvety box again and she pulled it out. Damn thing.

Slowly, she opened the box. There it was. Still there. Gleaming dully under her bedroom light. One solid diamond hovering over nine small channel-set diamonds. Beautiful.

Marriage is where the real fun is . . . Bliss . . .

She pulled the ring out and once again slipped it onto her finger, as she'd been doing all week. It felt heavy. Oppressive. Exciting. Frightening. Perfect. Terrible.

301

She held her hand out and gazed at it from a distance. It didn't look like her hand. She would never grow into that hand.

With an exasperated sigh, she yanked the ring off her finger and, as she'd done all week long, placed it back in the box and snapped the box shut. Ridiculous.

She shoved the ring back into the front pocket of her backpack and used her heels to stuff the whole thing under her bed.

One more day and she would be out of here.

SIXTEEN

Julia was sitting in the recliner when Claire came into the front room. Her feet were up and she was staring intently at the TV screen, which was set to a football game, the sound muted.

"This was the last thing he saw," Julia said, as Claire pulled out the piano bench and sat on it, facing the TV as well. "Weird, huh?" She turned her head and looked at Claire. "What a sad way to go. Alone like that."

Claire picked at the skin around her thumbnail. "He made his own bed," she said, holding herself back from saying any more. Again, the memory of him hitting her, not far from the very piano bench she was currently sitting on, rushed in on her. She pushed it away. She did not need to go there today. Not with that ring still burning a hole in her gut every time she thought about it.

"I always wanted to ask . . . is it true?

What you did?" Julia said.

"Not the Bradley thing again."

Julia shifted, curling one leg up so that the bottom of her foot rested against the calf of her other leg. "No, no . . . At the Chuck Wagon."

Claire chuckled, glanced up from her thumb, nodded. "Yeah."

Julia laughed out loud. "Holy shit, that must have taken guts!"

It had. It had taken more guts than Claire had ever known she had. Of course, there was more than just guts involved. Her face still smarted from where he'd hit her. Her heart still ached from Bradley's kiss. And her stomach still roiled from Maya's words — "Are you sleeping with her? You're screwing my sister, aren't you?" — as they'd caught up with her halfway across the soy field, anger piercing her eyes, nose running from crying.

Bradley had blubbered and tripped behind Maya, who was screaming obscenities at them both, all the way to her car. Claire had gone into the house. She'd changed out of her swimsuit and crawled into bed, lights off, her hair soaking pond water into her pillow, the shadows of evening creeping up and then over her as she lay there staring at the wall, trying to process all that had happened.

Had she asked for this? She'd never wanted to hurt her sister. She knew how much Maya adored Bradley. But she'd been letting him watch her, and why? For vanity? Because she liked the attention? How was that not hideously wrong?

But, God, she'd never meant for him to kiss her. She'd never wanted that.

After a while, there was a knock at her door, and her mom came in. She thought maybe Elise was limping just slightly, and her leg was bandaged up as if she'd merely cut herself shaving.

"You going to dinner with us?" her mom had asked.

"No," Claire said, sinking deeper under the covers.

"You sure? He's calmed down some," her mom said. "Had a few drinks. I'm sure he'd forgive you."

Claire sat up in bed, enraged. "Forgive me? All I wanted to do was borrow the car! That's it! How does that warrant this?" She gestured toward her cheek when she said that, then pointed at her mom. "I'll never forgive him. How about that? He can drink all he wants and forgive me all he wants, but I'll never forgive him. This is the last

305

time he hurts me. As of right now, he might as well be dead for all I care."

Elise said nothing. Just bowed her head for a few moments, then looked up again and asked, "You sure about dinner?"

Claire let out an angry burst of breath and flopped back against her pillow. "Positive."

"Well, we'll be at the Chuck Wagon, then," Elise said, and slipped out.

Claire lay in her darkened room for a while after she heard them leave, but she couldn't rest. How dare he be so magnanimous as to "forgive" her? All the beatings she'd had at that man's hands . . . all the insults . . . all the horrible days and nights . . . and he had the balls to forgive her? It was more than she could take.

She jumped up out of bed, threw on her shoes, and called her friend Michelle.

Half an hour later, Michelle waited in the parking lot of the Chuck Wagon while Claire marched inside.

They were sitting at a back booth, her father leaning across the aisle to talk to a couple at the table next to them. Their plates were scraped clean, their napkins tossed onto them as if in surrender. Her mom was looking in on the conversation, a smile plastered on her face. But Claire knew the smile was fake. She knew the well-placed laughter her mom let loose every time her father tried to be charming was for show. She knew her mom was beaten down and miserable and had all but given up. God, why didn't she? Why didn't she just give up and set them all free?

Claire walked straight up to their table, her chin held high, despite how small and nervous she felt. She didn't say anything, and it took a moment for Robert to realize that there was someone standing in front of him, wanting his attention. When he looked up at her, she saw the crinkled edges around his eyes disappear on a dime. Instantly, his face turned hard.

"I thought you didn't want to come," her mom said meekly.

"We're done with dinner. You're too late," Robert added, over his wife.

"I don't want to eat," Claire said icily, her whole body feeling flushed and on fire as she spoke. She nearly trembled with fear, looking into his face so close. "I just came to tell you that today was the last time you will ever lay your hands on me again, motherfucker." And with that, she mustered every ounce of reserve she had, pulled back one hand, and smacked him across his cheek so hard her wrist ached for a day afterward. The sound of flesh on flesh echoed throughout the restaurant so loud everyone went quiet. Even the waitress stopped and stared. Even Robert didn't seem to know quite what to do in the stillness.

But Claire did. She picked up the half-empty glass of soda sitting on the table in front of her father and chucked it, glass and all, into his lap, then turned and left the restaurant. She walked slowly, not wanting him to see how terrified she was of what she'd just done, and then hit the front door, and sprinted to Michelle's car, half laughing, half bawling, all the way to Michelle's house, where she stayed until she left for California one week later. She'd never spoken to her father again.

Maya had used Claire's absence as an opportunity to poison the well against her. Julia had tried to call a few times, always leaving mystified messages — *What happened . . . Why did you do this to Maya . . . Why are you breaking up the family* — but Claire, too indignant that she should even have to defend herself, never answered, and eventually Julia stopped trying, and it was done.

Julia laughed, throwing her head back against the recliner, as Claire retold the story about slapping him. Claire couldn't help it; she laughed too. Never in her wildest dreams would she have thought she would be able to look back on that day, one of the most horrible days of her life, and laugh. Never would she have thought the distance would be great enough, the perspective shifted enough.

"I'll bet the old bastard didn't know what hit him," Julia said. "Can you imagine?"

Claire's laughter dried up. Yes, she could imagine. She could imagine the way her mom held her arm close to her side while following Claire around as Claire packed to leave the farm. She could imagine the way her mom winced when she twisted just right. For years, Claire had held the guilt that her actions had most likely gotten her mom the beating of a lifetime when they'd gotten home that night. She'd never asked Elise for sure if that was what happened. She wasn't sure if she could handle the remorse if the answer had been yes.

"Where's Eli?" Claire asked, eager to change the subject, and proud of herself for using the kid's name.

"Outside," Julia answered. "With the little ones." She paused for a beat. "You know, I think something happened with him."

"What do you mean?" Claire asked.

Julia shrugged, picked up the remote, thumbed the TV off. "I don't know, really," she said. "It's just . . . he seems . . . lighter all of a sudden. You know, like hanging out with the cousins. He would've never done that before. But today he suggested it. And . . . we talked a little."

"About the suicide?"

"No, just about stuff. About opening gifts when we get home. He wants to go to Dusty's. He said he hopes he got a skateboard. That kind of thing. He's talking about things that are going to happen. In the future. That's got to be a good sign, right?"

"Did he?"

"Did he what?"

"Get a skateboard?"

Julia grinned. "No, but I called Tai and told him to go pick one up before we get home."

Claire snickered. "Spoiled brat."

Julia giggled too. "Not usually. And I kind of think that's part of the problem. He needed to be special more often." She shrugged. "I don't know. I'm probably just being hopeful. I'm still going to get him into therapy when we get back. We should've gotten therapy when we were kids, don't you think?"

Claire nodded at her thumb once again. She'd had therapy, not as a kid, but as an adult. Oh, how she'd had it. Session after session after session of it. She'd needed it. And she'd often wondered how she would have turned out had she gotten it when she was young. "There's no way Dad would've let that happen."

"If for no other reason than that people would've seen the bruises," Julia added. "It's kind of weird to think about. They'd have probably taken us away. Split us up. We wouldn't be here right now." She thought it over, then added, "Though one of us probably would think that's a good thing."

She was probably right. Maya would most likely think her life much improved if she'd never known she had a little sister named Claire.

"So what would you say if I told you I had a boyfriend?" Claire asked suddenly, wanting to connect with someone, wanting to share her secret. She cleared her throat. "Um, I guess sort of a fiancé. Kind of. Never mind."

Julia's eyes grew wide. "What? No, not never mind. You haven't said a single word all week. You're getting married?"

Claire squeezed her eyes shut tight and shook her head. As much as she wanted to share her secret with someone else, she suddenly wished she hadn't said anything. Life felt so much safer when she was the only one in her family who knew anything about her business. "No. Or maybe. I don't know. I've been so confused."

"What's confusing about it?"

Everything, Claire thought. *For starters, I have no idea what a good marriage looks like. I'm twenty-eight and have never had a successful relationship. With marriage comes kids and I don't know if I could even think of being a mom. Not to mention this is the first time I've ever been in love.* But she said none of those things out loud. "I just . . . I don't know if I'm cut out for marriage. I broke up with him."

Julia looked perplexed now. "So you're not getting married."

"I don't know," Claire answered miserably. "Just, see, okay, his name is Michael and he's an ER doc . . ."

There was the thump of a door slamming shut, somewhere off in the garage, it sounded like, and both Claire and Julia looked toward the door leading downstairs. Julia sat straighter, the recliner back squeaking upright with her movement.

"What the — ?" she said, as they heard muffled voices rising from the basement. Heated voices. Footsteps on the stairs.

"That's Maya," Claire said, and she

312

started to get up, as if she might leave the room, but the basement door burst open and she sat back down on the piano bench.

"Maya, please, just tell me what I did wrong," Bradley was pleading, as Maya stormed into the front room, her face stony, her body so rigid and erect she looked as if she was about to take flight.

Claire and Julia exchanged glances as Maya stopped midway through the room and wheeled on him. It was as if neither of them could see the sisters sitting in the room with them because they were both so consumed with their argument.

"Fine," Maya said. "You want to know? I'll tell you. You fucked Molly's dance teacher. Is that enough for you? Because it's enough for me."

Julia gasped, brought her hand to her mouth. Claire closed her eyes regretfully.

"What are you talking about?" he countered, but all three women could hear the guilt in his voice. He sounded like someone who knew he'd been caught.

"I'm talking about Amberlee, your little fuck buddy. Or should I say your *sister*? Mrs. Winsloop told me all about how sweet and helpful your sister is. How surprised I was to learn that you had a sister, Bradley. God, how embarrassing!"

He took two steps toward her, closing the gap between them, and reached for her tiny wrists, grabbed them. "Maya, please, you have to understand," he said.

She wrenched her wrists away from his grip angrily. "I don't understand, Bradley! I will never understand. I don't understand how you could do such a thing. I don't understand how you could do this to me. To your kids! She's Molly's teacher, for God's sake! Didn't you even stop to think how that might affect Molly? Or were you just so worried about getting into her pants that you didn't care?"

"It wasn't like that. I've been so scared."

Maya laughed, a sardonic bark. "So have you been scared, then, for ten years? Because I know Amberlee isn't the first, Bradley. I've just been too stupid or blind or, or, or whatever to face it."

In love, Claire thought. *You've been too in love.*

And, no, Amberlee wasn't the first. Claire knew it because Bradley had told her. Had broken down and spilled everything, in their old spot next to the pond, his breath puffing out in front of him like smoke against the moonlit sky. That's what he'd been doing all week. Purging. Maybe because he felt like he needed to, and like only Claire could understand what a tangle of emotions Maya could be. There had been others. Waitresses, colleagues met at conferences, even a months-long affair with a twenty-year-old intern that threatened to turn ugly. The girl wanted marriage. In Claire's estimation, that girl was lucky he was the one who got away.

Bradley didn't argue. Just stood in front of Maya, his eyes cast to the floor, one hand on his hip, the other stroking his upper lip contemplatively. Maya seemed to gather strength from his silence.

"I've known about them all along," she said. "Ever since Claire. Ever since the first one."

"I wasn't —," Claire began, but clamped her mouth shut. Now was not the time to insinuate herself into their fight. No matter how wrong her sister was.

"I could smell them on you, for God's sake. But I pretended I knew nothing. How stupid you must have thought I was."

"I never thought you were stupid," Bradley said. He looked up at her at last, his eyes watery. "I felt sorry for you. I pitied you for what I was doing to you."

This was the wrong thing to say. Claire knew it before the blood had fully gathered in Maya's face. Maya was not one to be pitied. Maya would never be okay with giving up that strength. Maya would see it as a loss of control, and if there was one thing Claire knew about her sister, it was that control had been the only way she'd made it through those bleak, dark years of childhood. What she could control, their father couldn't.

"Don't you dare pity me, you bastard," Maya said, her voice going dangerously low and ominous.

Bradley's eyebrows cinched together; he had the balls to look annoyed. "Stop with the name-calling, Maya, okay? We're both adults here. Let's discuss this like adults. I've apologized and I've broken it off and —"

"Don't tell me what not to do!" Maya shrieked. Julia jumped, pulling both legs up into the chair with her. She looked embarrassed to even be witnessing this scene. "Do not fucking tell me what to do!"

"Lower your voice. You're making a fool of yourself. Claire and Julia are sitting right here." He gestured helplessly toward the sisters.

"You!" Maya screeched, jabbing her French-tipped finger in his face. "*You* made a fool of me! You are not an adult. You're a cancer! You're a fucking cancer and you will kill me if I don't cut you out!"

Claire's heart sank. This, Claire thought, was the reason why she couldn't put that ring on her finger. This was the reason she couldn't say yes.

Thank God the children were outside and weren't hearing this. Her sister seemed like she was on the edge, screaming about cancer, raving about Bradley's "fuck buddy." Claire wished she could take it all back, turn back time to when she and Maya were friends. To a time before Bradley, when Claire could stand up and wrap her arms around her sister and tell her everything would be okay. That it didn't seem like it now, but a year from now she would look back on today and think, *Thank God I made it past that horrible time.*

"Stop it!" Bradley was yelling back, and for a second Claire and Julia simply looked at each other, eyes wide, as if they'd stumbled into something they wished they could get out of, but without any idea of how to exit the situation gracefully.

They began shouting over each other.

". . . can't believe I let you do this to me . . ."

"If you'd just stop yelling for a minute . . ."

". . . tried so hard to be perfect for you and you never gave a shit . . ."

"I didn't want a perfect wife!"

"I should never have married you! I wasted my life . . ."

". . . the kids will hear you if you don't stop screaming."

And then Maya, who'd been so steely as if to appear almost as a statue throughout this, finally broke down. Her voice came out in ragged chokes, tears raging from her eyes.

"Leave! Just leave!" she began screeching, pointing toward the door. Bradley was struck silent, his face red, his eyes bulging. He shifted his weight from hip to hip, breathing hard, but when he didn't move to her instruction, Maya stomped around him and up the stairs to their bedroom. A few moments later she reappeared at the top of the steps with a suitcase. She heaved it with a grunt and it sailed through the air and hit Bradley in the back of the legs with a mighty thump. "Get! The! Fuck! Out!" she screamed from the top of the stairs. "Go home, get your shit out of my house, and don't come back. Ever!"

She ended the last bit on such a scream that everyone in the front room — Julia, Claire, and Bradley, his back still to the stairs — flinched. Then she retreated to their room and slammed the door.

For a few minutes there was nothing. No

noise. No movement.

Claire didn't know what to do. Say something? What? What did you say after witnessing something like that? Go to her sister? As if her sister would have anything to do with her. Go to Bradley? He would be receptive — maybe too receptive — and the last thing she needed was to "side" with him. Pretty much nobody in the house would understand. Maybe not even her.

Finally, Bradley bent, turned and picked up the suitcase. Without a word, he walked toward the front door, pulled his jacket off the coat tree, and left the house. A few minutes later Claire heard a car door shut and the sound of an engine gunning and then gravel stirring under tires.

"What was . . . ," she began, but Julia shook her head at her sister perfunctorily, her eyes looking meaningfully to the door between the kitchen and the front room. Claire followed Julia's gaze and saw all three children — Eli, Molly, and Will — watching the scene.

"How long?" Claire whispered.

"Enough," Julia answered, looking down into her lap balefully.

Enough, Claire thought, *is too much.*

SEVENTEEN

His name was Michael and he was an ER doc.

Claire met him when she stepped on a shard of glass on the beach, slicing the bottom of her foot open during her roommate's birthday party. The pain wasn't too bad, probably because she was half-drunk, but the cut wouldn't stop bleeding and she was pretty sure she would need stitches.

"God, I'm sorry to ruin your birthday," she'd lamented over and over to Judy, her roommate, as she'd lolled in the front seat of Judy's car, blood leaking out onto a sponge that somebody rounded up from somewhere and rubber-banded to her foot. The sponge was filthy and it stank, and on a sober night Claire would have never put it on an open wound, but that night she was sloshy and carefree, trying to forget about her ugly breakup with Rob the Terminally

Boring Investment Banker two nights before.

"Don't worry about it," Judy said, slurring her words a bit, and Claire had a
distant alarm bell go off in her head about
her friend's ability to drive. "I was getting
tired of volleyball anyway."

"Yeah, but Ben was totally into you tonight."

Judy laughed. "We were probably about
half a minute away from a hard-core make-
out session."

Claire pushed her head back against the
seat again and closed her eyes. "God, I'm
sorry," she repeated.

"No big. He'll wait for me."

When they rounded the corner into the
hospital parking lot, Claire said, "Just pull
up to ER. I'll probably be here for hours.
You can go back to the party and I'll get a
cab when I'm done."

"You sure?" Judy had asked, and Claire
had nodded, pulling herself out of the front
seat, trying to steady herself while the
sidewalk was lurching and she was trying
not to walk on the ball of her foot.

But Claire hadn't needed to get a cab that
night. The adorable doctor with the dark
hair and tan, gentle hands who stitched up
her foot had offered to drive her home.

"Just don't tell anybody," he said. "I could get into big trouble."

Right away Claire knew that Michael was different from all the other men she'd dated, and it scared her. She'd always prided herself on the way she'd so efficiently protected her heart, at first by necessity, an eighteen-year-old, fresh off the farm, in a new, big city all alone. The vastness of California had frightened her. The people. The possibilities. They all seemed so dangerous, even deadly. She felt like she was constantly scurrying — scurrying to get groceries, scurrying to work, scurrying to the beach, just hoping to go unnoticed. The men, they were everywhere! And constantly on the make. She dated more men her first six months in California than she had her whole life in Missouri.

But she always feared them. When would one of them hit her? When would he call her fat or ugly, tell her she wasn't good enough? And would she have the guts to stand up to an abuser twice? Somehow she doubted it.

But as she grew more comfortable with her surroundings, she began to get more into a groove. She liked being unattached. She liked having that sheath of protection around her heart. She would be hurt by no one, because she would be damned before she'd let it happen.

She'd never fallen in love before, but even that first night, when he touched her foot so gently as he bandaged it, and when he helped her hobble into her apartment, Claire knew that Michael would be different. He had that soul — that one soul — that matched hers and that she would be unable to keep out.

He stopped by the following Monday.

She'd been cleaning, her hair mostly captured in a bandanna, her running shorts full of holes, when the buzzer rang.

"Who is it?" she shouted into the microphone, her voice still on louder-than-the-vacuum mode.

"Michael Bowman," came the answer.

Her brow furrowed. She tried to remember if she knew a Michael Bowman. The voice sounded vaguely familiar, but the name totally did not. Maybe he was someone she'd met at one of Judy's beach parties and she'd been too tipsy to remember having met him. She pressed the button on the buzzer to talk. "Do I know you?" she called down.

The voice responded, "Um, it's Dr. Bowman. From the emergency room?" He said the last as a question, as if he wasn't quite sure if that was where he was really from or not.

Claire's finger jerked away from the intercom button as if it were on fire. One hand involuntarily flying up to the bandanna on her head, she raced to her living room window, which stretched across the front of the building, allowing for a perfect view of the front stoop. She used one finger to split the Venetian blinds just slightly and peered down between them.

Oh, God, it was him. The hot doctor from the ER who'd brought her home Saturday night. The one she thought she'd felt a connection with. Standing there in scrubs and a gray T-shirt, his hair tousled and shiny in the sunlight. She watched as he leaned forward and rang the buzzer again.

Unsure what to do, Claire raced back to the intercom and pressed the button. "I'm here . . . um . . . just . . . can you give me a min . . . I'll be right . . . come on up."

She did something she'd never done before — pressed the button to unlock the front door to let a strange man walk right up to her apartment. Her heart raced with the danger of it all. And the excitement. There was definitely excitement. Something about him made her feel exhilarated and windswept, like she'd just gotten off of an amusement park ride.

Quickly, she glanced down at what she was wearing, and remembered that she hadn't even had time to brush on a little mascara. She looked like death on a platter. But he was already knocking on her front door; there was nothing she could do about it now.

She walked to the door, waited just a beat before opening it, then swung it all the way open with a smile. "Dr. Bowman! Hi!" She stepped aside to welcome him in. He stepped over the threshold awkwardly, his eyes pointed toward her foot.

"I just thought I'd check to see how you were doing."

"Great," she answered, though she held her foot up just slightly off the ground like an injured animal, because for some reason that felt like the right thing to do.

"Good. How's the pain?"

She shrugged, trying to ignore the flipping and turning sensation in her stomach. It was almost as if she could feel his . . . vibe . . . coming through the air toward her. She remembered being attracted to him in the hospital, but she'd also been drunk. To have the same — no, stronger — feelings with him nearby when she was stone-cold sober was surprising. "It's not bad. Sucks that it's on the bottom of my foot, though. Hard to do much of anything."

"Yeah," he said. "Mind if I take a look?"

At first she wasn't sure what he meant, and her face burned with the thought, *Please do. Look all you want.* Then she realized he wanted to check the wound. "Oh, sure, okay," she said and backed up to the futon and sat down, propping her foot up on the coffee table so that the bottom of it was facing him. He turned and closed the door, then loped over to the table, still never taking his eyes off of her foot, and knelt down.

"The wrapping help?" he asked, all business.

"I guess. It's kind of a pain to put a shoe on. And I miss the beach."

He grinned. "You love the beach, huh?"

"When you grow up your whole life in a dry, hot, muggy bowl of land, you love anything to do with water. The beach is like paradise to me."

He wound the bandage around and around until her foot was bare. She wiggled her toes in relief. Only then did he look up at her, just briefly, and she thought maybe she saw the same crushy fluster in his face as she guessed she probably had in hers. "You grow up in the Midwest?" he asked.

She nodded. "Missouri. You?"

"Omaha. I thought I recognized a Missouri accent."

"I don't have an accent!" she protested, giggling. "Missourians don't have accents."

"Oh, yes, they do," he said, poking and prodding around on her foot. For a moment she let herself imagine that he was giving her a foot massage, but the prick of pain she felt every so often when he hit a certain spot chased that image away.

"So you make house calls? How very nineteen-fifties of you."

He chuckled. "Only for special cases," he said. He glanced up at her and the glance, combined with his hands on her feet, practically melted her.

"Oh, well, what makes me so special?" she said, hoping that witty banter would make her sound much more confident than she felt.

But he didn't answer. Kept his head down and began winding the bandage around her foot, rewrapping it. Claire noticed that the tops of his ears were flaming red. "Looks good," he said, as if she'd never spoken. "Whoever gave you those stitches knew what he was doing."

Their eyes met again, his mouth set in that reserved little grin. When he finished, he stood up.

"Well," he said, "I guess I'll let you get back to . . . whatever you were doing."

She blushed, reminded of how dumpy she looked. "Cleaning," she said. "And, gee, thanks."

She walked him to the door, wanting nothing more than for him to stay.

"Actually," she said, touching his arm. "Really, thanks. It was nice of you to come check on me."

"And probably illegal or against at least a dozen privacy regulations. You're not going to turn me in, are you?"

His grin was contagious, as was his awkwardness. Claire felt silly, like a smitten thirteen-year-old, but she couldn't help herself. "Nope," she said. "I'm actually thinking of getting injured again because the service is so great."

He paused and her hand fell away from his arm as he reached for the doorknob. "Instead, you could just go to dinner with me," he said. "Look on the bright side — you might choke. If your goal is to get back into the ER, that is. I do know the Heimlich."

Claire laughed out loud. "Okay," she said, feeling pleasure well up in her chest. "Deal."

That had been almost a year ago, and

they'd been practically inseparable ever since. Michael was romantic and beautiful, and Claire loved to drape herself across him, wondering what the world must look like through those long eyelashes, wondering what the world must feel like on the other side of those soft, precise fingers. He made love to her the way he stitched her foot — like nothing else in his world mattered at that moment, like he wanted to memorize her, like he was afraid of breaking her.

She fell for him. Despite her efforts not to, she fell. He was everything she wanted to be, everything she wanted to have.

And the thought of that scared the shit out of her.

She began pulling away from him about a month before her father died. She'd hoped it would make things easier. That he would stray, find someone better, someone who knew a thing or two about how to treat him, how to act in a relationship. Her heart hated it, but she hoped he would fade away.

Instead, he proposed.

He'd taken her to dinner at a little Thai place they frequented, where Claire adored the tofu pad thai and he drank sweaty bottles of Singha and their table was so small their knees touched.

Claire had been brooding, so confused and frightened about the fact that even though she'd been pulling away he'd only seemed to grow more concerned about her, had only given her more space, and had done it lovingly rather than resentfully. She didn't know how to handle this, and feared that she would eventually have to break up with him, which she knew would break her own heart in the process. But better to break it now, she thought, than to wait for him to disappoint her later. To wait for him to beat her, call her names.

"So I've been thinking," he said after his second beer. Claire had dunked a spring roll into peanut sauce, but was caught holding it midway to her mouth as her stomach dropped. He'd sounded so serious. Maybe this was it. Maybe he was going to finally dump her. The thought both relieved her and brought tears to the corners of her eyes. She set the roll on her plate and looked down at the table.

"I don't blame you," she murmured, and wondered if it was too late to stop him from doing this. If maybe she'd made a mistake by pulling away from him. She reached for his hand, swiped it with her finger, not yet ready to let it go.

He dipped his head to try to look into her

eyes. "Blame me?"

"For breaking up with me," she said. "I've been asking for it."

He laughed, leaned to one side, and rooted around with his fingers in his front pocket. "I'm not breaking up with you," he said. He pulled out a box and set it on the table between them. Claire looked at the box, her heart thunked once, hard, and then she looked up at him. "I'm proposing," he said quietly, calmly, as if this was the most expected thing in the world.

He scooted his chair backward, palming the box and getting a very serious look on his face.

Claire jumped up out of her seat, the flimsy wooden chair flopping back onto the concrete floor behind her with a smack. Heads turned all around the restaurant and she felt even more panicked. This wasn't how she wanted to do this. Not with everyone watching. Not with him clutching a ring box and looking like a lovesick little boy. Not with her heart ripping into shreds inside her chest. Not with her wanting to lie down and die.

"What's wrong with you?" she asked.

He stopped, looked confused. "What do you mean? It's not five-star here, but I thought . . ."

"I've been so distant," she said, almost to herself, as if trying to convince herself that this proposal was not her fault. "I've been pulling away from you."

"You've been stressed. I haven't been taking it personally. I love you."

"Is that how it is, then? You just let someone treat you like shit because you love them? You just let them take and take and you let them abuse you and you let them betray you, and nobody is ever happy, because they're all in love? Doesn't that sound ridiculous to anyone but me? Isn't it wrong?"

He shook his head. "I don't know what you mean. You haven't treated me like shit. We're great together, Claire. I'll make you so happy."

"Don't," she said, her voice full of tears. She held out one hand toward him in a stop gesture. "I can't . . ." She took a deep breath. "Please don't ask me to marry you."

"Why not?"

She bit her lip. "Because the answer will be no. It's over, Michael," she said, and she had to rely on her ears to hear herself say it because her lips were too numb to fit around the words correctly and she couldn't feel them leave her mouth. It seemed surreal to her, this scene — gold lamé and the clinking of silverware against china and a Thai waiter rushing between the tables with pitchers of iced tea and Michael, the first man she'd ever allowed herself to love, holding a blue velvet box in one hand, his face a big question mark. She was not doing this. She was not breaking up with him.

Except she was.

"I'm sorry," she said, and picked up her purse and rushed out of the restaurant, bolted down the sidewalk before he could follow her, ducked through an alley to the next street over, and hailed a cab, which took her home.

And then flung herself facedown on her bed and sobbed for what seemed like a lifetime. She turned off her cell phone. Refused to check e-mail. Set the chain lock on her door. Slept.

She slept for what must have been three days, off and on. She would get up only to force a few crackers in her mouth, down a glass of milk or a bottle of vitamin water. She didn't shower, she didn't turn on the TV, she called in sick to work.

Her heart was broken, and she'd broken it herself. She loved him. God, how much she loved him. And it was for that reason that she couldn't marry him. If she had to choose one of them to hurt, she chose

333

herself. That's how much she loved him.

On the fourth day, she got up and show-ered, put her hair into a ponytail and went to work, waiting tables at a pizza restaurant a couple of blocks away. Her mind wasn't on her job and she was continually getting ripped by Billy, the manager with the porn-stache who she hated more than life itself. Her tips sucked, but she didn't care. All she cared about was that she wanted to hear Michael's voice, wanted to feel his soft fingers brush her legs, wanted to look into his eyes, kiss him, love him, make love to him. But she couldn't. She'd blown it. She'd blown it on purpose. She would have to live with the pain.

When her shift was over, she went straight back to her apartment, her eyes already drooping for want of sleep again. She knew it wasn't healthy to be doing this — that she should be going to the beach and swim-ming away the sadness — but she didn't care. Really, what in life was there to care about anymore? If there was something, she didn't know it.

She opened her apartment door and right off she could smell him. She lifted her nose like a dog, catching the scent of Michael's cologne on the air. The scent made her gut squeeze and cramp with loneliness. But also with curiosity. He'd been in the apartment.

"Hello?" she called out. "Michael?"

But there was no answer. She shut the door and moved into the room slowly, warily, looking for evidence of him.

She found it on the kitchen table. A vase with a single red rose in it, next to it a note, next to that the blue velvet box he'd been holding at the Thai restaurant four days earlier.

With shaking hands, she opened the note. It said: *Please at least look at it.*

She did. She looked at it and looked at it, touching the diamond, holding it under the light. Imagining it on her finger as Mrs. Michael Bowman. Or was it Mrs. Dr. Michael Bowman? She'd heard of some women doing that.

She never pulled it out of the box. She never tried it on. She only stared at it, tears streaming down her cheeks.

Hours later, the phone rang. It was her mom. Her father had died. She needed to come home right away for the funeral. Was she free?

Tearfully, she admitted that yes, she was free. Unfortunately, she was free as a fucking bird. Free to do whatever the hell she wanted. Not even a goddamn dog to board or cat to find a sitter for. She was nothing if not free.

And free felt like shit.

EIGHTEEN

Julia had gone outside, saying something about wanting to get fresh air, but Claire could hear the crinkle of a cigarette pack working under Julia's kneading hand in her coat pocket. She stifled a smile — Julia had always been the avoidant sister, the one to cut and run when the dirt got deep. Maya had always stuck around and wallowed in the pain; Claire had always fought back. But it was Julia who would find respite.

Bradley had left and Maya had been stomping around in the back of the house ever since. Claire sat in the living room alone, thinking about Michael, wanting him, while at the same time wanting to not want him. Maybe she would call him again later. Just to tell him she was okay. Just to apologize for hanging up so quickly earlier.

"Hello?" Elise came in from the sunroom, stomping slush from her boots. It had warmed up considerably outside. Pockets of slush were dotting the yard, snowmelt dripped in the gutter, and birds chirped along the top of the sheds and the barn. Elise had called out earlier that she was going outside to put out some more seed for the birds. She'd left humming "O Come All Ye Faithful," and it had occurred to Claire that they'd played no Christmas music all week.

"In here," Claire called from the piano bench. It was like she was riveted to that spot. It was an old relic of the McClure clan, that piano. One of her uncles or maybe great-uncles or God knew who used to play boogie-woogie like nobody's business. And church hymns. But that uncle or great-uncle or God knew who had long since left the farm, and had left his piano behind. Nobody in the Yancey family had ever played, although there was a time when Claire sorely wanted to. Robert would have never tolerated the noise, would have never tolerated the redundancy of practice, would never have tolerated a teacher's bill, so she never even asked. Still, the piano stayed, just like the ancient, dusty butter churn in the back of the pantry and the falling-down chicken coop and the rusted farm tools in the toolshed. They were as much a part of the family as Claire, Julia, and Maya were.

Maybe, in some ways, more a part of the family, because those things had happy memories attached to them, and Claire wasn't sure she and her sisters did.

Elise traipsed through the kitchen and out into the front room. She was still wearing her stocking cap, her cheeks two bright red patches from being out in the wind so long. "Where is everyone?" she asked.

"The kids are outside somewhere. So is Julia. Maya's upstairs. And Bradley left."

"Oh." Elise removed her gloves and dropped them into a box full of mismatched gloves by the front door. "Where'd Bradley go?"

Claire shrugged. To the airport, she supposed. Or maybe to a motel. Who knew? That was, oddly, something they didn't talk about during their nights down by the pond. All the things he had to tell her about Maya, and leaving her was never one of them. Claire knew it would sound unlikely to just about anyone — especially to Maya — but she believed that Bradley really did love his wife. He didn't mean to be hurting her. In his mind, he was able to separate his actions from his love for her. He was so genuinely frightened by the cancer.

God, the cancer. Her sister had cancer. No matter how many times she repeated that in her mind, Claire just couldn't grasp it. They were all supposed to still be children, not adults battling for their marriages, their kids, their lives.

She doubted anyone else knew. Bradley had told her that Maya was funny about spreading the word. She didn't want Molly and Will to know. She didn't want the babysitters to know. It seemed like the only two people carrying the burden were Bradley and Maya. Well, and some friend Maya had made. One who had cancer herself.

What a sad secret to be carrying around.

Claire quickly studied her mom, still standing in the front room trying to shake off the cold, gazing expectantly at her for answers. She didn't even know that one of her daughters could be dying. Shouldn't she know that? Was Maya being unfair? Was cancer the kind of secret you were allowed to keep, or were you obligated to share the news with the people who loved you so they could prepare for the day when they would have to say good-bye to you?

Probably Maya figured Elise was saying good-bye enough this week. "Maya kicked him out. I don't know where he went."

Elise paused. "Kicked him out? For good?"

Claire shrugged again. "I guess. He's been

cheating on her. Since day one. I think she's finally had enough."

"Well," Elise said, busying herself again, "who could blame her? Poor Maya. Those poor kids."

Claire said nothing. She wondered if she could blame her. Claire had always had a soft spot for Bradley. Had always enjoyed their talks by the pond, before he kissed her. And though she knew it was only going to start trouble this week, she'd been enjoying their talks again. Bradley listened to her. Bradley didn't judge her. And he was easy to talk to because Claire never expected anything from him. He couldn't let her down.

At the same time, he could never do anything right for Maya. She began their marriage so sure the other shoe would drop any second, she damn near threw it down herself. She gazed at him with disappointment in her eyes every minute of every day. She waited for his admission that he'd been the failure she'd always known he would be. She was so sure he would betray her, it really didn't make any difference if he did or didn't do it in reality.

He slept with those other women, in part, because in Maya's mind he had already done so.

Still. The woman had cancer. If nothing else, he lost points in human decency for that fact alone.

"Well, I suppose Maya knows what she's doing," Elise said. She perched on the edge of the recliner, where Julia had been just moments before, and tilted her head, gazing at her daughter. "I suppose I should have done it myself."

"Done what?"

Elise bit her lip, chewed for a second. "Kicked your father out." Claire noticed her mom's hands were shaking.

She had to work to keep herself from laughing. Did her mom even realize who she was talking to? In her mind, her mother should have kicked his sorry ass to the curb years ago. Maybe even years before Claire was born. The bastard had never done anything right for her, or for them, and to say good-bye to him would've made for a short while of pain and a long while of happiness, instead of the other way around. Well. Claire assumed, anyway. She guessed you could never really predict whether your actions would cause pain or pleasure down the road, could you? She would have never guessed that letting Dr. Bowman into her apartment to check on her foot would lead to her sniffling into a quilt every night by a frozen-over pond in Missouri snowstorms.

"It doesn't really matter now, does it?" Claire said by way of avoiding saying what she really felt. "He's gone either way."

"I suppose," Elise said. "But he may not have . . . well, things might have been different if I had."

Claire shifted. "Well, sure they'd be different. That's a given. But you shouldn't beat yourself up over it, Mom. He's gone. He's never coming back. It doesn't matter anymore."

"But you think I should have . . . let him go. You think it would have been all right to just . . . let him go."

Claire took a breath. "Yes," she finally said, "I do."

Elise seemed to take it in, her hands still shaking as they rested in her lap, her teeth still working her bottom lip, which was starting to redden around the edges. "I do too," she finally said.

Claire got up and walked over to her mom. She eased down onto the floor in front of the recliner and put both hands on her mom's knees. "Mom," she said softly, "nobody ever blamed you for what he did. He did those things himself. You were just as much his victim as we were."

Elise patted Claire's hands, tried on a

smile and failed. "Thank you," she said. "You girls were always so sweet to me. Even when I didn't deserve it. Even now, when I don't deserve it. I'm not as innocent as you think. And he left me that necklace. Why on earth would he do that, after all these years? I didn't get him anything."

Claire noticed that her mom's knees were shaking under her hands as well. "Mom? Are you okay?"

Elise gathered herself up tall, but the action didn't seem to have any real conviction to it. "Of course I am, dear. The funeral is tomorrow. It will all be over after that. I can forget . . . things . . . after he's been buried." She stared out into space for a moment — something she'd been doing more and more often — then turned to her daughter. "We need music, don't you think?" Claire watched as her mom pulled herself out of the recliner and sauntered into the den as if what had just happened hadn't been about ninety shades of freaky weird. Claire stayed on the floor, on her knees, listening to the rattle and shuffle of Elise digging out a CD, then a series of clicks, followed by Bing Crosby's voice belting out "Winter Wonderland."

For a moment, Claire allowed herself to be flooded with memories. She recalled ly-

344

ing on the den floor as a little girl, scraps of paper spread out in front of her, listening to this song over and over again while she drew pictures and scribbled poems. Feeling like the whole world was a blanket that rested over her and like there was no time more special than Christmas. The time of miracles. The time of love and joy and hope. The time to rejoice.

She could almost smell the lard melting. Could almost feel the birdseed running through her fingers as she helped mash the cooling fat and seed into a ball around a loop of rope that they would later hang from a tree. Almost heard Julia's proper voice and smelled Maya's perfume. Those memories were precious to her. The real gifts of Christmas. Too bad there were so few of them.

For she could also remember her father coming in from the fields in the middle of it, angrily shutting off the music while harrumphing about them being "leisurely," then going on to berate them until they cried and fled the kitchen.

As it had so many times since she came home, her mind wandered to Michael. What did he think about Christmas music? She'd never asked. Would he allow her to play it? Allow their children to sprawl on the floor and dream while listening to it? Would he rent a Santa suit just to put the gifts under the tree on Christmas Eve, even if she was the only one who would see him do it? Would he drink too much at a party and get flirty, make her giggle and slap at his hands in public?

For some reason she thought he would do all of those things. He would be merry, always merry. But she couldn't guarantee that she would. She couldn't guarantee anything about herself. She wasn't sure she even knew who she was now, much less who she would be in the future. Who wanted to marry someone like that?

After a while, she heard clanking of pans in the kitchen and she pulled herself off the floor, her knees cracking and popping as she stood. Twenty-eight was definitely not old, but she wasn't getting any younger, that was for sure. If she kept turning down marriage proposals, next thing she knew she'd be an old maid.

Did she really want to face a future alone?

She started toward the kitchen, her full intention to help her mom make whatever it was she was fixing. But her feet turned, practically on their own, and she found herself slowly climbing the stairs instead, and walking down the hall to Maya's room.

All was quiet behind the door, but she could hear movement behind it.

She knocked.

"What?" Maya said tiredly from the other side. "If it's you, Bradley, you need to leave."

Claire slowly, timidly, turned the doorknob and opened the door just a crack. "It's me," she said, peeking around the door with one eye.

Maya, hovering over an open suitcase and clutching a shirt in her hands, rolled her eyes and sighed. "What do you want, Claire?"

For a moment, Claire was transported back to her early teen years. Back when Maya had been a surly teenager, tiny and perky outside the house but a raging volcano inside it. Claire could think of a million times she'd stood at this very door, looking in on this very wallpaper with the little blue flowers and this very same dresser with the bottom drawer that always hung askew, getting the very same eye roll and sigh from her sister.

She opened the door and let herself in, standing awkwardly in the doorway.

"If you want him, he's yours," Maya said without looking up or missing a beat folding the shirt she was holding. "Congratulations."

"I never wanted him," Claire said, even though she knew that was, technically, a little bit of a lie. But her crush on Bradley really was ancient history. The moment he touched her lips with his, the crush was gone. Evaporated. And that was the truth. She'd wanted him as a friend far more than she'd wanted him as anything else.

Maya chuckled darkly. "Well, that makes two of us now. I hope the bitch gives him an STD."

Claire blanched. She knew this was something that worried Bradley.

What if I bring home some sort of STD and make her sick? he'd fretted the night before. *What if the cancer makes her more receptive to it or something? Can you still die from syphilis?*

You're not using condoms? Claire had asked him and he'd ducked his head so low his face was in total shadows. *Dude, that's sick,* she'd said, but honestly she'd been too caught up in her own drama — wishing too hard that he would just let her go outside to cry on her own for one stinking night — to really care. Now she worried on Maya's behalf.

"You should get tested," she said.

Maya dropped the folded shirt into the suitcase and picked up another, holding it still for a moment while she studied Claire with slitted eyes. "Why? Do you know something I don't know? Who am I talking to? Of course you do."

Claire swallowed, shook her head. "Not at this point, no. Sounds like you know everything."

Maya studied her harder, let the shirt flop against her stomach. "You seem worried. Is it because you have an STD and you've been sleeping with him?"

Now it was Claire's turn to roll her eyes and sigh. "No. I've told you a thousand times, I never slept with him. He kissed me, Maya. Ten years ago. That was all. I didn't ask him to. I didn't want him to. And nothing — not one thing — has happened since then."

Maya began folding again, only this time more angrily. "So what have you been doing sneaking around outside at night with my husband, then?"

"We haven't been sneaking out together. I've been going out to" — *cry, regret, wish I'd never said good-bye to Michael* — "clear my head. I have some things on my mind, believe it or not, that have nothing to do with you. And Bradley kept following me out there. I didn't ask him to. And nothing ever happened between us."

"Bullshit."

"Bullshit!" Claire was getting angry now. Until this point she'd ridden Maya's anger like it was something she'd somehow deserved, maybe because she hadn't pushed away the kiss faster, maybe because she'd initially had a crush on him, maybe because she knew that he liked watching her and she let her vanity get in the way and ate it up rather than telling her sister about it. But that was so damn long ago and she was a kid then and by God, she deserved forgiveness for poor choices, even if none of those choices really had anything to do with the betrayal Maya had been feeling for the past ten years. "You have spent so many years being pissed at me for something he was doing with other people. Have you forgotten the condom you found? It wasn't mine, and a part of you has always known that. He was sleeping with someone else. Someone from work. He has slept with dozens of women since you married him, Maya. And he's sleeping with Molly's dance teacher. But none of those people are *me*. You should be angry at *them,* Maya, not at me."

Maya slammed the shirt she was holding into the suitcase, then turned and walked right up to Claire. Claire was a full three inches taller than her sister, and Maya had kicked off her heels, a fact Claire noticed with a feeling something akin to shock when the top of Maya's head barely reached the bridge of Claire's nose. Maya never took off her heels.

"Then what have you been doing outside with him all week?"

"Talking to him. Listening to him talk, actually."

"About what?"

"About . . . you." Maya's mouth snapped shut and Claire could have sworn she saw something flit across her sister's face. Surprise? Fear? Triumph? She wasn't sure. Her voice felt tiny and unsure, all of the anger seeping out of it as if she were a balloon pricked by a pin and drifting around the room, getting smaller, smaller. "About the cancer."

"Wonderful," Maya said sarcastically, one hand on her hip. But her eyes looked wet and wide, as if she was frightened as she moved back toward the suitcase and reached in to straighten the shirts she'd placed in there.

Claire followed her toward the bed, sat down next to the open suitcase. "He's scared," she said. "He's scared of losing you."

Maya laughed. "Well, it's a bit late for

that, now, isn't it? He's lost me."

Claire nodded. "He's scared for the kids to lose you. He says you're the most amazing mom he's ever seen. And I agree. I could never be as good a mom as you are." Maya said nothing. Just kept folding. "And he said he was scared that he would lose you before he ever got the chance to be a good husband to you."

Maya tossed the shirt into the suitcase and picked up a pair of socks, folded them together, tossed them in on top of the clothes. "He had the chance. He had ten years of chances. He blew it."

"I agree," Claire said. "But I just wanted you to know that. That we weren't talking about me. We were talking about you." She paused. "Are you going to have to do chemo?"

Maya shook her head. "Just radiation."

Claire breathed a sigh of relief. "That's good news, then."

"Really?" Maya shot her a death glare. "Good news?" She went back to her folding. "Well, I hope you never get the good news that you have cancer, little sister."

"I just meant that it was good that you wouldn't have to have chemo. Why haven't you told anyone? Why haven't you at least told Mom?"

"Because . . ." Maya paused, let her arms go slack. "Because telling people would make it more real. And because I didn't want Bradley to see me as, I don't know, flawed and broken. I didn't want to give him an excuse to leave me."

Claire was quiet for a moment. How sad it must be to be Maya, to forever be afraid of being less than perfect. To hide herself away so nobody could see her human side. All this to hang on to a man who was never hers to hang on to. Not totally.

"I'm scared, too, Maya," Claire said. "I'm scared that you'll never believe me. That you'll never forgive me."

"This is probably the wrong day to ask me for that."

"When will there ever be a right day? I've been trying to get forgiveness for a decade."

Maya tossed a few more socks on top of the shirts and then zipped the bag closed. "Actually, you've been hiding out in California for a decade. I don't recall any phone calls or e-mails or anything. You know, asking for forgiveness."

I shouldn't have to ask for it, Claire thought. *Because I didn't do anything to deserve the blame in the first place.* But instead she said, "I was hiding out from Dad and you know it."

"Partly. You were also sending a message: 'Claire doesn't need anyone.' "

Claire had never thought about that before, but she knew Maya was right. She had been trying to prove she didn't need anyone, hadn't she? She'd been trying to prove that ever since she was a little girl toddling along after her big sisters just hoping for some attention, only to be yelled at to stop being a pest and go away. She'd been trying to prove that since the first time her father left a mark on her skin. She needed nobody. She was independent and they could all go fuck themselves for all she cared.

She was still trying to prove it, wasn't she? With Michael. By turning down the only man — the only person — who'd ever had a shot at really making her happy.

"I was hurt. And angry."

"And spoiled and selfish too."

"That's not fair, Maya. He never left you with black eyes."

Maya hefted the suitcase off the bed and set it on the floor, then picked up a child's suitcase and zipped it open. "He never left you with a sprained wrist. He never pulled out your hair."

"Yes, actually, he did pull out my hair. More than once."

"Okay, well, this isn't a contest, you know," Maya said, her voice rising. "He beat us. All of us. So the hell what? Why does that matter now? We're still alive and he's dead and who gives a shit?"

"I give a shit!" Claire shouted. "I give a shit because I can't marry the man that I love. It matters a whole hell of a lot to me. Right now."

Maya's eyes grew wide. "Well, that's not my problem," she said after a few minutes, but her voice was soft, sad.

Claire's heart sank. "Of course it isn't," she said. "And it isn't your problem that your nephew is suicidal or that our mom is totally freaking losing it, either. Because poor Maya, her husband slept with someone else so the whole world is about your problem. Boo-hoo."

Maya scooped out a handful of clothes from the suitcase and laid them on the bed. She started to say something, then stopped. "What do you mean my nephew is suicidal? Eli?"

"Never mind," Claire said. "I shouldn't have said anything."

"Yes, you should have. What's going on?"

"Nothing. And please don't tell Julia I told. I swore I'd keep it to myself." *Secrets,*

355

she thought as she said it. *We're all so full of secrets.*

At first, Maya looked like she might be inclined to argue, but she simply took a breath, closed her mouth, nodded, and went back to work. Silence stretched around them for several minutes.

Finally, "What about you? Are you scared?" Claire asked.

Maya continued working. Her movements were still angry, but her voice had softened somewhat. "Sometimes. When I think about the kids, I get a little sad. When I see how bad my friend Carla has gotten, I worry. Sometimes I wake up feeling like I'm being invaded, like I'm under attack, and I'm so helpless. That's the worst part, I think. Being helpless."

"Is the prognosis good?"

"As good as it can be, I guess."

"So the doctor thinks you'll live."

"He would never say that. Lawsuit city."

There was more silence, only this time, Claire noticed, it was not entirely uncomfortable. This felt like one of those rare times when she was invited into one of her sisters' bedrooms to listen to music and gossip about people from school, most of whom Claire didn't even know, but it never mattered because she was getting entrance into a very special place. A sisterhood in the truest sense of the word.

"Well, you look really good for —," Claire began, but Maya shushed her when she heard a noise, something like a siren coming from outside.

"That's Molly," she said, and both women rushed to the window, which looked out over the backyard and soy field and to the tree line and pond behind it. There, running across the snowy field, shrieking for her mother, Molly ran toward the house, stumbling every few steps as her boots slipped out from under her.

Claire and Maya looked at each other, and Claire could instantly see the worry on her sister's face. The screams ripping across the field weren't normal. The kid sounded absolutely frantic. Something was definitely wrong. Without speaking a word, both women bolted from the window, raced down the stairs, and out the back door toward the crying child.

"Molly?" Maya was calling as Claire sprinted past her toward the little girl. "Honey? What's wrong?"

"Will fell in!" Molly cried, panting, tears streaking her face. "Will and Eli together!"

"Fell in what?" Maya asked, finally catching up with her daughter and putting her

357

hand on Molly's shoulder, trying to shush her. But the little girl wouldn't calm down, wouldn't stop screaming long enough to tell her.

But Claire knew without the little girl saying a thing. She'd seen the extra set of footprints pressed into the snow after the first night here.

"The pond," she said, breathless, and bolted through the soy field, her feet unable to take her there fast enough.

Today had to be the day. There was no way around it.

The funeral would be tomorrow, and his mom had already told him that she would be packing their things tonight so they could leave straight from the cemetery. She wanted to get home. To Tai, to Christmas, to her students. And he couldn't blame her. If he'd had anything waiting for him at home, he'd be ready to get back to it too. The farm was really depressing. Which he found highly ironic, by the way.

So it had to happen today. He couldn't keep playing around with it. Couldn't keep getting interrupted. Couldn't take that chance. If he were to wake up in a hospital room somewhere, alive, he'd be pissed off. Or worse — alive and damaged, unable to try again.

He decided that his problem was that he was trying to be sneaky about it. Slipping out in the night and all that clandestine shit was action-movie-exciting but not very practical, especially around this place, where pretty much nobody stayed in bed, apparently. He looked too suspicious when he snuck around. Things would go off much easier if he just did it. Right in the middle of the day. Right in the middle of everything and everyone, just like he'd originally planned back home.

Pills would have been much easier. But the pond was a great second choice. It would take him quickly, painlessly, peacefully. He wanted to die, but all that suffering he could do without.

He'd spent most of the day making peace with his plan. He'd talked to his mom about shit that he wanted to do when they got back home, and even though he knew that their talk lulled her into this doe-eyed confidence that he was getting all better and oops, Mom, false alarm and I didn't really mean it and all that stuff, he still felt good about it. He wasn't terribly attached to his mom, but he liked the idea of their last conversation being a positive one. At least she would have that good memory. Even if she would figure out it was a lie.

He'd even gone outside and played with the little cousins for a while. He wanted to roll around in the snow one last time before he died. He had other things he'd like to have done one more time before he died too. Go to a water park. Eat a steak. Jerk off with one of the magazines his dad hid behind the toilet. But he guessed those things didn't matter anymore. Not really. Not when he was about to experience the bliss of being gone from it all.

The kids were cute. Followed him around like a couple of puppies. Will, especially. The kid couldn't say his words right and sometimes did some things that seriously made him look like a 'tard, but it was cool the way he mimicked every move Eli made, repeated everything he said. Molly was more of a bossy type. A know-it-all. A girl. But she was sweet, and she even kissed him on his cheek once when they were playing Snow City Avalanche (Will's idea).

But the cousins had gotten cold, had gone onto the sunporch to warm up. And he'd lain in the middle of the yard on his back, feeling the chill leak up through his coat. He'd stared at the sky, wishing it would just let loose on him and snow right then. Cover his eyeballs and gather in his nostrils, make him an abominable snowman. That would be the shit.

But after a while his thoughts went where they always went — to the place where he was miserable. Where he was relentlessly made fun of. Where he was a loser. Where he was lonely.

Where he wanted to die.

Slowly, slowly, he pulled himself up to sitting, and then to standing, and then he was walking, walking, walking, faster and faster, propelled by purpose, and soon he was punching through the tree line where the melting snow made a mud mess out of the banks around the pond.

He could see fading footsteps where Aunt Claire and Uncle Bradley had hung out last night. He wasn't sure what was up with them, but he was positive that it wasn't good, and that it had something to do with the root of why he ached so hard for a family that wasn't there. In some ways he couldn't blame his mom for being such a distant mom. How could she have possibly learned any better growing up in a family like this one? In that moment, he forgave her. He wished he would have left her a note telling her so.

His fingers started tingling, a sensation that traveled down the length of his whole body. Soon he felt both numb and hypersensitive, like every nerve ending was being jabbed by a sharp stick.

It was time.

Taking a breath, he stepped out onto the ice, his foot immediately sliding on the slick, melty surface. He wheeled his arms to keep his balance, and took another, more careful, step. And then another, and another, the ice creaking and cracking around him. The sound jazzed him, made him feel energetic. Creaking and cracking was always the sound of something exciting — broken bones, the bogeyman, coffin lids closing, death, death, death.

He kept his eyes closed, focused his energy on the steps he was taking. Step, step, step toward the middle, toward the end.

Soon he felt as if he'd walked long enough and opened his eyes to find himself not too far from the middle of the pond, where the ice was visibly thinner and slightly puddled in some spots. He smiled widely, said what he could remember of the Lord's Prayer just in case all that shit about heaven was real, and bent his knees to jump.

Thunk. Some cracking but not much to it.

Thunk! Harder this time. A crack snaking its way around the toe of his shoe. Very thin, singular.

Thunk!! He put some muscle into it. Pulled his quads up high on the takeoff, landed with his heels. A loud crack resounded and a spiderweb of cracks surrounded him. One more and he'd be through.

"Avalanche!" he heard, and snapped his head around.

The little cousins were on the ice again. Right where he'd caught them before. Will was at the top of the smaller-but-still-there drift, ready to jump, Molly on the bank right behind him.

"NO!" he boomed, but even though his voice was loud, Will had already left the mound and was in midair. He wouldn't have been able to stop himself if he'd tried. Will landed on his butt on the ice, just hard enough to poke a small dent down into it. His eyes grew wide, startled, as the back of his pants got soaked, and he scrambled to his feet. But rather than run off the ice, in his panic Will ran straight toward the middle, arms outstretched for help.

"Eli!" Will cried.

"Stay there!" he cried back, trying to get to his cousin, but the adrenaline that had been racing through his veins moments earlier was making him shaky and he kept slipping and falling to one knee as he tried to close the gap. "Stop! The ice is breaking!" he yelled, and those were the last words he was able to get out as his left foot slipped in one direction and his right in the other. He went down, first on a knee, then onto his belly, just a few feet from Will.

The ice opened and the pond swallowed them both.

At first he was only aware of a feeling of being shocked. Had he not been holding his breath already, it would have surely been swept away from him in a gasp.

He opened his eyes and could barely see anything. The pond was murky and brown, and the ice cover and dim sky made it almost appear black. He whipped his head around wildly, searching for his cousin, but in his panic he could see nothing. He racked his brain to remember what color Will's coat had been — red? Yes, red. Definitely red — but he saw nothing red under the water.

His lungs quickly felt as if they might burst and he clamped his lips together tighter, wanting to keep every bit of air that he could. He looked up, saw the ring of light where the hole they had fallen through was and kicked toward it, straining against the ache that was starting to set into his bones. The cold. It was so damn cold.

He broke through the water and took a deep, ragged gasp of air, coughed, took another.

Distantly, he heard Molly screaming, and hoped she was staying off the ice. *Please don't let them both die because of me,* he thought, and the very thought of Will dying under the ice squeezed his heart with such fear that on his next breath he dove back under.

This time he felt calmer . . . or maybe he was feeling sluggish. The cold was doing it to him, he was sure. His arms and legs had begun to feel leaden, like it would take far more strength than he had to move them through the water. He struggled, felt jerky, felt like giving up, like closing his eyes and letting himself sink into the sediment at the bottom.

But then a splotch of red just below him caught his eye.

Will!

Mustering every ounce of strength that he had, he flipped his legs up behind him and kicked toward the patch of color, stretching his arms out, his fingers splayed to catch whatever he could of his cousin, to get a hold.

After what seemed like forever, his fingers finally brushed up against the collar of Will's coat and he forced them to close. He clamped down and righted himself, then looked back up toward the ring of light, which seemed so impossibly far away, he was sure he'd never make it.

It was the cold that was doing this to him. It was what he had been counting on, after all, wasn't it? Cold that would seep into his very bones. Would make him stop moving, make him stop fighting.

Make him die.

NINETEEN

Claire wouldn't know this until later, but her bare toes were already cracked from the cold and bleeding, leaving trails in the snow, even before she got to the tree line.

She didn't care about her feet, or about anything other than racing through the soy field as quickly as she could.

Her nephews were down in that pond — the pond she knew in and out, up and down, like the back of a mermaid's fin — and she had to get to them.

She should have said something. That was the thought that kept circling, circling in her head as she dashed past the beehives. She should have told Julia that she thought Eli had been going down to the pond at night. That she'd seen footprints and that she'd thought she'd seen him in their father's recliner at night too. That he'd been acting weird, testing his luck, testing his life, on the ice.

But she hadn't. She hadn't done it, and why? Because there was a part of her that thought maybe he was just being a kid sliding around on the ice the way she did when she was little? Maybe. But she knew better. She knew, after one glance at Eli four days ago, that he wasn't just a normal kid who thought of and did normal kid things.

So why didn't she do it? Why didn't she tell like she'd said she would?

Probably because if she told, it would mean she was involved. It would mean she was part of this family, part of a whole. And being part of a whole scared the holy living shit out of her, didn't it? Maya was right. That was why she ran away to California ten years ago. That was why she preferred one-nighters with douche bag guys she'd never even look at twice in a sober moment. And that was why she was running away from California now.

That was why she'd broken up with Michael.

She had to stay disengaged, because being a part of a whole was scary. Being a part of a whole could mean hurt. Being part of a whole could get you knocked on your ass at the bottom of the stairs with two black eyes.

But, God, how she wished Michael was there right now. For Eli, but also, more important, for her. She needed him. Even if that need scared the ever-loving shit out of her. Because she hadn't realized it until she was sprinting toward the tree line with her heart in her throat, but facing life without him scared her even more.

She plunged into the trees, her feet and arms pumping, her breath pulling in and out in great puffs. She felt numb all over. Not from the cold, but from fear. She could hear Molly's cries, thin and distant, and Maya's shouts not too far behind her, but nothing coming from ahead. Not a sound from the pond.

She bulldozed through the thicket, not worrying about branches hitting her arms, her hands, her face, not worrying about following any sort of trail — really at this point just a barely worn path where mushrooms would crop up in the fall and squirrels would skitter during the spring and summer. She saw the edges of the pond up ahead. She thought she heard a splash. Maybe a ragged grunt. A breath, maybe? A sound of life? The thought propelled her even harder. She ran faster, faster than she'd ever run before. Faster than she'd ever even thought she might be able to run. Her feet sank into the mushy snow and she thanked God that she'd been running on a beach every day for ten years, and momentarily had a sense of purpose. *Maybe this was the real reason I was led to California,* she thought. *To prepare me for today, for this very moment. Maybe this was predestined.*

Claire wasn't a religious person by any means, but she guessed that God wouldn't predetermine the death of two children. No way. This had to be a failure on someone's part. Maybe Maya's and Bradley's. Maybe Julia's. Probably her own.

Or maybe this was just what happened when you let yourself into the Yancey Farm. You got hurt. Maybe the place was cursed.

She heard the splash and grunt again, a breath being expelled and then sucked in, just as she pulled up onto the bank, her heels pushing deep holes into the mud as she ran.

She didn't stop or even slow down, though she tried to be aware, to take everything in.

There was something on the ice. Something red. A child's coat? Dear God, Will's coat? Soaked, and discarded next to a jagged hole about four feet across.

Not far from it was Will, waterlogged and shivering, pale, in his shirtsleeves, coughing. He lay on his side on the ice near the bank, his cheek pressed up against it. *Hypothermia.* The word blared through her mind. He was so little; it wouldn't take long, and all kinds of bad things happened with hypothermia, right? Frostbite, heart attack? Death?

She whipped her head around. Eli was nowhere to be found. She'd heard a grunt, a breath, some splashing a few seconds before. Was he still in there? The water had to be thirty degrees, and who knew how long Eli had been in it? He might not last much longer.

Whose child did she choose? Which sister? Julia, who had confided in her, who was silently suffering this very possibility every day, that her son might die? Or Maya, the one who had just lost her husband, the one cowering from cancer, the one who had only moments before finally begun to trust her, to let her in, the tiniest bit?

The choice seemed impossible and unfair, but in the end it was the fact that Will was still breathing that made her turn and rush toward the hole in the ice.

Her whole world got grainy and slow, like she was seeing everything in a dream or through a strobe light. Like one of those ridiculous bars Judy was always making her go to, where they'd wear children's glow necklaces and drink potent mixed drinks out of tall plastic mugs that flashed blue, green, red lights as if a parade were coming through.

She felt as if she couldn't see, couldn't take it all in, but later she would be able to recall every vivid detail, every tick of every second perfectly. It would keep her up at night. Rack her body with sobs.

She fell to her knees next to the hole and plunged her arms into the water. She felt something that might have been hair, but not enough to wrap her fingers around. She dropped to her belly and stretched so that her arms were submerged up to her shoulders. This time she thought she might have bumped against skin, but it was cold, so cold, and she couldn't be sure what she was feeling. She thought something brushed against her arm. A hand? Was that a hand? But then nothing more.

She heard Maya coming close, her cries and sobs and gasps all intermingling into one ugly sound. It was the sound of a terrified mother. The sound of worst fear, realized.

"Will!" Maya shouted. "Oh, my God, Will!" Claire glanced back. Her sister was on her knees on the edge of the ice, pulling Will into her lap, her face frantic and horrified. "Where's Eli?" They seemed to be the only words she could wrap her mouth around. Over and over again. "Where's Eli?

Where's Eli?"

Claire braced herself for the cold. She felt it in her chest. Grief. Dread. Fear. She sucked in a great lungful of breath and ducked her head, raised her arms and pointed them toward the hole.

And then she slipped headfirst into the water.

TWENTY

The water was so cold her immediate reaction was to want out. To scramble back up the side of the broken ice and call for help. To give up, let fate take over.

Her yoga pants, so restricting just a few hours ago, felt like nothing against her skin. No protection. No warmth. Her feet stung and ached and floated little trails of blood through the murky water. Her arms felt heavy and slow.

Still, she angled herself downward and opened her eyes, searching for a sign of her nephew. Bubbles would be nice. Bubbles would be miraculous.

She didn't see him.

She looked up toward the top again, hoping he'd found the air pocket that always seemed to reside between the ice and water. Hoping she'd see kicking legs, a head tilted up, sipping in oxygen. But again she saw nothing.

Claire knew every centimeter of the pond, and she knew that where the ice had broken was above a fairly shallow portion of it. Deep enough to swallow two children, for sure, but shallow enough to reach the bottom in one breath.

Using every ounce of strength that she had, she kicked straight for the bottom. God willing, she wouldn't find Eli there. God willing, he'd be hiding out in the woods or back home in front of the fire by now and this all would have never happened at all. A dream. A really, really bad dream.

Please don't do this to Julia, she prayed as she kicked her ever-slowing legs, propelling her toward the bottom of the pond. *Please don't rip my sister's heart out.*

But then she saw him. He almost seemed to pop up in front of her out of nowhere. He was flailing, his eyes wide and panicked. He was holding out his arms toward her like a toddler wanting to be picked up. His lips were pursed tight, small bubbles leaking out of them and floating over his head. His eyes seemed to be telling her that he couldn't hold his breath much longer, and that he couldn't get up top again for more. More important, they told her that he wanted out. He wanted to live.

She kicked extra hard, reaching for him,

feeling like she was going nowhere through the water.

Just hang on, Eli, she pleaded inside her head, the fear and dread she'd been feeling before now looming so large it almost felt as though it was pulling her down. *Please hang on!*

She stretched so far her shoulders ached, her fingers splaying and grabbing until they found his hands, his elbows, his shoulders. She gripped him, praying that her fingers would bend and clutch and not let go. To her relief they curled and she was able to drag him toward her.

She pulled him up against her chest with one arm, noticing for the first time how thin he was. Still just a boy, really.

And as she got her feet onto the ground underneath her and pushed herself back up toward that light spot in the ice, her lungs full to bursting, wanting to take a breath so badly, mightily pulling through the water with her free hand, everything in her world seemed to slow down.

Fronds and sediment floated around her, unmoving. Fish wove through the weeds nearby. Sounds, muted and melted, drifted down into the water in bangs and creaks. Eli's hair drifted up in front of her face; his scarf waved like a flag.

And she realized, with something akin to a punch to the chest, that this was the first time she'd ever held him. Her nephew. Her sister's little boy. Her blood. She'd never gathered him into a sticky hug as a toddler, and here he was turning into a young man. A very troubled young man. And she wanted nothing more than to turn back the calendar pages, to go back to when Eli was born, to be there for her sister. For both of her sisters. Time had marched in on the wave of anger and grudge, had swept an opportunity out of her hands like a finger snap, and had left her empty before she'd even realized that it was ticking.

The thought filled her with horror. How many things had she lost over the past ten years? How much love, how much warmth would she never get back? How many more things would she lose if she kept herself closed off from love?

She couldn't do it. She couldn't go through life alone like this. She wanted Michael. She wanted love. She wanted time to leave her with sweet memories, not empty handfuls of missed ones.

She broke through the surface of the water without even really trying. Automatically her chest heaved in a breath and expelled it back out again, and thank God for involuntary bodily responses, because she may have never breathed again.

Breaking through the water was like walking into a chaotic room. There was screaming — Molly's and Julia's — and sirens in the distance, though Claire thought they might be heading across the old soy field toward them. There was a rough coughing, frayed around the edges, and Claire realized only vaguely that the sound was coming from Eli, who was frantically clawing at the ice around the hole. Julia was lying on the ice in front of him, sobbing, pulling on his arms, trying to free him without breaking the ice further, and Claire, still in the water, was pushing him, though she had no foothold to give her any strength. There was shouting coming from Elise and hands reaching and Eli sliding on his belly across the ice to safety and Maya repeating, "Oh, thank God, thank God, oh, thank God . . ."

And Elise called, "Back here!" to the paramedics who had finally arrived and were slogging through the tree line with their equipment.

Claire pulled herself out of the water, not caring when the ice she was clutching broke loose and dumped her back in. Barely even noticing how big the hole had gotten as she pulled herself up again and this time freed herself, breathing heavily, shivering, unsure exactly what had just happened and who had saved whom.

He was still alive.

Not that he cared.

Not that he wanted to be.

Not that he should have been.

But he knew he was because he could hear the clock from his bedroom ticking all the way in the den and he could feel the tag of his flannels scratching up against the small of his back and he could still feel a little bit of a tingle in his pinkie finger. Frostnip, the doctor had called it. Made him sound like he belonged in a freaking Christmas carol.

He was breathing. In, out. In, out. His heart was beating. *Ka-thud, ka-thud, ka-thud.* He was alive.

They had tried to keep him in the hospital, but he'd begged his mom not to make him stay. He was fine. He was cold, but he was warming up and he was fine.

He'd heard her repeat those very words to his dad on the phone later. He'd given them a hell of a scare. Nobody knows what they were doing on the ice, no. It was just an accident. A very frightening accident and they were all very lucky. And he was a hero! He'd saved his cousin's life!

But he knew better. He knew he was no hero. He knew it wasn't an accident. He knew he'd caused it. And he was fine.

Goddamn it!

He was fine and his little cousin was still in the hospital and they were saying things like hypothermia and frostbite and needing to watch him for a couple of days and there was nothing he could do to take it all back.

Nobody could get ahold of Uncle Bradley. Aunt Maya had tried. She'd called his cell phone over and over and he hadn't answered it. She'd begged him on his voice mail to call her back.

"Please," she'd cried into the phone. "Something has happened. Will's in the hospital. Please, Bradley. Call me." But he didn't, and they had all eventually left her and Will there at the hospital and gone home and just slowly drifted off toward their beds.

And he was here. Alive. Reliving what had happened in his mind over and over again. His cousin's coat coming off just when he got him to the top of the water. And his cousin splashing back down into the pond again, leaving him there clutching a stupid empty coat and crying like a baby. Watching his cousin sink to the bottom of the pond and going back underwater after him, his arms and legs feeling like they'd been plugged with lead. And finding his cousin again and dragging him up by one arm and pushing his cousin out of the water but unable to pull himself out no matter how hard he tried. And then drifting down, which should have been exactly what he wanted, should have made him happy and calm because it was finally going to happen. But instead of letting death take him, he'd panicked and headed back up to breathe, over and over again, until his body physically couldn't do it anymore. He'd swum toward his aunt Claire, afraid, afraid, afraid of dying, and being thankful.

Thankful to be saved.

Fuck.

Everyone was asleep. Nobody left their bedrooms tonight.

Except him.

He couldn't sleep.

He was alive and he shouldn't have been.

He curled up onto his side and felt the wool of the recliner press into his cheek. He stared out the window, where the moon shone down brightly onto the head of the snowman he'd built with his little cousins earlier that day.

Tears snaked out of the corners of his open eyes.

He stayed that way until morning.

■ ■ ■ ■

DECEMBER 27
THE DAY OF
THE FUNERAL

■ ■ ■ ■

"He was only surprised
for a few minutes."

TWENTY-ONE

Elise didn't expect Maya to come to the funeral. She figured her daughter would stay at the hospital by Will's side, waiting for news on whether or not the cold had done any permanent damage.

Elise had cried herself to sleep the night before. The poor boys. Her poor daughter. She'd lost Bradley, almost lost her son. Tragedy upon tragedy, and what if she'd never manipulated the girls? What if she hadn't been greedy about getting them all in the same house for Christmas? What if she'd told them the truth, that the funeral had always been set for the twenty-seventh? Would this have not happened? Would they have shown up last night, tired and jet-lagged and whole? Instead, her lie had brought them in early. A family had arrived five days ago, but only one of them — Molly — remained at the house this morning. A family damaged, depleted.

In this way she felt responsible for the things that had happened with Maya this week. And a loop of should-haves and might-haves and could-haves filled her brain all night long. She should have told the truth. She should have had the pond filled in years ago. She should have been watching the kids more closely. Not to even mention the biggest should-have of all, the one about the night Robert died — what she should have done that night — but she still wasn't ready to face that one.

But whether she should have or not, she didn't do any of those things, and that was the important part.

Out of habit, she rolled over to her left side to avoid Robert's snoring in her face, then once again caught herself, remembering that he was gone. He wouldn't ever be snoring in her face again. Or making her have sex during her period. Or smacking her for some perceived wrong. When would she stop forgetting this? When would it be just a normal fact of life that her husband was gone? She forced herself to turn over to her other side and look at his pillow. To touch the sheets on his side of the bed. She picked up the pillow and held it to her face, smelled it. It still smelled like him, and the scent stirred up feelings in her.

She missed him. As crazy as that sounded, she did. Not the mean bastard she'd been married to for so long, but the boy who'd wooed her with wood carvings and wildflowers plucked from their field and lavish dates where she felt like royalty. Had he been planning to bring that boy back? Was that what the necklace had been about? She wished she knew.

He had been good to her. For a long while, he'd been good to her.

But the drinking had started and the girls had been born and he'd been so stressed and angry all the time and he'd been bad to her. For an even longer while. So would it really have mattered if the pendant was an apology? She guessed not. There was such a thing as too little, too late, and she supposed Robert had passed that point long, long ago.

She pulled herself out of bed and took a quick shower, then dried her hair and slipped into a black dress, the same one she'd worn to her mom's funeral years ago.

When she got to the kitchen, she was surprised to see Maya sitting at the table, erect and vacant-eyed, dressed in a beautiful black pantsuit neatly pressed and hugging her curves. She was sipping a coffee and staring out into space. Elise could hear Molly playing in the den, the Christmas tree rattling every so often.

"I wasn't expecting you to be here," Elise said, pouring her own coffee. "Surely you're not going to the funeral today."

Maya's eyes barely shifted. She didn't move. "My father died," she said flatly. "I have to go."

Elise joined her at the table. "Honey," she began. "Will —"

"He'll be fine for a couple of hours," Maya interrupted, her eyes finally meeting her mom's. "He's sleeping anyway. They've got him on pain medication. His fingers are still hurting pretty bad. And his ear. The one that was pressed down on the ice."

"What are the doctors saying?"

"That it's possible he could lose some of his left pinkie and some of that ear. It'll take a few weeks to know for sure."

Elise nodded, sipped her coffee. It seemed horrible to her, how a little boy could be perfectly healthy one minute and losing fingers the next. But he was alive. At least he was still alive.

"We're going back to Chicago tomorrow morning as planned. Bradley is already there, which is why he wasn't answering last night. He was on a flight . . ." She trailed off, went back to her stare, but Elise noticed that her daughter was swallowing, and swal-

lowing again. "I've got . . . an appointment . . . on Thursday, and now this, and
Bradley's already moving his things out . . .
How am I ever going to do all of it by
myself?"

"I'll help you," Elise said. "I'll try to get a
flight in the morning. So I can be there. Do
what you need."

Maya seemed to be struck by this offer.
She shook her head. "I don't know what I
need anymore."

Elise reached over and touched her daughter's elbow. "I know, honey."

Maya jerked her elbow away, pulling it to
her side protectively. "No, you don't know."
She leveled her gaze at her mom again.
"Mom, my appointment is radiation treatment. I have breast cancer."

Maya's face began to crumple with grief,
but all Elise could do was sit back in shock.
Cancer? On top of everything else, Maya
had cancer? How did she not know this?
Why had no one told her? Forget everyone
else — why hadn't Maya told her?

"Oh, my God, Maya," she whispered.

Maya blinked, her head making fast little
shaking movements as she lifted her face
upward to try to keep the tears from falling
over her lower lids. She swallowed, took a
deep breath, used the pads of her fingers to

dab at the corners of her eyes, and gathered herself.

"I've lost everything," she said. "I'm being punished and I don't know why."

"You haven't lost everything," Elise said, though she knew her words would fall on deaf ears. Of course Maya felt as though she'd lost everything. Wouldn't she herself feel the same way? "You still have the kids. You have to be there for the kids."

"What if I can't? What if the cancer is worse than they think?"

Elise had no answer for that.

Last night, sitting in the uncomfortable vinyl hospital chairs, a jittery Julia had confided to Elise that Eli had been trying to commit suicide. Julia had wondered aloud if that was why he'd been on the ice, if this had been a suicide attempt and Will had just innocently gotten mixed up in it. Eli wasn't talking and nobody knew exactly what had happened, but still Julia worried.

Elise had been dumbstruck that one of her grandchildren was contemplating killing himself, and even more dumbstruck that this was knowledge that one of her daughters had and hadn't shared with her.

Now to find out that Maya had cancer . . . it was almost as if her wondering about her daughters had been answered. There were secrets. Tons of them. What more did her daughters keep unrevealed? What more were they sitting on? Keeping her out of? What other secrets would she discover?

And would they find out hers?

TWENTY-TWO

The funeral home was more crowded than Elise would have thought. She'd had no idea her husband had so many friends, although she had often, over the years, wondered if some of the old cronies that clogged up the funerals out there in the boonies were actually friends of Joe Dale and if he didn't beg them to come out to make a good showing. A ministry to the hopelessly unloved, if you will.

Clem Hebert and his wife and the other ladies who'd taken them to dinner at Sharp's were there, as were a couple of men she recognized as having helped Robert fix some fencing a few years ago. Others she recognized from in town but didn't know their names. She supposed he knew some from poker games, some from restaurants or bars, and some from the farm store that he frequented. She supposed that no matter what brand of son of a bitch you were, you still gathered a handful of followers by the time you were sixty-seven years old.

Joe Dale greeted them at the front door with a smooth "Good afternoon, Elise, ladies," and a small, contrite bow of the head perfected by years of handling the grieving. "Right this way."

He led them into the little chapel room where Robert's casket was, shining under the lights and surrounded by flowers and plants. She could see his forehead and nose poking out over the lip of the open casket. and immediately felt woozy and as if she'd better sit down before she fell down.

"Mom? You okay?" Julia said softly, putting her hands on the small of Elise's back. "You look a little wobbly."

"I'm fine," Elise said, trying to smile away the queasiness that had settled in. She glanced at her daughters.

Claire had appeared in the kitchen this morning in her Hollywood sunglasses and had not taken them off since. The doctor had checked her out and released her. He had not given her anything to help her sleep, to rest, and Elise doubted that she had done either of those things last night. In many ways, her youngest daughter seemed more distraught by what had happened than anyone else had.

Maya had sat down in the last pew, her arms and legs crossed primly, her gaze straight ahead.

"If you'd like to spend a few moments with the departed," Joe Dale said, "you will have some time after all the guests leave."

Elise nodded somberly, and as calmly as she could, she strode to the front of the room. She looked down into the casket. Gazed at him — at his tie, at the rouge on his cheeks — and tried to feel something, anything other than shame. And then she realized . . . she didn't even really feel that.

She touched his lapel, smoothed it with her palm. "Oh, Robert," she whispered. "I guess I should apologize. I do feel bad about the way it all ended. But I really do think I would do it again, that's the thing."

Soon Julia was standing next to her, her hand resting on the small of Elise's back once again. "He looks like a wax figure," Julia said. "Not that I expected him to look good or anything."

"He looks so small in there, don't you think?" Elise whispered. "He always had such big shoulders. But he looks like a little old man in there."

"I don't know, Mom. He looks the same size to me. Just not angry. Maybe that's what's throwing you off."

Mourners started to file in, and Elise took her spot, with Julia, next to Robert's casket, to shake hands and give hugs and thank people she barely knew or didn't know at all for coming to join her in saying good-bye to her husband. Julia must have known almost nobody who came through the line, but she held her own. She was charming and poised, and Elise could see a side of her she had forgotten existed. They called her Queenie for a reason. Something had been off about Julia all week — now that Elise knew about Eli, she supposed that was what it was. But how her daughter could turn her charm on like flipping a switch she would never understand. She supposed it was Julia's own defense mechanism, learned to help her survive Robert's wrath.

Claire didn't join them. She sat in the front pew, sunglasses on, with Molly on her lap, holding Eli's hand. Elise couldn't tell what her daughter was thinking and feeling behind those giant glasses, but she could see the hard set to her jaw and knew that she would not be joining the receiving line anytime soon.

If ever.

Sad organ music played and people clutched tissues and a group of old farmers chatted quietly, respectfully, in the back and a couple of children nosed through a cookie platter just outside the chapel door. After a while, the music stopped and once again Joe Dale appeared and took Elise by the elbow, leading her to the front pew, where she sat between Eli and Julia. Maya stayed in the back pew by herself.

"Welcome," Joe Dale began, and Elise felt her eyes fill with tears. Not tears of sadness. Oh, no, those tears would come soon enough. Those tears would wash over her in a wave. Those tears would stretch back decades and would leave her raw and hollow and regretful.

These tears were different.

Robert was dead. Her husband of forty-seven years was gone. There was tinsel on the tree and poinsettias on the porch and nobody would get drunk and beat her tonight.

These were tears of relief.

TWENTY-THREE

The service was short, the preacher going on about shadows and valleys and all the typical funeral things.

Nobody who knew Robert rose to speak, so even his eulogy was stale and ordinary, and Elise couldn't help but feel some amount of smug satisfaction that nobody was going to stand up and talk about Robert Yancey as if he were some sort of saint. It was bad enough to hear that he might be heaven-bound. If anyone deserved a short trip on a long escalator downward, it was that man.

So when the preacher began talking about Robert being someone who loved the outdoors and gathering over a good meal with good friends, until he got to the child of Christ part, it almost sounded like a dating ad. She wondered if he would also claim that her dearly departed husband enjoyed long walks on the beach and French poetry.

After the service, everyone filed out except Elise and her daughters. Even Eli had dutifully taken Molly to the cookie tray, both of them silent and looking wrung out. It was going to be a rough patch for poor Molly, her family broken, her brother and mother sick. And rough for Eli as well, Elise suspected. She hoped her daughters were prepared to be there for their children. That was where she'd always fallen down, in taking care of her daughters. In protecting them. She hadn't done enough of it and she knew it. If she had a regret in this life, it was of not taking them away from their father, rather than not taking herself away from him.

"We'll give you a few moments," Joe Dale said, and left, closing the door behind him.

Elise dutifully went back to the casket, said an internal good-bye and stepped away.

Julia stepped up next, peered into the casket for a moment, then backed to her mom's side. They looked out at Claire and Maya, who had both stayed in their spots at opposite ends of the chapel.

Maya simply shook her head no, slowly.

Claire stood, walked over to the casket, looked down, and said, "Fuck you," then walked away. Elise was surprised that she didn't feel scandalized by it. In fact, she felt a little triumphant.

The ground was soft and slushy. The snow had melted a good deal, and their high heels sank into the ground as they walked, all except for Maya, who seemed to know how to float above treacherous ground in her heels. Probably because she had worn them so much.

The wind had kicked up and they huddled against themselves as they traipsed to the grave site, hugging their coats tight around them, ducking their heads down into their collars. Julia lit a cigarette and smoked it on the way, then gave one each to Claire and Maya, who both took them gratefully.

They sat in folding chairs under a canopy that had been hastily erected, but did a nice job of keeping the wind out, and listened as the preacher read from the Bible and said more generic things that had nothing to do with the man who was Robert Yancey. The children hung in the back of the crowd, Molly twirling in circles, her little skirt fanning out around her delicately.

They sat in silence. They nodded their appreciation to the preacher. They nodded to Joe Dale. They stayed in their seats, shoulder touching shoulder, as everyone filed away.

It was done.

After everything, it was finally done.

And that was when Elise finally broke down, sitting with her daughters, remembering all the times the girls' cries and pleas had broken her heart and she could do nothing about them but hope that they wouldn't be horribly tainted for life at the hands of her husband. She sat with them now, three grown women who all held pain in their eyes. Who all had secrets and who kept their feelings and thoughts locked away.

She wanted them back. Not for Christmas, but forever. She wanted that relationship she'd never been able to forge with them, thanks to him. She wanted to be there for Maya as she nursed Will, and herself, back to health. She wanted to be there for Julia as she sought help for her son. She wanted to be there for Claire, who looked so haunted Elise wasn't sure that it was only yesterday that haunted her. She wanted to be there for them at last.

She wanted to know them, and she wanted them to know her. She wanted to be rid of this secret that was making her act crazy and felt like a brick wall between her and her daughters. If she expected them to speak, she had to do so first.

"I did it," she said at last, her voice creaky and small. She cleared her throat and repeated herself more forcefully. "I did it."

"Did what?" Julia asked. She squeezed Elise's hand.

"I killed him."

There was a beat of silence, and then Claire leaned forward. "Holy shit, Mom," she breathed. "What happened?"

"I'd had enough, and I wanted him gone," Elise said. "So he's gone."

Claire stood, faced them. "What did you do?"

So, sitting in a folding chair next to the man's fresh grave, Elise recounted to them how Robert had died that night.

She'd been in bed, reading, just like every night. Reading, and hoping he was drinking enough to pass out in his stupid recliner, just as he'd been doing lately. As much as it sickened her to wake up to the stench of his acrid breath barreling out of his body and stinking up the front room every morning, at least when he was passed out in the recliner he wasn't terrorizing her in the bedroom.

She must have dozed off, because she remembered picking her book up off of her chest when she heard the *thunk* from down in the front room. It was a sound she recognized, like someone had sat up real quick in the recliner and knocked it back to sitting position. She opened her eyes and listened for more, hoping that he wasn't coming to bed. He'd be angry that she'd fallen asleep with the lights on and wasted electricity.

But then she heard a cry, a kind of strangled *yargh* sound and a wheezy cough. And then her name, only it took him several tries to get it out. "El . . . Eli . . . Eli . . . El . . . Elise!"

She was scared. Was there an intruder in the house? A murderer? She strained to hear more, not moving a muscle for fear of drowning out an important noise such as footsteps climbing the stairs. But there didn't appear to be the sound of any sort of struggle going on. Just Robert making those strange guttural noises and the squeak of his recliner moving around.

At last she got out of bed and crept down-stairs.

"Robert?" she asked, and when he didn't answer, walked into the front room with her heart in her throat, barely breathing because she was so frightened.

But she rounded the corner and saw him there, his face so red it was purple, both hands clutching his chest. He was holding his breath.

"Robert?" she asked again, coming into the room, startled. "What's wrong?"

"Help," he choked out, and he reached for her.

Without thinking, she ran for the phone in the den. She picked it up off its base and carried it into the front room, her finger hovering over the "9."

When she came back in the room, she could see that his pain had only intensified. His cheeks bulged in fear and his fingers scrabbled at his chest. His breathing was coming out in raspy gulps. And looking at him, she realized she was looking at someone having a massive heart attack. If she didn't get help for him, he could die. In fact, from the looks of things, he probably would die.

He looked so pathetic. So frightened. Practically pleading for mercy.

How many times had she pleaded for mercy and not gotten any from him?

How many times had she looked pathetic, been clutching at a body part in pain, been frightened and needy?

And how many times had he kicked her while she was down?

His bulging eyes seemed to take her in and know exactly what she was thinking, because they'd gotten a fearful look to them. He'd thrashed in the chair a bit as if to get up and grab the phone from her, and then he'd gone unconscious.

"I'm sorry, Robert," she said, pulling the phone to her side. "You don't deserve my help."

She'd climbed the stairs back to her bedroom, taking the phone with her, and locked the bedroom door behind her. She never knew if he regained consciousness, if he died right then, or if he suffered for hours first.

They sat in stunned silence, their faces turned toward their father's casket. Elise sniffled into a tissue, feeling miserable and responsible and as if her daughters would never again want anything to do with her. At last her secret was out. Nobody seemed to know what to say.

Then a sound from the end seat punctured the silence.

A snicker.

Elise, Claire, and Julia all turned, leaned forward, to look at Maya, whose shoulders were shaking. Elise's eyes grew wide.

"I'm sorry," Maya said, covering her mouth with one hand, but her giggles seeped out between her fingers. She tried to compose herself, cleared her throat, pressed her lips together. "You didn't kill him, Mom. You're not a murderer." The other two daughters nodded in agreement.

"You can't be held responsible for some-one else's heart attack," Julia said.

"He died of natural causes," Claire added. "Bacon killed him. Bacon and booze and a terrible temper."

"Who's to say the paramedics could have saved him anyway?" Maya said. "You let him go. You should have done it years ago."

Maybe they were right. What if she hadn't heard his cry that night? What if she'd slept just a fraction more soundly, or awakened two seconds more slowly? What if she'd searched for her slippers or stopped to tie her robe? What if the ambulance hadn't ar-rived in time, if the CPR didn't work, if he'd died on an operating table early the next morning? He would be no less dead, and she would be no more at fault.

She liked the way it sounded, that Robert was dead, but she didn't kill him. She just . . . let him go.

He may have been the shy boy who'd carved that hummingbird box for her, the one who'd called her *beautifullest,* the one who'd promised to love and honor her. But he was also the one who'd pulled her hair, who'd pushed her down the stairs, sprained her wrist, sneered when she cried. He was the one who'd hurt her daughters — the people in this world she loved more than anything. He was the one who'd driven them away, made them lock up their hearts, made them forge secrets and keep them from her.

He needed to be let go. And she'd let him go.

There was a beat, and then Claire started laughing. "How surprised the old goat must have been when he ordered you to do something and you actually didn't for a change."

"But he was only surprised for a few minutes," Maya said, then lost her composure again and joined her sister's laughter, and even Julia's mouth tipped up in a little smile. But abruptly Maya's laughter turned to sobs, so gut-wrenching they sounded painful. "I'm sorry," she said, "I'm sorry. I'm such a mess. I just . . . everything that's happened . . . I'm scared . . ."

Claire rushed to Maya's seat and knelt in front of her. She reached up and rubbed her sister's arms, repeating, "It's okay. It's going to be okay, Maya." Soon they were all sobbing again, and to Joe Dale they might have looked as if they would miss his friend Robert Yancey as much as he would. But they were mourning something much deeper. The loss of a father. Of a husband. Of sisters. The loss of their own childhood.

The loss of so many years, spent up and wasted with pain and anger.

They had so many years' worth of tears to cry.

Slowly, Elise pulled herself to standing and walked over to the casket, shining and pristine with a spray of red roses adorning the lid. She reached into her pocketbook and pulled out the necklace Molly had found in the Christmas tree branches, which she'd tucked in her purse at the last moment. She held it up and watched the pendant swivel at the end of its chain. Such a mystery, that necklace. But the man — there was no mystery about him. Even if he'd been trying to apologize with this gift — even if he'd been saying he wanted to start anew — Elise knew it wouldn't have been long before she was nursing a broken bone, or a broken heart, a broken soul again.

The pendant, the mystery, it didn't matter. The man was a monster, and she should have rid herself of him years ago.

She dangled the necklace over the casket. "I'm sorry, Robert," she said. "It just doesn't work that way. Too little, too late." She opened her fingers and let the pendant fall. It landed on the casket with a rattle and slid over the side, down into the yawning grave below.

Julia stood, wrapped her arm around her mom, and pulled her close, leaned her head against Elise's. "It's okay, Mom," she whispered. "We're here. We're all here."

TWENTY-FOUR

Elise didn't get to taking down the tree until after she'd gotten back from Chicago.

She'd flown home with Maya and the children two days after Robert's funeral. By the time she got back, the Colorado blue spruce was brittle and browning. It no longer carried the smell that God intended. Her mother would have been frantic with worry. Would've been expecting it to spontaneously combust any minute.

Still, when she got home from Chicago, from the frenzy of heartache, during which she tried so helplessly to be there for her daughter who was grieving the loss of her marriage in between difficult doctor's appointments, she left her bags by the front door and went straight to the spruce and stood in front of it, pondering her own heavy heart.

When Maya's shock had worn off and the realization that her marriage was over had finally arrived, it hit her with such a force as to dissolve her. Elise's daughter was empty, drifting about with wet eyelashes and a sunken look that suggested a part of her had disappeared with Bradley. She scarcely spoke, couldn't do anything for the poor children, who seemed lost as well, couldn't lift a finger without needing to go back to her dark bedroom and lie down for hours.

Elise tried her hardest to help out. She kept on top of Will's pain pills and daily visits to the doctor, as the blood vessels in his fingers slowly repaired themselves. She sat with the children during Maya's radiation appointments and played with them when their mother arrived home, tired and crabby. She took down the Christmas tree and helped the children open up all their new toys. She made sure the kids bathed and dressed and she arranged for them to spend some time with their father, who appeared to be living with a colleague just a few blocks away. She cooked dinners that nobody ate and vacuumed floors that nobody walked on.

Will was doing better every day, but Elise stayed on, tending to her daughter's shattered life the way she'd tended to the farm as a child — a set of unwelcome, yet satisfying, chores to do. Nobody was waiting for her to come home. She could stay as long as she needed.

But after three days, a bald lady in a pink T-shirt came to the door, carrying a bag loaded with supplies. Cleaning supplies, comfort food, bottles of wine. The poor thing looked so shrunken, Elise stepped aside and ushered her in, taking the bag off her shoulder and carrying it to the kitchen for her.

"I'm so sorry I couldn't get here sooner," the lady said, following oh so slowly behind Elise. "I've been out of commission lately. But I've rallied once again . . ."

Maya, who had heard her friend's voice, flew off the couch and into the kitchen, wailing like a siren and holding her arms out like a child. They fell into each other's embrace, rocking and crying so that Elise knew it was time for her to go, time for her to let Maya's friend take the reins.

Now, standing in front of the Colorado blue spruce, many of its needles under her feet on the floor, more sleet clicking against the windows, she felt very alone. But peacefully so.

"I suppose I'll go ahead and take down the tinsel, Robert," she said, even though she knew he wouldn't answer.

She started to reach for a strand of silver,

but her hand fell away. Instead, she leaned over and plugged in the lights, knowing, but not caring about, the danger of doing so on such a dry tree. She stood back admiring the twinkling lights for a moment, hands on hips, reflection on her face, and then eased herself down to the floor.

She lowered herself onto her back and scooted under the tree, looking up through the ornaments and the lights and the tinsel, and gave a sigh of relief.

Epilogue:
December 24

One Year Later

Claire was, of course, the first to arrive. Elise stood on the front porch, leaning forward onto her toes, arms wrapped around her shoulders against the wind. It was a cold day, but sunny. It had not snowed yet in Missouri, and, much to the chagrin of the white Christmas wishers, it was not going to snow anytime in the near future. Just icy cold and wind whipping across the plains, sinister and deadly.

Elise chuckled as her daughter tossed a fistful of crumpled bills over the cabdriver's seat and pushed open her door . . . only to see Michael reach over the seat behind his new wife's back, gather the bills and straighten them, then add one to them and hand them to the cabdriver with a handshake. He stepped out of the opposite side of the cab and came around next to Claire, picking up her beat-up backpack in one hand while carrying his duffel in the other.

They both wore sunglasses. They both wore jeans.

They both waved, almost in sync, to Elise as the cabbie backed away. Elise waved back.

They had been married only a few months. A Vegas wedding. They'd flown her in for the ceremony. Immediately Elise had liked Michael Bowman, finding him sweet and patient, the slow and easy side that Claire didn't have and desperately needed. He gambled a little, teased his new mother-in-law a lot, and doted on Claire as if he'd been given a rare and precious gem to keep. And the most amazing thing? Claire let him. Sometimes it looked as if it might actually be painful for her youngest daughter, but grudgingly, she let him. She needed him. Elise could see it in her eyes, in the way she gripped his elbow when they walked side by side, in the way her fingers curled desperately around his when she said her vows. In the way she cried while saying them.

Claire loped up the sidewalk, crinkling her nose. "When are they ever going to take care of that shit smell?"

Elise laughed. "I don't smell it." She held her arms out and folded her daughter into them. She smelled Claire's hair, kissed the top of her head. It still felt strange for her to make these gestures, but with big change comes discomfort. Her therapist had told her that, over and over again since Robert's death. Elise understood, and she was willing to withstand the anxiety.

"Maya and Julia here yet?" Claire asked, unraveling herself from her mother's arms and stepping up on the porch.

"Julia should be here any minute. Maya's flight comes in tonight. Hi, Michael!" She quickly hugged her son-in-law as a greeting.

"Great to see you, Elise! What's this rumor I hear about mulled wine?"

"It's on the stove. Come on in."

They had barely sat down when Julia and Eli arrived. Eli had gotten a haircut, Elise noticed, and his acne had gotten worse. The result was a face that was so angry with lesions it jumped out at you, looking throbbing and painful. He sat at the table next to his mom, his arms crossed and mouth shut, surly. He hadn't changed much. To hear Julia tell it, in private, he had gotten worse after falling through the ice. He'd become almost inconsolable at times, suffering nightmares, begging for her to let him die, pressing knives to his throat at the dinner table, threatening to jump out of the car on the highway. She'd taken him to a psychiatrist, who'd hospitalized him, medicated him, then suggested he spend more time with Dusty, so Julia had clamped down on her own heart and sent her son to live with his dad. Slowly, he'd been making progress. Though they all figured he would never be that smiling, curious child again.

"Where's Tai?" Elise asked once everyone got settled.

Julia looked somber. "His research project just couldn't be put on hold. He stayed behind to work on it."

"On Christmas Eve?"

Julia shrugged. "That's exactly what the marriage counselor said."

Elise frowned. Julia hadn't mentioned marriage counseling before. Her daughters all still had some secrets, she supposed. They were working on that, but old habits die extremely hard. She would ask about the counseling later, when Eli wasn't around, because she had resolved to test those habits, and those secrets, the day Robert died, and she wasn't about to give up on her daughters now.

Later, Maya arrived with the kids . . . and Bradley. This was a surprise to no one. She'd warned everyone that they were giving it another shot.

"It's tentative," she'd told Elise on the phone. "I don't know if I trust him completely, but I'm willing to give it a try. For the kids."

Molly looked so much older, and Elise was taken aback at how much of a difference a year could make. At eight, the little girl was already wearing clear lip gloss and shoes with tiny, clicking heels. She looked like a miniature version of her mom, right down to the pinched expression and tense shoulders. Will padded along behind her, her little shadow, who eyed his surroundings warily, as if he might get hurt by making a wrong move. He'd managed not to lose any body parts to frostbite after all, but his nervousness showed the confidence that he'd lost in his fall through the ice, and Elise wondered if he'd gained a timidity that would follow him through life.

"We're going to Jamaica after Christmas," Molly announced to the room in her precise, somewhat aloof manner.

"Kingston," Maya added, setting her suitcase on the kitchen floor with a huff. "We're leaving straight from here on the twenty-eighth. Doctor says the relaxation will be good for me."

There were some changes about Maya — the long hair clipped short, the lack of bangles snaking up her arms, the assertiveness, the sneakers. Elise figured Maya had

419

entered a portion of her life where she would take no shit from anyone. She'd lost her husband for a time, she'd almost lost a child, she'd beaten cancer. She had been to the gates of hell, then had turned around and trudged back to reality with her shoulders squared. Nothing would scare her now. Nothing would beat her.

The girls began to chatter about Jamaica. About swimsuits and parasailing and beach volleyball. Claire talked about a trip she and Michael had made there. She made some suggestions and laughed over vacation dramas, and they all chatted over one another, sipping on mulled wine and hot chocolate and passing a plate of cookies back and forth between two poinsettias.

Elise stood by the stove and crossed her arms, looked out the window at the chicken coop she'd repainted and filled back in the fall. Tomorrow morning they would eat Essie's and Maria's and Chickie's eggs for breakfast. They would slather biscuits with crab apple jelly from the crab apple tree in the front yard, jelly that she'd canned herself during the summer, along with beans and yams and jars and jars of homemade pickles.

She'd sold the back acreage, along with the pond and the soy field and the beehives, her daughter's bloody foot trails outlining the boundary of what once belonged to distant aunts and uncles. She'd kept the barn and the pasture, and planned to buy a couple of cows in the spring. She'd kept the garden and had welcomed the sweaty, hard, backbreaking labor all summer long. She'd farmed enough vegetables to feed herself all winter, and enough to give to the new family that had filled in the pond and built a tidy farmhouse on the land. And she'd filled the chicken coop, her lovely birds her friends and confidantes.

She'd spent days finding, and cutting down, the perfect Colorado blue spruce and loading it up with lights and ornaments and fountains of tinsel. She'd been busy for weeks making plans with her daughters. This time they would come of their own accord. This time she would not need to lie to get them, and keep them, home. This time they would come and fill the floor beneath the tree with gaily wrapped gifts. With excited chatter. With warm meals and wine and "O Come, All Ye Faithful."

This year they would have Christmas.

■ ■ ■ ■

CONVERSATION
GUIDE:
THE SISTER SEASON

JENNIFER SCOTT

■ ■ ■ ■

This Conversation Guide is intended to
enrich the individual reading experience, as
well as encourage us to explore these topics
together — because books, and life,
are meant for sharing.

A CONVERSATION WITH JENNIFER SCOTT

Q. The Sister Season *is set on a family farm outside Kansas City, Missouri. It's such a real place and the details of the natural world are so lovingly observed, from the birdhouses nailed crookedly to the old trees to the ice freezing on the pond while the fish continue to swim among the reeds underneath. Why did you choose this setting? Have farms played a significant role in your life?*

A. My parents owned a small piece of pastureland in rural Pleasant Hill, Missouri, when I was young. Across the road, a close family friend owned, and lived on, a small amount of farmland. Between the two families we had just enough space to house a few cows and chickens, a couple of geese and ducks, a barn cat or two, a large garden, a pond, and some fruit trees.

Growing up, I spent my Sundays on that land, helping to work in the garden, hanging out in the barn, wandering around the orchard, plinking the keys of an old upright in the living room, or churning ice cream on the back porch. It was hot and buggy, or dead and frozen over, there was no TV or any electronic entertainment, and there was usually work to be done.

But, for me, it was also a place of dreaming, and a place of great comfort. A place where I could tell myself stories, where I could jump and climb and sing at the top of my lungs. It was a source of comfort food and cozy Christmases, an outlet for my creative self. And, yes, it was also a place of dark corners and unforgiving seasons, and there seemed to be stories to imagine in every nook and cranny.

That farm became a part of me, a place I still mentally retreat to when I want an image of peace. I've always wanted to set a story on a version of that farm, and to me the setting of *The Sister Season* is almost a character unto itself — a very beloved character I've known my whole life.

Q. *There are four different women we follow fairly closely in this book — the sisters Julia, Maya, and Claire, and their mother, Elise. You do a wonderful job portraying each woman in sympathetic, complicated ways, but were some of these female characters harder to write than others? Do you have a favorite among them?*

A. Oddly, my answer to both questions is the same sister: Claire.

Claire was the hardest to write, because she was so closed off on the inside, yet had this outward image of being easy and carefree. In a way, Claire is the most tender of the three sisters, yet is inwardly the most impenetrable. This dichotomy of Claire's personality made the writing of her story a bit of a difficult dance.

Yet at the same time I had the most hope for Claire. I related to her the easiest — the youngest sister, artsy and blithe on the outside but easily hurt and guarded within — and I trusted her. I knew that she was ultimately going to be the one to set healing in motion. If any of the sisters could push past the hurt and begin moving them all toward the future, I knew that sister would be Claire.

Q. Julia's son, Eli, is given his own sections within the book, which you label "Attempts." Why did you set him off this way? Why not weave his story into the book in chapter form the way you did with the women?

A. Eli's story is set up as a mirror of what is going on with the women. He is continually attempting to give up, and is continually failing at it. There is always something standing in his way of completing that final death, and in the end it is love that keeps him alive.

The same thing is happening to his mother and aunts. They have tried to give up on one another, on their family. They have attempted their own sort of death — the death of the sister bond. But there is something standing in their way, something keeping them from successfully letting go. Just like with Eli, it is ultimately love that keeps their bond alive.

For this reason, I wanted to set Eli's story apart from theirs. In a way, I felt like I was pausing to take a breath and to study their reflection in Eli. Overall, *The Sister Season* wasn't about Eli at all — it was the three sisters' story — but at times the two journeys were very close to one and the same.

Q. You also write fiction for young adults. How does writing for adults differ from writing for young adults? Is one more draining, or more rewarding, than the other?

A. Really, in terms of process, there isn't

much difference. I'm not even thinking so much about genre while I'm writing. I'm simply telling the story that wants to be told. Sometimes that story features women in their late twenties or early thirties and deals with marriage and aging parents and parenting struggles. Other times the story that wants to be told involves high school lockers and boyfriends and scandals at parties.

But in the end, they're all stories about love and loss, conflict and friendship, the struggle to connect, and, ultimately, the great reward in gutting it out until that connection is made. Because of that, I see them as simply different sides of the same coin, and I love them equally.

Q. What's next for you in your writing life?

A. The only thing I can say for certain is that I don't know and I like it that way! I'm a big fan of trying new stories, new styles, new genres, and I never say no to a story that's tickling the back of my brain, wanting to be heard, without at least giving it a try. Because of that, I'm always experimenting.

That said, I have special places in my heart for women's fiction and young adult fiction, so I fully intend to continue writing

in those genres for many, many years to
come.

QUESTIONS FOR DISCUSSION

1. Within this book a family comes together for two events — to bury a father and husband and to celebrate the holidays. Why do you suppose the author wanted to mingle these two events? What is gained, and lost, with this decision? Have you yourself had experiences where grief and joy were commingled?

2. The family's reactions to both of these events are somewhat unexpected. Their feelings about gathering for the holidays seem ambivalent at best; it's certainly not the typical joy-filled big family gathering. Likewise, their experience of Robert's death is not primarily one of grief. As we learn more about the family's history, does this make sense? Have you yourself experienced events — perhaps holidays — where your own feelings didn't match what you were "supposed" to be feeling?

3. There are three sisters in this book, and in some ways their personalities seem determined by their birth order. Julia, the oldest, is a successful professor; Maya, the middle sister, struggles to define herself; and Claire, the youngest, is the rebellious free spirit. In your own life, where do you fall in birth order among your siblings and how do you think this shaped your personality — if at all? In what ways do the sisters, and you, buck the trend?

4. Elise has a complicated relationship with her daughters. When Claire arrives home Elise imagines hopping off the steps, wrapping her arms around her daughter and maybe even crying. But instead, "for reasons even she couldn't understand, the idea of rushing into her daughter's arms never translated into the actual motion of doing so." Yet by the end of the book, when Claire arrives one year later, Elise "held her arms out and folded her daughter into them . . . It still felt strange for her to make these gestures, but with big change comes discomfort." Do you agree with Elise? Does change bring discomfort? Have you shared her experience of doing one thing in your mind but another in reality? And what does her different reaction say about the ways her

relationship with Claire has changed? The ways Elise has changed?

5. Throughout much of the book Elise carries what she feels is a terrible secret. When she reveals this secret, do you have the same reaction as her daughters? Do you fault her? Do you understand her? How does her handling of the gold locket reflect her feelings and play into her own character growth?

6. Each of the sisters is hiding something that she eventually shares with the others. What are these secrets and what does the sharing of them do for each sister? Why has this sharing taken so long? And what do you think this says about the nature of sisterhood — its fractures, its endurance?

7. You might say Claire makes one decision about her relationship with Robert (to end it), but the sisters make a different decision about their relationships with one another. How do we decide when to end relationships versus when to mend them?

8. Two of the women in this book are children, but they also have children of their own. How have Maya's and Julia's relationships with their parents influenced them as

parents themselves?

9. Eli stands as the most articulate of the third generation of the family in this book. Would you say he's a sympathetic character? In what ways is he central to the plot?

10. What role does the epilogue play in this story? One year later, is the family where you thought it would be? Are there unanswered questions — and if so, what do you imagine happens next?

11. Although *The Sister Season* deals with a family coming together for the holidays, the working title of this book was *Solstice*. What new context does this bring to the story?

ABOUT THE AUTHOR

Jennifer Scott also writes award-winning young adult fiction as Jennifer Brown. *The Sister Season* is her first adult novel. She lives in the Midwest with her husband and three children.

The employees of Thorndike Press hope you have enjoyed this Large Print book. All our Thorndike, Wheeler, and Kennebec Large Print titles are designed for easy reading, and all our books are made to last. Other Thorndike Press Large Print books are available at your library, through selected bookstores, or directly from us.

For information about titles, please call:
  (800) 223-1244

or visit our Web site at:
  http://gale.cengage.com/thorndike

To share your comments, please write:
  Publisher
  Thorndike Press
  10 Water St., Suite 310
  Waterville, ME 04901